This book is dedicated to all of my friends and family, without whom none of this would have been possible.

CHAPTER 1

I t was precisely 11pm when he realised he was going to die.

He knew this for two very different reasons. Firstly, the crowd he'd been running with was into something heavy. Something bigger than the usual robberies and low-level drug peddling he'd been used to. It had been two years since he'd first been offered the job; a one-off, they'd told him. That was many jobs ago. It was just his rotten luck that he'd ended up here, now.

The second reason? He'd been tied to a chair and was staring down the barrel of a sawn-off shotgun.

He could hear the faint sound of a distant clock as he made another futile attempt to prise his hands from the ropes that had been used to bind him. It was useless. He grimaced as the coarse material chafed away at the raw skin around his wrists. His heart slapped against his bruised ribcage, three beats for every tick.

Although he couldn't see his captor's face, he could sense him smirking behind the balaclava. A shuffling sound to his left caught his attention. He couldn't see who it was, but he knew they all answered to him. The invisible presence carried an aura of control. He'd seen it before. Probably wouldn't see it again.

'Look...'

The hand that struck him was gloved, but it did nothing to dampen the impact on his face. Tears streamed from his swollen eyes as he settled back into silence, his vision jarred.

'I want a name,' a voice called out from the darkness.

'I don't know what you mean,' he replied, fighting to keep the tremor hidden from his voice.

'This is... unfortunate.'

He didn't recognise the voice, nor the accent. It sounded Eastern European but he couldn't be sure. Like some kind of evil Bond villain. If he hadn't been so sure he was about to die, he would have laughed. They must be ignorant, he felt. People in these parts knew not to mess with the crew he was running with. Once the boss found out about this there'd be hell to pay.

Not that this lot seemed bothered though.

The go-between had told him there would be minimal fuss. He'd gone straight to the pickup point at the Port of Tyne, just as he'd been ordered. He'd been on time and had done everything asked of him. Baz had seen them coming and nicked off in the van, the prick. Apart from Baz, who he'd never liked much, he'd miss the lads. But not as much as he'd miss Suzie. He'd promised her he'd be done after this last job. He'd sworn it. He'd even told the boss. Well, he'd asked. He'd found himself some other work. Less dangerous, they'd told him. Didn't matter now.

'The name,' the voice said again, this time right next to his face.

He could feel steel against his throat, pressure being slowly applied until he was sure they'd drawn blood. He felt the nausea creeping up through his stomach. There was no way out for him now.

'I've given you everything I know!'

'You're lying,' the European said. 'I'm told you northerners are made of strong stuff. Let's test that theory, shall we?'

He screamed as the blade left his throat and began sawing through the bone of the baby finger on his left hand, just below the knuckle. He wasn't afforded the luxury of passing out. On and on it seemed to go, his screams reverberating around the warehouse. Once it was over, he looked down at the bloodied stump where his finger had once been and threw up on himself, his sobs reverting to whimpers.

'The name!'

A single candle fluttered in between himself and the European who was now sitting opposite, pointing the gun. Other than that, there was only darkness.

He knew there was no way out now. All he could do was protect Suzie. 'Fuck *the name*. When the boss finds out about this your life won't be worth spit.'

The warehouse fell silent, the only sound the rustling of the European's collar as he turned his head, staring back into the darkness.

'Ankegren, bring me the pliers.'

CHAPTER 2

In nearly ten years of police work, not a lot surprised Detective Chief Inspector Jack Lambert. When he'd received the call about two bodies being discovered, he'd had the same rush of adrenaline he'd encountered numerous times before. However, shocked he was not.

Until now.

Stamping a half-smoked menthol into the damp earth, he sighed, resting a palm on his throbbing forehead. Detective Sergeant Watkins paced up the hill towards him, pale faced, his shock of wiry, ginger hair bobbing up and down. Sheets of rain lashed the grassy knoll, mimicking the sombre mood of the crime scene. Jack had forgotten to bring a coat.

'Yep, two of them,' Watkins relayed. 'One male, one female.'

'What do we know?'

'Not a lot,' he replied, his voice rising in pitch as it often seemed to do when he was nervous.

The wind was picking up now. Jack ground his teeth together in frustration; just one of the many things he'd inherited from his estranged father. Weather like this wasn't going to make their job any easier. Still, South Shields wasn't exactly known for its exotic climate.

'Show me.'

They followed the muddy path towards the hastily erected white tent. Navigating the uneven terrain proved difficult, the easiest route having been cordoned off due to the presence of potential tyre marks. A mixture of uniformed police and medical teams in white overalls darted about, trying to solve their latest mystery. South Shields' famous foggy coastline was doing its job today, sending a thick, grey paste their way.

Ducking into the tent, Jack was met with the animated chatter of the investigating team. He squinted at the patchy grass, faint sets of footprints moving in short bursts from the centre.

'Detective Lambert.'

Even in drab white overalls it was hard not to be taken aback by the striking looks of pathologist Rosie Lynnes. Half the force would have killed for the chance to have a shot with the auburn-haired stunner. Jack Lambert had been the one cop to charm her, but then he'd managed to break her heart. Having had enough of living in denial, he had come clean about his sexuality nearly a year ago. Far from finding himself liberated from the mental prison he'd put himself in, he had retreated into his shell. The pathologist, for her part, seemed to have an unhealthy hatred for him now. He couldn't say he blamed her. It didn't help that he'd specifically requested that she attend the scene of these murders.

'Rosie.'

'Put these on,' she said, casting a swift glance over his appearance, 'and follow me.'

While wishing he'd taken the time to shave that morning, he stepped awkwardly into the SOC suit, the material proving itchy as always. He'd gained a few pounds in the last year and, at a stocky six feet two inches, he found that most people took him for a bouncer rather than a police officer. They were only half wrong. He followed Rosie towards the centre of the tent as he wrestled with the zip. When he finally got to grips with it he focused on breathing through his mouth as the scent of rotting bodies hit him. It didn't do much good. Death always had a way of overcoming such methods. Watkins started retching. It happened to the best of them. The young, newly-promoted DS certainly had potential. If he could keep his professionalism intact, he'd make a fine detective, Jack thought.

He moved closer and kneeled over the corpses.

'I'd estimate no more than around twelve to fourteen days since the time of death, but that's a rough estimate. It's not certain.'

Even Rosie's perfume couldn't mask the stench.

'Any good news?' he asked.

'I'm afraid not.'

'Cause of death?' he asked.

'I'll need to conduct a proper examination.'

'You must have some idea?'

'If I were into guesswork,' she said, cuttingly, 'I would say strangulation.'

'Both of them?'

'Yes.'

Watkins appeared to Jack's right, sweat beading down his face as he gasped for fresh air. They stared into the ditch that housed the two corpses. Both were in the early stages of decomposition and stripped naked. Jack noted the red hue that both bodies had taken on, which backed up the theory that it was days rather than weeks since they had died. Both of the bodies were on their side, with the woman's arm wrapped around the bloated torso of the man. Odd that it should be that way round, he thought. Jack focused his mind, aware that even the tiniest detail at the time of discovery could prove vital to finding the killer. Although ages were difficult to determine, he guessed both of them to have been somewhere between twenty and thirty. Certainly younger than his own thirty-five years.

'We'll need an ID as quickly as possible,' he said, dragging himself back up.

'Should I start looking through the missing persons list?' Watkins asked.

'You don't need me to tell you how to do everything, Watkins,' Jack snapped. 'Yes, of course, and get onto the lab.'

They left the shelter of the tent and headed back out into the tree-lined area of Cleadon Hills. Although the cold air slapped him in the face, he was glad to be able to breathe normally again. The smell, on the other hand, would take days to wash out of his clothes.

Gazing around the scene, he felt his hopes for a quick resolution dwindle. The area was remote and the chances of anybody having seen anything would be slim to none. Still, protocol existed for a reason, even if he had gained a reputation as someone who liked to ignore it.

'Let's start door to door enquiries.'

Watkins nodded. 'So, what do you think?'

Jack's experience had taught him to look at everything and rule out nothing. It also told him that when more than one body was involved, it was generally bad news.

'I think we're in for a difficult winter,' he sighed. 'Have we questioned the bloke who found them?'

'Yeah. He's a dog walker. Comes here all the time. He's being treated for shock,' Watkins said, motioning toward a nearby paramedic van.

'Bit of a cliché,' Jack said.

He watched as two medics flanked a middle-aged man who was wrapped in a blanket nursing a warm drink. His dog, a young-looking Labrador, lay close by, looking as glum as Jack felt.

'Detective.'

He turned. 'Jane.'

DI Jane Russell strode over with what some might call concern etched onto her face. Jack knew it was all an act though. Still, it didn't pay to mention it to her. Despite being on the same team, she had a habit of making things all about her. A fine policewoman, yes, but selfish. And Jack couldn't stand selfish people.

'I don't know why you're here.' Her grey eyes narrowed. 'We've already secured the scene and bagged up potential evidence.'

'Edwards wanted an extra set of eyes on this,' he replied, holding her gaze. 'Plus, I've been assigned SIO.'

The detective's pencil-thin features scrunched up, ageing her by at least ten years. 'Yes... well... just don't contaminate the scene... guv.'

She strode away, casting a cursory glance over her shoulder. Having not long made DCI, Jack was determined to stay involved in the investigation process. He'd be damned if he was going to put his feet up and delegate everything away like his predecessor. Jane Russell would just have to deal with it.

'What's up with the Bulldog?' Watkins asked as she began barking orders at a nearby PC.

He shrugged. 'Who knows?' Turning to take in the scene once more he added, 'but I don't like this one bit.'

The DS began swinging his gangly leg around, kicking at the loose dirt. 'What's got you so spooked?'

'Stop that.' He crunched an ibuprofen down and dry-swallowed it before continuing. 'Somebody dug that ditch up. Somebody who knew where the bodies were and wanted us to find them.' He fixed his eyes on the sergeant. 'I've seen nothing so far to suggest that we're dealing with anything other than one sick bastard, and sick bastards are usually the worst kind of killers to find.'

At the corner of the field, a small crowd had gathered, aware something serious was going on. As the two detectives left the scene, only one man amongst the nosing throng was aware of what had happened. Suppressing a smile, he feigned concern, the images of the bodies he'd dug up dancing through his mind on a happy repeat. A quick check of his watch told him it was almost time. They'd both be waiting, hoping he'd change his mind and let them go. Unfortunately for them he'd be unable to comply. After all, he had a schedule to stick to.

And this was just the beginning.

CHAPTER 3

Jack was greeted by a young desk sergeant as he waded through three policemen wrestling a drunken teenager with a penchant for facial piercings and foul language. He was early for work but his 5am wake up was a lie-in for him. Once a big case ignited, sleep became a luxury he couldn't afford.

He glanced at his watch. 'Eight am? They start earlier and earlier, don't they?'

'Or stay up later,' the desk sergeant replied. 'Oh, before I forget, sir, Superintendent Edwards is looking for you.'

Jack forced a smile before pushing through the double doors into the main station. He began a slow ascent to the second floor, each step proving heavier than the last. A summons from Detective Superintendent Logan Edwards was something nobody looked forward to. Unlike most, he wasn't frightened of the gaffer, but he didn't trust himself to keep quiet when being spoken down to; a habit he'd developed whilst messing about at secondary school.

By the time he'd made it to his office, his lack of breath had convinced him to get back on the bike. If he wasn't careful he'd end up like his father, approaching retirement with a waist size comparable to his age. Given that his drinking habits were also starting to resemble his old man's, he would have to be careful with his lifestyle. For some, working the doors had led to strict sobriety; for Jack – in his previous line of work – it seemed to have had the opposite effect.

'Where have you been?' A flushed-looking Watkins met him at his office door.

'At home. It has just gone 8am.'

'Yes but...'

'Lambert!' Edwards' voice boomed from the end of the corridor.

'I'm not here,' he whispered to Jack, before attempting to enter the office.

'Wait right there!' the superintendent shouted, lumbering towards him.

'Sir?' Watkins squeaked.

Jack suppressed a smile. Edwards' love of instilling fear in others was legendary. Sooner or later it would probably catch up with him, though. Modern day policing wasn't what it had been. So far, he had stubbornly refused to change.

'You're not paid to kiss my arse every day, sunshine. Now, go and make Detective Lambert and me a cup of coffee. Black no sugar.'

'Actually, I'd prefer mine with milk and sugar,' Jack interjected.

'Nonsense. You're a man. Men drink black coffee without sugar.' He turned on the DS. 'Are you still here?'

Watkins shuffled off as they entered Jack's chaotic office. Edwards was renowned for his hard-headed attitude and, truth be told, was a dinosaur working in the wrong age. Rumour had it they were counting down the days to his retirement, hoping he could leave with some dignity still intact. If he wasn't careful, that day would happen sooner rather than later.

'Look, I... sorry about that man comment, I didn't mean anything by it.'

Jack swallowed his irritation. Edwards never broached the subject of his sexuality but their lack of social contact in recent months told him all he needed to know about his boss's thoughts on the matter.

'Don't worry, you aren't my type.'

Recent case files lay strewn over an old oak table, complete with numerous coffee stains. His bin was overflowing with crumpled up notes and empty cups. Although he smoked with the window open, the unmistakable smell of tobacco still clung to the room like a young child to its mother's breast. If Edwards noticed it, he didn't say anything.

'Here,' he said as he pulled a seat out from under the table and knocked a layer of dust from it.

'Dear God, Lambert,' he said. 'It's a wonder anything ever gets solved round here with an office like this.'

He resisted the urge to point out the state of *his* office. 'What do you want?'

'This double murder.'

Jack nodded, taking a seat opposite the DSI. 'Nasty business.'

'Don't worry, I'm not expecting it to be solved right now. But we are going to be giving a press conference.'

Jack nodded, annoyed at the intrusion into his case. It wasn't the first time. 'I see.'

'Now, I know you aren't the biggest fan of these things but, as the senior investigating officer, I don't see why you should get off lightly.'

'Shouldn't I be making those calls?'

The giant superintendent leaned forward, dark, bloodshot eyes focusing on him. His face bore the scars of alcohol abuse; burst blood vessels crisscrossing his face like an intricate road map. Unkempt grey hair framed his round face, his double chin making him look like a drunken Father Christmas. 'Look, I know you aren't the most comfortable performer in front of journalists.' Jack was sure he saw the beginnings of a smirk. 'And I know after that business with the Newcastle Knifer last year you aren't exactly flavour of the week.'

He felt his stomach give a twinge as Edwards uttered the nickname of the man who'd stuck a knife in him just over twelve months ago. The scar across his chest served as a reminder of the near-botched job of apprehending the multiple murderer who'd been terrorising Newcastle's nightlife. Missed leads and the subsequent press fallout had cost Jack a lot of kudos with the public and media. It didn't seem to matter that, in the end, he'd been the one to catch him.

'That's an understatement,' he said. 'And do we have to use the tabloid's nickname for him? He had a real name.'

'But you have to face these things,' Edwards continued, ignoring Jack's comment. 'How do you think I got to where I am today? You have to be thick-skinned and be able to get on with all types of people.'

The door to his office opened. Watkins stepped through carrying two overflowing mugs.

'And what do you call this, sergeant?' Edwards thundered.

'Well... coffee, like you said.' His eyes darted to Jack who did his best to remain straight-faced.

'Did you not hear Detective Lambert specifically ask for milk in his coffee?'

'But you said...'

The superintendent stood up, his giant frame looming over the pale-faced policeman. 'Are you calling me a liar, boy?'

'No, sir.'

'Good, because that would be very bad for your career. Now, piss off and get Detective Lambert another drink!'

Logan Edwards grabbed the two cups from a shaking Watkins before ushering him out of the room.

'Where was I? Oh yes,' he continued. 'Always make the effort to get on with people. I'll keep both of these, seeing as you're a fussy drinker. I'll see you in an hour.'

Jack leaned back in his chair and gazed at the ceiling, his finger subconsciously tracing the outline of his scar. They'd spent months hunting the Newcastle Knifer, aka Leonard 'Dazza' Watson. What had started out as a series of night-time armed robberies had developed into a plethora of knife crimes, with each victim being slashed across the stomach before being finished off in gruesome-style by the twenty-five-year-old local murderer. The longer the hunt went on, the longer the press saw fit to lambast the police for failing to do their jobs. Instead of being labelled a hero for putting his life on the line and eventually capturing the perpetrator, they'd branded Jack incompetent and out of his depth. Yes, there'd been missed opportunities but there was no doubt in Jack's mind who the main instigator was in terms of turning public opinion against the police.

David bloody Robson of the *Newcastle Chronicle*.

Camera flashes exploded around him as he followed Edwards into the press room. Watkins stood by his side, still not having quite recovered from his earlier run-in with the superintendent. Jack had managed to talk him out of filing an official complaint against the DSI. He hadn't taken much persuading. Watkins never did.

Jack took a deep breath, steeling himself for what was about to happen. Sweeping his gaze across the room, he noticed Robson sitting in the front row, slim fingers running across a newly-grown black pencil moustache. The journalist caught his gaze and offered a toothy smile before carefully placing a recording device on the front table.

'Ahem,' Edwards cleared his throat. A hushed silence went up around the room. 'Let me just start by thanking you all for your time,' he began.

Jack could see the big man grinding his teeth at having to play friends with the press. Everybody on the force knew he couldn't stand them. The press did too. Still, even Edwards wasn't daft enough to get on the wrong side of them.

The DSI spent the next five minutes filling them in on what had occurred, stopping short at the intricate details of how the bodies were found. Still, the journalists weren't satisfied, each member of the assembled scrum firing questions at the panel.

'Do you have any leads?' 'Has anyone been brought in for questioning?' 'When was the exact time of death?' 'How were the bodies found?'

Edwards straightened up, perspiration beginning to wash down his brow. 'If you have any queries, please direct them to Detective Chief Inspector Jack Lambert. Our DCI here was one of the first on the scene and will be the SIO on the case.'

Jack stepped up to the platform, resisting the urge to punch his boss. 'Any questions?'

A sea of hands shot up in the air.

He managed to field most of them, each reporter seemingly happy with his responses. By the end of it, he felt satisfied that he hadn't botched up in front of the cameras but was conscious of the fact that he still hadn't shaved or worn an ironed shirt.

'If that's all...'

'Actually, I have a question... Detective,' David Robson cut in.

He'd sat quietly throughout the briefing, choosing instead to chew on a battered old pencil.

Jack bit down on his tongue. 'Of course.'

'Seeing as the estimated time of death was nearly two weeks ago, and that they were both positioned in some kind of ritualistic way, what is Northumbria's police force going to do to alleviate public fears that this may not be a one-off event?'

The room jolted back into life, reporters launching to their feet, as he stood rooted to the spot.

'No further details will be released at this time!' he shouted above the chaos.

Out of the corner of his eye, he saw a smiling Robson make a slithering exit from the room, pencil still in mouth.

Jack practically dragged Watkins back to the office.

'What the hell was that all about?'

'Beats me,' the DS stuttered.

'Unless he committed the murders himself, which would be an immense stroke of good luck, he's being fed information from the inside. I want it sorted.'

DS Christensen entered the room. 'The gaffer wants to see you in his office immediately, boss.'

Jack acknowledged the Scandinavian-born officer, inviting him in. 'Please say you have some good news?'

Christensen shook his head. 'Not yet. I contacted the lab an hour ago to try and chase up those IDs, though.'

That was what Jack liked about the squat, Boris Johnson lookalike; he didn't need prompting to get on in an investigation. Unlike his double, he rarely put a foot wrong, his sense of humour being akin to that of a cyborg. Everybody on the force knew they could rely on him. Barely an inch over five foot, he had the look of a blond hobbit, and walked with a slight limp. Nobody ever said that to his face, though, such was the aura the man carried.

And nobody wanted to know why he had the limp.

'Good, keep me posted.'

Never being one to back down, Jack decided to face up to Edwards straight away.

'What the hell was that about?' the DSI thundered, slamming his meaty fist on the desk.

Jack pulled a seat from the debris that was strewn across the room and planted himself opposite the DSI. 'Isn't it obvious?'

Edwards lashed out again, sending a set of papers flying across the table. 'Someone is taking backhanders from the press, Jack. I want a name. Get it done, or I'll find someone else to do it for me.'

Jack held his ground. 'I always do, don't I?'

The DSI snorted. 'There's always a first.' He leaned over the desk, his stale breath slapping Jack in the face. 'What's to say it isn't you?'

He bristled. 'That's a hell of an accusation, Logan, especially given the length of time we've known each other. You might want to consider what your next words are very carefully.'

His superior officer raised a surrendering hand. 'Fair enough, I didn't mean anything by it.'

Jack stood to leave. 'And lay off Watkins, he's a good policeman. He doesn't need you rampaging around having a pop. Sooner or later, unless you learn how to treat people with a bit of respect, you'll be turfed out. And if you keep going the way you are, you won't have me to deflect things any more.'

'Fine,' Edwards said, slumping into his seat.

Acknowledging the DSI's backtrack, he left the office. Although the run-in with his superior officer had done nothing to stem his oncoming headache, he knew it wasn't really the telling off that had got to him. Somebody had leaked key details to the press, violating serious police code. It wasn't anything particularly new in some regards. Hell, even he had cosied-up once or twice to help get some information on key suspects. This was different, though. There was no doubt about it, somebody had made a big error of judgement. Had they done it for money? Were they being blackmailed?

When he got the chance, he would have to pay a visit to David Robson, shake him down for information. For now, though, he had a meeting to attend.

'Right, you all know why you're here,' Jack told the assembled officers.

'Because we are the best!' Watkins beamed.

'The A-Team,' DC Gerrard added.

Jack smiled. He liked DC Claire Gerrard. Bundles of enthusiasm and a straight-to-the point attitude had earned her a fearsome reputation as an up-and-coming officer on the Northumbrian force. Her staunch feminism often put her at odds with Edwards, but he was old hat. Claire Gerrard was the future. Even though they were superior to her in rank, Jack could tell that both Christensen and Watkins admired her strength of character.

'Aye, something like that,' Jack replied. 'Let's see if we can use some of that spirit to catch this son of a bitch.'

'Shouldn't be too hard with our skillset,' Watkins added.

Christensen merely nodded.

Jack eyed them all. Each of them had their own strengths and they complemented each other well. Watkins had excellent intuition and a calming effect on people, even if he sometimes lacked the conviction to act on his gut instinct. Christensen was a no-nonsense officer, precise and dutiful no matter how mundane the task. With Gerrard's unflappable confidence he couldn't have wished for a better group of people to work with.

The fact that one of them could be a mole didn't sit right with him, though. He trusted them all implicitly. Or, at least, he thought he did. He'd need to be certain who it was before confronting them, that was for sure. In the meantime, he'd play his cards close to his chest.

'Where's DI Russell?' Watkins asked.

'She'll be along later,' Jack said.

The group didn't react. Jack's personal issues with the Bulldog didn't make for an ideal working relationship, but he was the first to admit she was a skilled officer. He was in no doubt she would ultimately be an asset as the investigation moved forward.

'Right, guv,' Gerrard began. 'Just to recap, we have two bodies, as yet unidentified, in Cleadon Hills. Based on what we know, it looks like the killer murdered them, buried them, then came back and dug them up.'

'Leads?' Jack put to her.

She shook her head. 'Nothing yet. The dog walker is clean, and the surrounding area is sparse so witnesses will be at a minimum.'

'Still,' Christensen said. 'It does mean that anybody acting peculiar up there would have been noticed had anybody been about.'

DC Gerrard nodded, continuing to take the lead. 'Indeed, which is why we are focusing on speaking to local residents again to double check if anybody saw anything.'

'It's the right call, obviously,' Jack said. 'But our guy is smarter than that. We can assume he has operated in the early hours of the morning to avoid being seen. Still, let's double check that. Any updates on those IDs?'

'Not yet,' Christensen said. 'We've been searching the missing persons list, though and I'll get back to you when I know more.'

The room fell silent as they processed the information.

'Okay,' Jack continued. 'Did anybody notice anything odd about the scene, any details that stuck out?'

'Yeah,' Watkins interjected. 'Why was the woman's arm around the man's body?'

DC Gerard rolled her eyes. 'Is that so hard to believe?'

Watkins shrugged. 'In a way, yes.'

'I agree,' Jack said. 'I think it's significant. I don't know how yet but I'm sure it is in terms of his thinking.'

'So, what do we think?' Christensen mused. 'Jilted lover?'

Jack wasn't so sure. 'It's too early to tell but let's hope so.'

'Why, guv?' Gerrard asked.

He paused. 'Because, if it is, it means it won't happen again.' They fell silent as the implication sank in. 'Now, let's go, we've got work to do.'

'Yes, guv,' they replied in unison.

Jack watched as the team moved into action. It felt good to have the full group back together again, even if it was under such grim circumstances. Unfortunately for them, they were now a man down. Jack's friend, the profiler and psychologist Frank Pritchard, was no longer around. When the Knifer case was over, Pritchard had retired from the force with immediate effect. Although they'd never spoken about it, he knew Pritchard blamed himself for missed opportunities. It didn't matter that Jack was in charge and that, ultimately, the buck stopped with him. In Frank's eyes it was his own shortcomings, which he put down to age, that had led to unnecessary killings in Newcastle City Centre.

What he wouldn't give for the old man's insight right now.

CHAPTER 4

J ack managed to sneak in to his office unnoticed, despite the furore that had taken hold of the station since the double body discovery. The bacon sandwich he'd wolfed down before work had done nothing to temper his searing headache. He hadn't been able to shift it for some time. Once this case was over, he was determined to see a doctor about it.

'Take a look at that!' Watkins exclaimed from behind a crumpled red-top newspaper. 'What I wouldn't give for...'

'Enough!' he pleaded, massaging his temples.

He'd done his best to avoid the newspapers but had failed when he saw his own mugshot plastered across the front of the *Chronicle*. It was a bad photo, capturing the very moment he'd been hamstrung by David Robson's question. Hell, even Jack would have believed himself to be incompetent looking at that. The double body discovery had been sufficiently gruesome enough to make the national news, albeit after some new EU fallout and American posturing over Iran. As for *Look North*, it was their main story, and all fingers were pointed at him. He might as well have been the murderer for all the press cared.

Grinning, Watkins handed him the newspaper, the picture of a scantily-clad blonde woman with large, blue eyes staring through him.

'Who is she?' he asked.

'Nell Stevens.'

'Am I supposed to know this person?'

Watkins spat his coffee out. 'Do you not watch that talent thing on Channel 5?'

'No, please enlighten me.'

'It's a reality TV thing,' Watkins continued. 'She won a place in that new girl band, Da Girlz.'

'Da Girls?'

'With a z,' he coughed, eyes wandering back to the page.

'Well, once the novelty wears off, I'm sure she can continue her modelling career,' Jack said.

'She does look good in a thong.'

'Wonderful.'

'Anyway, that's not the point.'

'Then what *is* the point?' Jack asked, his patience scraping away.

'The point is she's downstairs waiting to speak to somebody.'

'And you're only just telling me now?'

He grinned. 'Seems as if she's gotten herself a stalker. She was out round the Quayside the other week when some bloke approached her and got a little too close for comfort. Since then, she's been receiving some dodgy mail.'

Jack leaned back and began tapping his pen on the table. It wouldn't be the first time somebody famous had attracted a stalker. Most of the time it came down to jealousy. Sometimes it was just a bloke with a crush. His eyes glanced back over the paper on his desk.

'So,' Watkins continued, 'what do you say?'

'What do I say about what?'

Watkins rolled his eyes. 'Can I do the questioning?'

'Yes, but I'll sit in with you.'

'Oh aye,' Watkins eyeballed him. 'I mean... sorry.'

Jack waved him away, aware that the disclosure about his sexuality was still a topic most of the force were struggling to get their heads around. The two detectives left the office and entered the reception lobby, only to be greeted by a gaggle of flashing cameras.

'What's this all about?' he asked the desk sergeant.

'They followed her in,' she said, motioning towards a small entourage that was sitting waiting near the front window.

'I can see that,' he snapped. 'Get them out of here.'

Blushing, she stood up. 'Right, you lot!' she screeched. 'Out! Now!'

Jack was impressed. Smiling, she sat herself back down as the media scrum waddled out with their cameras between their legs.

'Hello,' Nell Stevens greeted him, pale, penetrating eyes searching his. 'I'm sorry about that, it's an occupational hazard.'

It was hard to believe he was looking at the same person who he'd just seen in the newspaper. For starters, she was wearing clothes; but her expression didn't match the smiling, happy Geordie girl from the tabloids. Dark rings circled her eyes, her gaze flitting its way across the room in nervous starts.

He smiled. 'If you'd like to follow me I can take a statement from you.'

They settled into an interview room on the first floor of the station. Nell Stevens sat, hands fiddling with a bright red handbag. Her nails looked immaculate, reminding him of his ex-wife's fascination with nail polish. Clearing his throat, he pushed the image to the back of his mind.

'Why don't you start at the beginning and tell me what's been going on?' Watkins suggested, switching the recording device on.

'Okay, Mr?'

'Stephen Watkins.'

'It's Detective Sergeant Stephen Watkins,' Jack interrupted. 'Let's keep this professional.'

'Stephen,' she continued. 'I was invited to the Quayside the other weekend...'

'Date?'

'No, it wasn't a date.'

Watkins smiled. 'I mean, what was the date?'

'Oh,' she blushed. 'November tenth.'

'Then what happened?'

'I was dancing in Blue Bamboo, with some friends, when this bloke shoved into me, like...' she began, a tremor in her voice. 'He started getting a little hands-on and my security guards had him tossed out.'

Jack raised his eyebrows and resisted the urge to roll his eyes. 'You have security guards?'

Nell Stevens shrugged. 'You can never be too careful.'

Apparently not. 'Did you get a look at him?'

'Not really,' she said. 'It was dark and it all happened so fast.'

'I see,' he said. 'What leads you to believe that he is the one who has been sending these threatening letters?'

Her gaze met his. 'It has to be. I had no trouble until after that.'

Jack sat back. There were a number of possibilities. Could be a scorned ex. Could be a deluded fan. Could be Mr Hands-on from the bar. Still, he felt it was a long shot to link the two instances. Though he was well aware that you could never rule anything out.

'I've brought the letters here for you to read,' she said, fishing about in the expensive-looking handbag.

'Thank you,' Watkins said, taking the small bundle from her. 'There's a few here.'

'I've been getting one every day,' she said, her eyes taking on a pained look. 'Please help me, I'm not making it up. I'm scared, Stephen,' she said, placing her hand on his arm.

'It's still Detective Sergeant, Miss Stevens,' Jack stated.

'We'll do our best, miss,' Watkins spluttered, his face going almost as red as his hair. 'Meanwhile, if anything else happens, don't hesitate to contact us.' He offered her his contact card.

Jack cornered Watkins afterwards. 'You take the lead on this one but keep me informed. I'll let you do the hard yards,' he said, motioning to the bundle of letters.

'Will do, guv.'

'And let your head lead you, not your...' he said, motioning to Watkins' groin.

'Of course,' Watkins replied, smiling.

Jack left him to it and decided to grab a drink in the canteen. It was empty, save for a couple of PCs. He made his way to the counter where Doreen, a wrinkled chain smoker from Aberdeen, greeted him with a grunt. Her weathered face was almost as haggard as the upholstery.

'Aye?' she asked.

'Orange juice and a brownie, please.'

She eyed his stomach. 'That's three quid,' she said, planting his food onto a grey, plastic tray, complete with food stains.

'Someone call the police,' he joked. 'There's been a robbery.'

Blank face. 'What?'

He left her to it and found a seat at the far edge of the canteen. Pulling out a stool, he sat himself down, taking a large bite out of his chocolate brownie. It was dry, but it'd do. *The diet can start another day*, he told himself.

'Mind if I sit here, guv?'

'Sure.'

DC Gerrard sat down opposite him and placed a bottle of Sprite on the table. 'Is it true Nell Stevens was just here?' she asked, taking a gulp of her lemonade.

'Yes, she's got herself a stalker apparently,' he replied, motioning towards her drink. 'I thought you were all about jasmine tea and boiled water?'

She shrugged. 'Just because I do yoga and run twenty miles a week doesn't mean I can't allow myself a treat once in a while. What's your excuse?'

She had a point. 'Fair enough.'

'So, how's things with what's-her-face?'

'Who?'

'Ginger lass.'

'Rosie? I don't know, how would you feel if your partner left you because he was gay?'

'I'd be supportive,' she replied.

Something told Jack that wasn't strictly true. 'Anyway, don't concern yourself with my private life, focus on the case.'

'I'm a woman, Jack, I can do both.'

'Is that not a bit sexist?'

She took another sip of lemonade. 'Not when it's empowering towards women.'

He pushed his brownie to one side. Suddenly he didn't feel so hungry.

'Look,' she continued. 'I'm only telling you this for your own good. You look like shit.'

'Don't hold back.'

'Thanks, I won't,' she continued. 'It's like you aren't even bothered any more. When was the last time you had a shave? And don't get me started on your lifestyle. Brownies and cigarettes?'

He bashed the table. 'That's enough. I'm too busy trying to solve murders to think about pruning myself. I'll hear nothing more on it.'

'Fine,' Gerrard said. 'Don't say I didn't warn you.'

He tried to change the subject. 'We any further forward on those IDs?'

'Don't think so,' Gerrard said. 'Last I heard, DS Christensen was still putting the frighteners on the lab techs. It's a grim situation, like. Reminds me of the Knifer case.'

He didn't need further reminding about the Newcastle Knifer. The slow progress of that investigation had probably cost the lives of at least two innocent victims, not to mention the prospect of Jack ever being promoted into the top job. Those scars would heal in time but the ones on his chest would be there for life. It wasn't enough that it had forced Pritchard into retirement and put Jack on the sick for six months.

'That David Robson is a right twat, isn't he?' Gerrard said. 'I saw the press conference. He well and truly set you up, guv.'

She was right. Nobody Jack knew had a good word to say about the journalist, even his own colleagues. Still, he always seemed to get the jump on the rest of the press when it came to issues involving the Northumbria police force. He'd have to remember to pay the man a visit at some point.

'I...'

'Boss!' Christensen came barrelling into the canteen, papers in hand. 'I've just got off the phone with the lab.'

'Tell me we have some news,' he said, pushing his juice to one side.

The DS nodded. 'We have an ID.'

CHAPTER 5

Jack assembled the group together in the MIR and motioned for Christensen to break the news to them.

Christensen stood in front of Jack, like the first kid finished in an exam, waving his paper around. 'The man is Travis Kane, thirty-one, works for a local removal company. He's on the database. Nothing major, but enough to have his DNA on record.'

Jack looked around the room. 'Go on.'

'Jessica Lisbie, aged twenty-six, a local girl who was reported missing a few days ago by her mother. She matches the picture,' he said, holding up a printed photo of a smiling young woman. 'We'll have to get the parents in to view the body, though.'

'Why was Kane on the system?' Jack asked.

Christensen shuffled through his notes. 'Assault on a drunken night out.'

'So, other than that, seemingly squeaky clean,' Watkins mused.

Christensen nodded. 'So it seems.'

'You not sure?' Jack asked.

'Just seems to me, boss, if somebody has been done for assault, then they aren't what I'd call clean.'

Jack smiled. Christensen hadn't earned his reputation on the force by accident.

'There must be a link between the two of them.'

'Lovers?' Gerrard suggested.

DI Russell scoffed. 'Unlikely.'

'Why is that?'

The Bulldog motioned to the picture. 'Have you seen him? No, he's definitely not her type.'

'Who knows what her type was?' Jack said. 'But there has to be a link somewhere. Find it.'

DI Russell cast him an icy stare. 'If that's what you think.'

Jack dismissed her. 'It is. We need to move, now.'

Jack stared at their photos once more as he was getting into the car. Jessica Lisbie seemed an attractive woman; slim build, dark hair, pretty features. Travis Kane, on the other hand, looked like a thug who put a lot of thought into how he looked. The mugshot the police had of him showed him to be broad-shouldered with a number of visible tattoos. At first glance, Jack wouldn't have placed them together. Still, what did he know about love? His track record didn't exactly qualify him as an expert.

'Is the FLO on route?'

'Yeah, she's meeting us there,' Christensen said, pulling out of the station.

'Good.'

Family liaison officers were a detective's best friend in a situation like this. If you got a good one, they could be a godsend when a relative of the deceased lost their composure. Grief did strange things to people. Jack could understand that; he'd suffered his own losses over the years.

Not through murder, though.

They spent the majority of the journey in silence and Jack found himself able to watch the Newcastle scenery in peace. The bustle of the city centre, complete with multiple stag dos and drunken youths, thinned out into a leafy suburb as they headed to Lawson Street on the outskirts of the city. Gripping the edge of the seat, he dropped the window a notch, and mentally prepared himself to break the worst news a parent could ever wish to hear. Having a young daughter of his own, despite the limited access he had, made him acutely aware of how horrific this would be.

'Any word from the pathologist?' Christensen broke the silence.

Jack shook his head. 'Not yet. I'll probably pop in after here and put a rush on it.' He was sure he saw a twitch of a smile on the DS's face. 'Something funny?'

'No, boss.' He cleared his throat. 'Just... good luck with that one.'

Ignoring him, he stared out of the window. When it came to Rosie Lynnes, he'd need more than luck.

As they pulled up outside twenty-seven Lawson Street, they were greeted by a young-looking FLO. The lack of lines on her face suggested she was a recent recruit, with an assortment of freckles and a well-styled brown bob adding to her pixie-like appearance.

Jack introduced himself.

'Gemma,' she said in a mouse-like voice. 'Nice to meet you. Nasty business all this, isn't it?'

Indeed it was. Despite having done this numerous times before, Jack still hadn't found the magic formula for delivering bad news. The best he could do was to be open and honest, offering his own condolences.

The Lisbie property was a modestly-sized semi-detached house. A silver Renault Mégane sat on the drive, various ornaments decorated a tidy-looking garden, which looked like it had been mowed recently. A large bay window sat at the front, at the right of a bright, red front door. Two windows stared down at them from the second floor, blinds closed on both. At the top of the house, a small, circular window perched from the rooftop, looking out from what must have been some kind of attic space.

'I'll do the talking,' Jack said as they made their way up the path.

Christensen pressed the doorbell and, seconds later, yelping could be heard in the passageway. A shadow appeared through the frosted glass, before the door flung open, revealing a middle-aged woman holding on to an aggravated West Highland White.

'Can I help—' She stopped short when she saw Jack's ID badge. 'Paul, come down here!' she shouted up the stairs, before turning back to them. 'Oh my God, what's happened?'

Jack cleared his throat. 'Hello, Mrs Lisbie, my name is Detective Chief Inspector Jack Lambert, may I come in?'

Lynn Lisbie directed them through to the living room where they broke the news to her. They sat in silence for what seemed an age before she eventually spoke.

'Would anybody like a cup of tea?'

'Mrs Lisbie, are you okay?' the family liaison officer asked. 'You've just been given some shocking news.'

The mother of Jessica Lisbie merely smiled before straightening her cardigan and heading through to the kitchen. Jack motioned to the FLO, who took leave to follow her through. Paul Lisbie had sat stony-faced as they broke the news that every parent must dread hearing. Only a slight tremor in his leg betrayed any emotion within him.

In the silence, Jack took the opportunity to look around, noticing numerous picture frames dotted about a mahogany mantelpiece. Upon closer inspection, he surmised that Jessica must have had a younger sister. Near the front window, a huge, widescreen TV was mounted to the wall. A busily-patterned cream wallpaper design greeted him from every side of the room, a spotless chestnut-brown carpet finishing the picture. The silence stretched on as Jack shifted on the leather three-piece he was now perching on.

'Mr Lisbie,' he began. 'I'm...'

'For goodness' sake, woman!' he erupted. 'What are you doing?'

Moments later, Lynn Lisbie returned, shaking hands placing a small tea tray onto the coffee table. The FLO followed suit, bringing in a tin of assorted biscuits.

'Paul here likes his tea black, but I prefer milk and sugar,' she fussed.

'Mrs Lisbie...'

'Jessica, though, she loves... loved...' She began to sob.

'I'm so very sorry,' Jack said.

'Don't make a scene,' the father said.

Jack noted Paul Lisbie's temper and his wife's inability to look him in the eye. He swallowed his anger and grasped the seat.

'What happened?' Lynn asked.

'There's no easy way of saying this,' Jack began.

'It's the bodies from the ditch, isn't it?' She clattered her cup onto the saucer, sending a stream of tea over the edge.

'I'm afraid so.'

'There were two of them,' Jessica's father said, his icy gaze piercing through him.

'Yes. The other body was a... Mr Travis Kane,' Jack said, bringing out his notepad. 'I'm sorry about this but it's important that we talk to you about Jessica. Any information we can put together may help us catch the person who did this.'

Jessica's father nodded, reaching over with tattooed hands to pick up his cup. His red pallor suggested he liked to indulge in something stronger than tea. Lynn sat, dabbing her eyes with a cotton handkerchief, her own features bearing a striking resemblance to those of her daughter.

Jack leaned forward. 'Mr and Mrs Lisbie, do you know who Travis Kane is?'

'Never heard of him,' Paul grumbled, rising to grab a half-full bottle of whisky from the corner cupboard, and pausing to throw back a generous helping.

'She never mentioned him at all?'

'No, I'm afraid not,' Lynn said.

'Do you know if Jessica was in a relationship?'

'Not that we know of.'

'Were you close?' he asked.

'She's our daughter!' Paul thundered. 'Was...' he tailed off.

'How long did you wait before reporting her as missing?'

'I don't know, a few days. Jessica doesn't live here any more,' Lynn began, eyes flitting over to her husband. 'She wanted her own space. For the past few months she's been renting somewhere in Jesmond with a friend.'

Christensen, who had been furiously scribbling notes down, spoke. 'Do you know who this friend is?'

She shook her head. 'No, I'm sorry. You don't think they...'

'There's nothing to suggest that,' Jack said. 'We just need to get as full a picture together as possible.'

The FLO placed a hand on her shoulder and Lynn smiled, taking a deep breath.

'What about her sister?' Jack asked, motioning to the mantelpiece.

'Ruth is working abroad on a placement,' Lynn told him.

Jessica Lisbie's father stood, moved over to a side cabinet, and poured another glass of whisky. 'I want to see her,' he said.

'I...'

'Now!' he thundered, smashing the tumbler against the living room wall.

Jack started, shocked by the sudden outburst. Christensen sat, unruffled, as whisky dregs crawled down the wall.

'Paul!' Lynn shouted. 'Just stop it.'

Having concluded their inquiries, they'd taken a look at Jessica's old room, which now seemed to be used for storage. All in all, the trip had proved fruitless for the investigation though. Jack swallowed the disappointment at not having found out more but clung to the hope that her other residence – and flatmate – might prove more useful. Paul Lisbie had made a mumbled apology and left the room following the whisky incident, returning afterwards to see them out. After saying their goodbyes, the FLO had remained with the family to co-ordinate a visit to view the body when the time was right.

Away from the stifling atmosphere of the house Jack glanced up at the sky. The clouds were moulding together into a thick, grey sludge, reflecting his own mood. Sighing, he took out a cigarette and lit up.

'Thought you were going to give those up?' Christensen said.

'You my nurse now?' he replied, offering him one.

Rain began pitter-pattering on the pavement as Christensen waved him away and fished out one of his own. Jack pulled up his collar to battle against the elements as they set a quick pace back to the car, the DS limping ever so slightly.

'What do you think then?' Christensen asked.

'Don't know yet,' Jack said. 'The father has a temper though… and I wonder what happened for their relationship to break down.'

'You think he's implicated in some way?'

'I doubt it,' Jack said. 'He might have a short fuse, but that doesn't mean he's a murderer.'

Christensen nodded, taking a long drag on his cigarette. 'Wonder if Watkins had any luck with Kane.'

'Let's get back to the station and find out,' Jack said, buckling himself in. 'Meanwhile, I want to get a search of Jessica's flat sorted and try to question her flatmate. She may well have been the last person to see her alive.'

They began the short journey back to Northumbria HQ, the city centre traffic becoming hectic as people finished work for the day. Jack took the time to reflect on what had happened so far. There was always the hope that Watkins had uncovered something when talking to the Kane family. Still, doubt was gnawing at his insides, adding to the growing concern he had over just about every aspect of the case so far. Something told him they were going to be in for a difficult time.

CHAPTER 6

'He's been missing for days now,' she said, hands playing with a sodden handkerchief.

She'd been hysterical since arriving at the station over half an hour ago. Jack would have given the task to somebody else but Watkins' lack of information from Travis Kane's family had caused a lull in the investigation. It turned out Travis wasn't close with his family either. As for the link between the victims, his estranged parents had no clue as to who she was. He'd not been reported missing and his employers just thought he had done a runner, given he had a penchant for being unreliable.

Realistically, he could have done with some time to sort out his mounting paperwork, even if only to satisfy Edwards. Not that he ever got on top of his own. Still, policing to him wasn't about ticking boxes, it was about solving crimes. He'd deal with the fallout later.

'Miss Willis...' he began, dragging a calloused hand through his unkempt hair.

'I haven't come here to exchange pleasantries,' she spat. 'Just get out there and find him!'

She folded her arms, covering a swollen belly. Despite the baby weight, Jack got the impression she wasn't leading the healthiest of lifestyles. Dark rings circled her eyes, jet black hair having been scraped back into a ponytail, complete with a bright pink scrunchie.

'Has he disappeared before?'

'I've already told you this, no!'

'Had you argued?'

She shrugged, sallow eyes on anything but him. 'No more than usual.'

'Was he ever violent to you?'

She shifted in her seat. 'No, my Liam is a canny lad.'

'Can you think of any reason why he might have gone missing?'

She shifted again, her gaze falling upon him. 'Look, he's been hanging out with a pretty rough crowd. I've told him hundreds of times before that he needs to get out of that stuff, especially with a baby on the way...' Her voice trailed off.

She was barely eighteen, but something in her face told him she'd lived more than most people twice her age. Lines had already begun making their appearance well before their stage cue. He'd heard this story many times before. Chances were, the bloke had grown sick of the arguing, gotten cold feet, and left. Still...

'Which crowd?' he asked.

'I'm not supposed to say,' she tensed.

'Suzie, how am I supposed to help you if you can't be honest with me?'

'I don't want any trouble.'

'Nobody does. But if Liam is caught up in something then we need to know about it.'

She bit down on a heavily-manicured fingernail, seemingly weighing up her options. 'He works for Dorian McGuinness.'

'Ah.'

'Just when I thought things couldn't get any worse,' Jack said as Watkins manoeuvred the car through the city centre.

'I thought you two were friends?' the DS quipped.

He snorted. Jack had what you might call a 'professional' relationship with Dorian McGuinness, aquatic shop owner and local gangland boss. Back in his younger days, when he was bouncing, he'd come across McGuinness and done some work for him. Once he'd decided to join the force, though, he'd been keen to avoid all of that, not wanting to ruin his chances of a successful career. He'd been honest with him and Dorian had offered to keep the job open should he ever decide police work wasn't for him. In fact, he even once offered to stick him on the payroll. Jack had politely declined and made it clear that he wasn't to be asked again. As it was, his ties with the McGuinness crew had made him the unofficial go-between when questions needed to be asked. It was this uneasy arrangement with which Jack was wrestling as they neared their destination.

'Look, if you want to keep your bollocks, let me do the talking. You just stand there and look hard.'

'Me, hard?' Watkins squeaked. 'Why?'

'Because he can smell fear. And, trust me, he'll use it against you.'

'Could you not have brought Christensen?'

'No, he's busy. Just think of this as useful training.'

They left the car down a grubby side street, not far from the Gate, a central hub in Newcastle's boisterous nightlife. It was also a central pain in the arse for most of the police who had to work the area on a weekend. Jack shivered against the elements. He'd read they were in for a tough winter this year. He could practically hear Watkins' teeth chattering as they approached the shop. The DS was right, Christensen probably would have been a better choice, but he was busy following up an incident near Central Station which had occurred the previous night.

Cheap, wooden, wind chimes rang out as he opened the door to 'McGuinness Aquatics.' The smell of fish food hung heavy in the air, mixed in with the unmistakable scent of potent marijuana. The drugs were an issue they could deal with another time. Right now, they had more serious things to discuss. As they made their way inside, two aisles greeted them, both leading to a small serving counter at the back. A man sat there leafing through *The Sun* newspaper, shaved head appearing above the pages.

Arnold 'Tank' Mohan, complete with cheap aftershave.

Jack cleared his throat as they approached, squeezing past a plethora of tropical fish. Tank didn't look up.

He decided to try a more direct approach. 'Hello, Arnold.'

The man grunted and dropped the paper on the desk, leaving a double-paged spread of Nell Stevens gazing up at them. The headline read: Stunner Stalked as Police do Nothing!

'What do you want, pig?'

Jack stared him down.

The man known as 'the Tank' glared at him, each eye a different colour. Stubble lined his square jaw, a faint knife scar visible on his left cheek. Nobody was certain how he'd gotten the nickname, but Jack had heard it was due to his explosive temper, which had led – amongst other things – to him storming a local gym and beating a rival gang member half to death. He'd been a key cog in McGuinness's inner ring for as long as Jack could remember.

'Who the fuck is that?' Tank motioned to Watkins. 'Looks like a ginger rat.'

'Hey!' Watkins started.

'I'm looking for Dorian,' he cut in.

'Who?'

Jack sighed. 'Come on, Tank, we can do this the easy way or the hard way.' He hoped it'd be the former; sure, he could handle himself, but a fight with Arnold Mohan on enemy lines wasn't something he fancied right now.

'What you want the boss for?'

'Some fish, obviously.'

The squat man snorted, thumping a heavy fist down on the table. Anybody who cared to think about it knew the fish shop was just a front for the local mobs' array of activities. They'd spent years trying to tie Dorian McGuinness down to something, but nothing would stick. Edwards had known about Jack's loose affiliation with the gangster and had hoped to exploit it. However, McGuinness was too smart for that.

'Supposing he was out?' Tank sneered.

'Then I'd come back with a warrant and drag him in for questioning; and he'd most definitely find out whose fault it was,' Jack told the heavy.

'Wait here,' he grunted, heading through a blue drape.

'Why do they call him Tank?' Watkins asked.

'No idea,' Jack said. 'And why are you whispering?'

The DS cleared his throat. 'Dunno.'

Seconds later a scraping sound could be heard from behind the drape. Jack tensed. He made to warn Watkins but was too late as the giant Rottweiler hurtled through the curtain and lunged for him. He'd forgotten about the guard dog.

'Get it off me!' Watkins shrieked, crashing to the floor.

'Lucy, come!' Tank shouted, reappearing in the doorway. 'Seems you brought along your own bitch,' he chuckled, dragging the salivating dog back by a heavy chain.

'So, is Dorian in or not?'

'Aye, he's through the back; you know the way.'

The two detectives headed through into a dusty corridor laced with numerous wooden crates. Jack loathed to think what was in those boxes, but thought better than to check; at least not without backup.

'Detectives, how can I help you?' Dorian McGuinness greeted them as they entered his dark office laced with cigar smoke and various pieces of expensive art.

Apart from the smog, however, it was remarkably tidy. A small window sat to the left with iron bars cut across it. Dorian was sitting at a large oak table, glasses perched on his long nose, flanked by two heavies, one of whom was holding a joint.

'Hello, Dorian,' he said. 'I have a few questions to ask you.'

'Jack, I've not seen you in weeks. You don't call, you don't write, what's a man to think?'

The heavy to the left snorted and Dorian turned his stare upon him. He didn't take long to compose himself.

'I've been busy catching criminals.'

The mob boss let out a booming laugh before straightening down his suit jacket, which covered a purple dress shirt that was open halfway down his hairy chest, a gold medallion finishing the picture. His jet-black hair was slicked back from his massive forehead, giving him a distinctly seventies disco look. Dorian McGuinness certainly wasn't like most crime lords in the area. First of all, he maintained a fairly public persona, even campaigning to be a local councillor at one point. He almost won, too. McGuinness also happened to be an openly gay man in a world that wasn't exactly socially liberal. Still, nobody was likely to hassle him about it. Jack had heard stories about one rival who'd been brave – or stupid – enough to have a go at him. Rumour had it, Dorian had chopped off his manhood, and fed it to him, remarking that they now, 'both eat cock.'

Jack could well believe it.

'So, tell me, why are you here?' His eyes narrowed, pleasantries seemingly finished with.

'Liam Reed.'

Jack sought to look for any trace of reaction from the man. If he did know something, Dorian McGuinness was far too well versed to give it away.

'I know Liam, he does the odd job for me.'

'Delivering fish?'

The booming laugh came back. 'Something like that.'

'He's gone missing, is all; still, I'm betting you already knew that.'

His tone darkened. 'I sincerely hope you are not pointing the finger in my direction, Detective.'

'When did you last see him?'

McGuinness shrugged. 'A few days ago, maybe a week.'

'Do you have any idea what might have happened to him? His fiancée is very distressed.'

'Ah, Suzie, she is a nice girl. Punching above his weight, I'd say.'

The charm was lost on Jack.

'So you don't think much of him?'

'I never said that.'

Jack studied the crime boss. 'I don't suppose you're going to help me out on this one, are you, Dorian?'

McGuinness raised a large hand to his designer-stubbled chin and scratched, light reflecting from the small window off his gold rings. 'Liam's disappearance has been brought to my attention.'

'Maybe he wanted an out.'

'Detective, you offend me.' He grinned. 'If any of my staff wish to leave, they need only ask.'

'Did Liam ask?'

'He might have.'

'That can't have pleased you much.'

'Not at all, as long as an employee works his period of notice. Liam understood that. I was happy for him to leave. Fish selling isn't for everyone,' he added, smiling.

'Well, if you hear anything, you have my number,' Jack said, turning to leave. 'Oh, and I notice you've had a pretty large delivery. Business booming, is it?'

McGuinness smiled, showing an assortment of gold teeth. 'My business always booms, Detective. You see, there's just no competition left.'

They were back in the car before Watkins spoke. 'What do you think?'

Sporadic splotches of rain had begun landing on the windscreen as Jack pulled out a cigarette. Gazing at the nicotine stick, he decided against it. McGuinness's office had given him a weekly fix. The wind had picked up, sending litter flying across the road from where they'd parked. A council worker, struggling with his luminous hood, went scuttling after it.

'He's an excellent liar, but my gut tells me he hasn't done anything to the bloke.'

'That's a relief.'

'Is it?'

'Well perhaps he's just run off,' Watkins said. 'Maybe the pregnancy put the frighteners on him?'

'I hope so,' Jack sighed, popping another paracetamol. 'Because if somebody else has done something to him, you can bet Dorian McGuinness isn't going to let it lie. He'll be conducting his own, private investigation. And you can bet your house on him dishing out his own particular brand of justice.'

Jack just hoped that they could get to them first, before the war started.

If it hadn't already.

CHAPTER 7

It was 6.30am when the phone rang. Throwing the covers back, he tried to recall what he'd been dreaming about. His usual Newcastle Knifer dreams had been replaced by a new set of dark visions. Since the discovery of the two bodies in the ditch nearly a week ago, he'd not been able to scratch the images from his mind. He'd lost count of the amount of times he had woken up in a cold sweat, dead bodies reaching up out of the ground to pull him down.

'Hello?' He yawned into the receiver.

'Jack, it's Louise.'

If Louise was ringing him, it must be bad. Having started a brief relationship when they were both in their early twenties, they soon found out she was pregnant. Although they both knew they weren't right for each other they had made an effort because of Shannon. Then he'd met Rosie and he thought that was what he wanted. He could still remember the night he broke the news to her; she'd merely nodded and left, taking their daughter with her. They'd been amicable since then but rarely had any conversation outside of family matters. Deep down, though, it had all been a charade. He just wished he hadn't pulled Rosie into it.

'What's happened?' he asked, suddenly alert.

'It's your father,' she replied.

After fishing for the details, he replaced the receiver and threw last night's clothes on. He brushed his teeth with a newly-bought electric brush, quickly adding some spray before heading downstairs. Ten minutes and one scalding cup of coffee later, he was outside in the crisp morning air, heading over to the Freeman Hospital. Pushing through the slow, automatic doors, he felt his chest tighten as memories of his mother's long illness came flooding back.

'Hello, Dad,' his daughter greeted him on the ward.

'Shannon, honey, it's good to see you,' he said, offering her an awkward hug.

He noticed the tenseness of her body. Pulling away, he looked her over. She'd grown up so much in the last year, he thought, and he'd missed most of it. Sure, the job was demanding, but he had to do better before it was too late. Her usual bright pink clothing had been replaced by a more Gothic look and, judging by the colour of her cheeks, she'd started wearing make-up too; at eleven years old.

'He's in here.'

'You've grown your hair,' he commented.

'It's been like this for ages, Dad.'

They entered the ward, four of the six beds occupied by old men with varying levels of sickness. The first housed a man who looked in his mid-fifties, heavily tattooed, with an oxygen mask on. A family sat by the next bed – in sorrowful silence – as a frail-looking man lay asleep. Various machines and mounted TV sets gave out faint sounds, a mild respite to the sick and dying. Jack suddenly felt very warm. The fact that the hospital had allowed them in outside of the usual visiting times told him all he needed to know.

His father was lying in a bed by the window. He was asleep, his breaths coming in short, sharp gasps. He tried to suppress the sadness he now felt as he looked upon the man who had raised him, but who was practically a stranger. Quietly, he pulled up a small plastic chair and sat by the edge of the bed.

'Hello, Jack,' a familiar voice greeted him from behind.

'Louise,' he said. 'You didn't have to come.'

'I'm here for Shannon,' she snapped, then – her face softening – added, 'but if there's anything you need...'

They settled into an uncomfortable silence. Jack sporadically picked at the grapes someone had brought in for his father. He loved grapes, but they felt tasteless to him as he sat with the three people who, just a few years before, had been the people closest to him.

He noticed that Louise had also grown her hair, much like Shannon's. Shannon had inherited her mother's striking looks, green eyes and jet-black hair. Divorce had obviously served her well. Not that he was bitter. Even though they'd both been unhappy, the breakup had been his fault and his fault alone. The look in Shannon's eyes told him she agreed.

'How's Jeremy?' he asked, referring to her partner.

'Don't pretend like you care,' she said.

'Can you two not get on for just one day?' Shannon scolded.

He looked to his daughter, all grown up. It used to be him that told her off.

'You're right,' Louise sighed, placing a hand on her arm. 'I'm sorry about Harold.'

He glanced to his father. It was probably a good job he was asleep. He loved Louise like she was his own daughter. He probably wished she was. When they'd divorced, he'd blamed his son, the last remnants of an already strained relationship cut forever. His father had never wanted him to join the police force, preferring a trade such as a carpenter or electrician. 'Real work,' as he'd put it. Harold Lambert would have preferred his son down the mines, but Thatcher had seen that one off. Jack's disdain for reactionary politics, coupled alongside a career with 'the enemy,' had put paid to any pleasantries between them. When he told his father that he was gay, the old man had merely snorted, picked up a newspaper and told him he could see himself out.

Hence Louise finding out about his admission to hospital before he did.

His father roused. 'Carl?'

His eyelids forced open, the whites of his eyes having turned a dark shade of yellow, much like the rest of his skin. If he didn't get a new liver soon it would be too late.

'No, Dad, it's me,' he said, placing a hand on his father's clammy arm.

The old man squinted at him. Carl, his younger brother, was off globetrotting on some biochemical adventure as the head of a major corporation. He got to travel, earning five times what Jack did. A job to be proud of, apparently.

And he was straight.

'Ah.' The old man coughed, before closing his eyes.

At 10am Jack arrived at the station, his mood as dark as the black coffee he'd picked up along the way.

'Where have you been?' The desk sergeant stopped him.

'In hell,' he sighed. 'Why?'

'Edwards' meeting, remember?'

No, he hadn't remembered. Necking the caffeine hit, he binned the cup and hurtled up the stairs.

'Detective Lambert, how nice of you to join us.' Edwards eyeballed him.

The whole room turned and stared. Jack ignored the passive aggression and planted himself next to Watkins who had saved him a seat.

'Where were you?' he whispered.

He shrugged. Getting into his family history wasn't something he was interested in right now. Glancing around the room, he saw there were a dozen or so officers who had been summoned to attend the meeting. They all looked how he felt. Edwards' meetings were legendary in that everybody would rather be out on nightshift, getting puked on by a drunk outside the Crown and Anchor, than listen to one of his monotonous rants.

'As I was saying!' the DSI bellowed, narrowing his eyes in Jack's direction. 'I know we all have busy caseloads right now, but this double murder has to take priority. Since the press got hold of the story, the public have been drummed up into a frenzy. We need results and we need them fast.'

His superior officer grabbed a morning paper from the table he had propped himself onto, holding the front page up for all to see. The image of the grassy knoll – where they'd discovered the two bodies of Jessica Lisbie and Travis Kane – appeared front and centre.

'Detective Inspector Jane Russell has an update on the Travis Kane angle. Jane, if you wouldn't mind filling the officers in on the details.' Edwards motioned, shuffling out of the way.

This was news to Jack. As senior investigating officer he should have been the one calling the shots and, indeed, they were already chasing up leads on the male victim. He glared towards the DSI who was looking anywhere but at him.

DI Jane Russell sprang to her feet and hopped up to face the room. Seeming to take a dislike to the patch of table that Edwards had been leaning on, she scooted across to the other side and placed a light blue coloured folder on table before clearing her throat.

'Thank you, sir,' she said, straightening down her suit jacket and glancing over the assembled officers. 'I took the liberty of preparing a few pictures to help go over some of the key details and keep people focused.'

As if on cue, the lights dimmed and the silence was broken by the sound of a projector whirring into life. He could feel the room give a collective groan as she fished about in the folder.

'Fiver says somebody gets caught sleeping,' Watkins whispered.

'You're on,' he replied. 'And make it a tenner.'

The Bulldog clicked the control, a gruesome picture of the two, bloated corpses flashing up in the process. Jack heard somebody gasp a few rows back. Up ahead, DC Gerrard seemed to be casting an interested look over the images as a number of other officers settled in for the show.

'These are the bodies that were found just days ago in Cleadon Hills, South Shields. As of right now, we have very little to go on but I'm hoping that will soon change. After putting a rush on the lab, we have identified the victims as twenty-six-year-old Jessica Lisbie and thirty-one-year-old Travis Kane. Whilst Jack is leading the investigation into the female deceased—' he saw a grimace work its way over her pointed-features '—I have been speaking to the family of Mr Kane.'

Although the DI was talking, Jack was unable to take his eyes from the bodies on the screen. It was almost as if he were back in the tent, looking at them for the first time. The scent that had hit his nostrils reappeared in his psyche.

'Although not ideal, the press leaks may now work in our favour.' Jack zoned back in to the briefing. 'If it helps in getting witnesses to come forward, we might be able to get the ball moving with regards to possible suspects. Personally, I feel that I can handle this situation perfectly well, but...'

'Ahem,' Edwards cut in. 'The investigation will be operating under DCI Jack Lambert's command. Hopefully we can draw a swift conclusion to this one before they send in extra help.'

Jane sent daggers his way but, for Jack, the feeling was mutual. Still, there was no point in getting too upset about her need to massage her ego. Her ambition was what ultimately held her back.

Edwards was right, though. Although they had a large and well-drilled force, they didn't want outsiders to be called in. The press would have a field day. Something similar had happened down in Manchester, not long ago, and the entire force was struggling to repair the damage it had done to its public image.

'Also,' Edwards continued, 'as you know, our usual criminal profiler is currently unavailable,' he said, referring to her pregnancy. 'So, as of tomorrow, Frank Pritchard will be temporarily coming out of retirement to help us.'

Jack smiled. He'd been the one to suggest they bring Pritchard back in. Expecting a straight 'no' from the psychologist, he'd been surprised by the old man's enthusiasm at the idea of coming back. Having him back would feel like a blast from the past, the two of them having worked closely on a whole host of cases in years gone by. Edwards, unable to see past old school methods of deduction, was not the man's biggest fan.

'Anyway, as I was saying,' DI Jane Russell continued, flicking to the next picture, a close up shot of the bodies. 'Things are probably going to start moving pretty fast. Let's just hope everybody can keep up.' She shot a cursory look towards Jack.

'Thank you, Detective.' Edwards stood up as the lights flickered back on.

'This is going to get interesting,' he mumbled to Watkins.

'That's one way of looking at it.' The DS grinned.

'Thank you all for your time,' Edwards said, breaking up the meeting. 'Oh, and Harriet?' he called to the back of the room. 'If you want to sleep, do it in your own time, not mine.'

'Shit,' Jack cursed, fishing out a ten pound note.

'Just so you know.' DI Russell cornered him as he stood to leave. 'I'm perfectly capable of leading this one up without you. There's no need to busy yourself with it.'

'Well, I like to keep myself busy. Keep in touch, Detective.' He moved past her, towards the front. 'I'll be expecting daily reports on my desk by 9am.'

He was sure he could still hear the grinding of her teeth, long after she'd left the room.

'What's crawled up her arse?' Watkins asked, holding up his winnings.

'Same old,' he said. 'It's real, don't worry.'

'And where the hell were you?' Edwards collared him.

Jack held his posture. Although he was a touch over six foot, and not exactly skinny, Edwards' frame dwarfed his own. He'd known the DSI for many years and, whilst others thought him incompetent, he'd always had a grudging respect for the man and his methods. At least he was consistent in his approach. He'd be damned if he was going to be treated like some kid on work experience, though.

'Logan, I don't have to account for my every movement,' he told him. 'But, seeing as you're curious, I was visiting the old man in hospital.'

'Ah... is everything okay?' he backtracked.

'Not really, but he's been ill for some time,' Jack said. 'You mind telling me what all that was about?'

'Look, she asked if she could get up and speak. You weren't here...'

'Let's get one thing clear,' he snapped. 'Either I'm SIO or I'm not. I can deal with Jane and her God complex, but I don't need you undermining me as well.'

Edwards shrank back, placing a hand on his forehead. The man looked like he was about to keel over. 'I need you two on side, here,' he said. 'The ACC is up my arse on this one, not to mention the new PCC.'

PCCs, or Police and Crime Commissioners as they were commonly known, were a recent initiative from the government. Not happy with the already sickening levels of Americanisation in British society, they'd stolen the idea of 'sheriffs' from their Atlantic neighbours. The new Northumbria PCC had a reputation for being hands-on, constantly hosting meetings with officers to discuss public grievances, no matter how large or small. If the ACC was getting hassle, there was no doubt the DSI would be next in the firing line.

'Let me do my job, Logan.'

Edwards shook his head. 'It's the ACC, I swear. I have faith in you, Jack, I always have. But we're all under pressure here.'

Jack brushed him off. 'If there's nothing else I have a dinner date to get to.'

'Who's the lucky lady? She got cracking legs?' Edwards winked. 'Ah, sorry.'

'No, he most definitely doesn't.'

Jack found him sitting on a stool by a large side window. He made a beeline for him, cracking his knuckles as he approached. Taking a deep breath, he tried to remain calm.

'Ah, Jack, it's good to see you.' David Robson held out a clammy palm.

He declined it. 'Save the niceties, Robson.'

So much for calm. He ordered a J2O and a side of onion rings before settling down for the private chat that the journalist had requested. Jack had wanted to speak to him anyway but, as it turned out, Robson had contacted him first. He glanced over at his host, the familiar twitching moustache manoeuvring around his upper lip.

'Look, I'm sorry about the press conference.' He held his palms up. 'But it is my job, you know.'

'Who's the mole?'

Robson shook his greasy head. 'You know I can't give that information out, Jack... even if there was one.'

He stood to leave. 'Then we are done here.'

'Wait!' the journalist pleaded. Jack noted the tremor in his voice. 'Maybe I can help you.'

He took a swig of juice. 'I know how this works, Robson. What is it you're after?'

Indeed, he did know only too well. David Robson had done a great job of making the entire force look foolish over the Newcastle Knifer case, Jack in particular. Pritchard always used to say that there were two types of journalist. One, the moral journalist, of real use to the police, genuinely caring about the welfare of the public. Two, the selfish journalist, only concerned about his or her own pay cheque, no matter what the cost to others. David Robson definitely came under the latter.

The reporter picked up his whisky tumbler and swirled it around before taking a small sip, moisture lining his mouth as he cleared his throat to speak. 'I'm in a spot of bother.'

Jack resisted the urge to laugh. 'So, what's that got to do with me?'

Both men paused as the barmaid brought the onion rings over, plonking them down in front of Robson. He made to grab one before Jack swatted him away.

'Well... you're a policeman, aren't you?' he stuttered. 'Sworn to protect and serve.'

He shrugged. 'Depends what mood I'm in.'

'Look, I know you're looking for somebody who used to work for a certain... aquatic shop-owner.'

Jack lowered his voice and felt his temper rise. 'How do you know that?'

The shift in Robson's usual cocky demeanour was remarkable. Sweat was beading from his brow, his eyes darting about the bar.

'Look,' his voice lowered. 'There's a war coming to these parts and it's coming soon.'

'Over what?'

'Territory.'

Jack shrugged. 'So someone is moving in on McGuinness's patch. What's that got to do with me?'

Robson paused, bringing a hand across his forehead. 'Because when the bodies start piling up, you'll be left picking up the pieces.'

Jack thought about it. Robson was right; if another gang decided to encroach on Dorian McGuinness's patch, he'd be certain to react. Sometimes it's better the devil you know.

'So how are you involved?'

He pulled at his collar. 'I dug a little too deep and they know that I know something. It's only a matter of time before they come for me.'

'And what do you know?'

'I'll be a dead man if I speak about it. I shouldn't even be sat here with you now.'

Jack reached for an onion ring but found his appetite had deserted him. There was no doubt that Robson was spooked, which didn't happen very often. Still, he couldn't exactly set up surveillance outside the man's house twenty-four hours a day. Pushing his food towards the journalist, he stood to leave. 'Do you know what has happened to Liam Reed?'

'No.'

Jack nodded, the look between them giving him all the information he needed. Liam Reed was long gone. The question was, who was next?

CHAPTER 8

Jack spent the night stewing over what Robson had told him in the bar, feeling unsure of his next move. They'd have to start watching McGuinness closely. That was easier said than done, though. Dorian McGuinness was no mug. He would be alert to anything unusual and, if he really was hiding something, Jack didn't want to frighten him into doing anything rash.

Six years ago, the police had reason to believe that McGuinness was involved in protection racketeering – still did, in fact. But back then they had a witness who was willing to testify in court. However, two weeks before the trial the witness mysteriously had his kneecaps realigned after a bar-room 'altercation.' After that, he refused to talk and the case collapsed.

'We need to talk, guv,' Watkins said, greeting his boss as he entered the bustling MIR.

'What is it?'

'Nell Stevens? Looks good in a thong?'

Jack waved him away. 'I know. What about it?'

'There's been another incident.'

'Tell me,' Jack said.

'Well, there's been a break-in. Nothing was taken but we're running checks on potential fingerprints. Whoever it was smashed up the place.'

'Does she not have some kind of top-of-the-range security installed in her home?' Jack asked. Most local celebrities did.

'Sorry, did I not mention it wasn't her house?' Watkins said.

'Not her house? Then which bloody house was it?' he snapped. 'Details, Watkins.'

'Her mother's.'

Jack sat at a nearby desk and gathered his thoughts. If the stalker had attacked Nell Stevens' mother's house, then it had to be somebody she knew. It wouldn't take a genius to find which mansion the younger woman had purchased. But the mother? Something wasn't adding up. Pausing, he focused on what he already knew. Nell Stevens had found fame, fortune and, potentially, a stalker. She goes to a well-known bar on the Quayside and meets with unwanted attention. After this, she starts receiving threatening notes. Now there's been a break-in, but at her mother's house, not her own.

'What are you thinking?' Watkins asked.

'I'm thinking look into it and keep me posted.'

'Surely this is below your pay grade?'

'Let's just say it's piqued my interest,' he replied. 'I would imagine the break-in at the mother's house was a coincidence.'

'She doesn't think so.'

Jack shrugged. If the stalker had taken the time to break into her mother's house, the odds were that he knew her prior to the reality show being aired. However, if she already knew the perpetrator, then surely she would have recognised him in the bar. He scratched at his ever-growing beard, lightly tapping the desk with a chewed biro. Either there were two stalkers, his theory on her knowing him was wrong *or...* no idea.

He massaged his temples, trying to fit the pieces together. Was there something he wasn't seeing? Either way, they had to investigate the break-in. Watkins could sort it out but, like he'd said, his interest had been piqued. Plus, the lack of headway in the double murder case was beginning to bother him. He needed the distraction.

'I see police work still doesn't agree with you,' a familiar voice said. 'You've aged about ten years since I last saw you.'

Jack smiled. 'Pritchard, it's good to see you.'

The stout criminal psychologist took his hand in a warm embrace, his eyes looking as alert as Jack had seen them for some time. By the end of his distinguished career with the Northumbria force, there'd been a distinct lack of life in the old man; in no small part down to the gruesome Newcastle Knifer case. Last time Jack had seen him, though, the profiler had been cultivating his own crop of vegetables. It seemed as though his time away from the force was doing him good. He'd put on a little weight, but he'd always been 'big boned' as he'd called it. His usual small, square glasses were perched on the end of his wide nose, cheeks a little redder than he'd remembered them.

'Well, you know me, always wanting to help.'

'Let me bring you up to date,' he said, handing Pritchard a thick folder of documents once they arrived at his office.

'I see you still like to keep things untidy,' he replied, leafing through the contents.

Jack motioned to the murder wall, as he called it, at the side of the office. Pictures of Travis Kane and Jessica Lisbie lined the whiteboard, pre and post death. Around them, he had made a plethora of notes, searching for some link between the two of them. So far, he'd had no luck. Just what did a twenty-six-year-old marketing graduate have in common with a thirty-one-year-old removal man?

'We've had no leads, as such, so far.' Jack forced his eyes away from the pictures of dead bodies. 'That's where I'm hoping you can come in.'

Pritchard replaced his glasses and moved the folder contents aside. 'Well then I'll need to see the bodies.'

Jack was glad that Rosie had already completed the autopsies prior to them visiting the morgue. It wasn't that he was unable to cope with the cutting up of dead bodies, merely that he didn't want to have to spend his time there in awkward silence. The discomfort wasn't lost on Pritchard, who had taken great joy in ribbing him about it on the way there.

'Rosie,' he greeted her, forcing himself to meet her gaze.

'DCI Lambert,' she said, emotionless. 'Frank, it's good to see you again, I'd heard you were coming back.'

The profiler smiled. 'Yes, it seems the force is lost without me.'

You're not wrong, Jack thought.

The three of them pushed through the double doors into the examining room. The chronic smell of detergent and death created a potent mix, every surface seemingly scrubbed to within an inch of its life. As they approached the two bodies, Jack could practically taste the bleach.

Rosie, suited and booted, pulled the pale, green sheets back to reveal the two victims. 'I'll cut to the chase,' she said. 'Estimated time of death was correct. I'd put it between three and four weeks ago from where we are now.' She moved round to the other side of the table, facing the two of them. 'Toxicology reports show nothing untoward. That doesn't mean there isn't something there, just that it's not been detected so far. I maintain the cause of death was strangulation.' She pointed to the neck of Travis Kane. 'Judging by the nature of the bruising, I would say the killer used his hands. I say *he*, it could be a she, but the marks are consistent with a larger specimen. Given the lack of evidence under the fingernails, one can assume they were bound at the moment of death, which is confirmed by the ligature marks on both wrists and feet. It all looks very neat. The girl—' she motioned to the corpse '—has a broken nose, but I'd say it was a fairly old injury; older than a few weeks, anyway.'

Jack moved around the table to get a better look, brushing Rosie's arm by accident. In a flash, she jerked away, fumbling over some papers. Pritchard raised his eyebrows before gazing down over the victim.

'Any signs of sexual abuse?' Jack asked.

The pathologist shook her head. 'There's nothing to suggest any sexual activity took place.'

'Oh, there was definitely a sexual element to it,' Pritchard said.

'I'm sorry, Pritchard, but if there was, I'd have found traces.'

The old man waved her away. 'Not in that sense,' he said. 'But, our killer definitely derives sexual pleasure from this.'

'Go on,' Jack urged.

'Well,' he started, before his phone began ringing. 'I'm sorry,' he said, fishing it out. 'I have to take this.'

Jack noted the look of panic on Rosie's face as Pritchard left the room. As the silence grew awkward, he looked down at the almost peaceful-looking body of Jessica Lisbie, no doubt in stark contrast to the moments leading up to her death.

'So, how have you been?' he asked her.

'Really?' she sighed.

'Well what am I supposed to say?'

She shook her head. Truth be told, he had no idea what he wanted her to say. All he could muster in himself were feelings of regret at how things had turned out.

'Just because things are bad between us, doesn't mean I don't still care.'

'Well you have a funny way of showing it,' she said, pausing. 'Look at what you've done to me,' she said, tears forming in her eyes. 'This is what I've become.'

He made to move towards her.

'No!' she shouted. 'You don't get to be that person any more. Besides,' she said, straightening. 'I've met somebody. He's called Alan. He works in counselling and, more importantly, he's not you.'

'I...'

A flustered Pritchard walked in, the look on his face telling Jack he knew he'd arrived at an awkward time. He cleared his throat, leaning over the edge of the table as Rosie turned away from them both. Jack was pleased she'd met somebody. She deserved to be happy. He couldn't say the same for himself.

'So, as I was saying, the killer derives sexual pleasure from this, for sure. The fact that he's put them in a grave is suggestive enough. The fact that he has returned to dig them up proves he takes pleasure from it. He's gone back to the scene of the crime to relive what happened.'

'I'm starting to like this less and less,' Jack said.

Pritchard eyed him. 'So you should. The neat nature of the killing and burial tells us he's organised, calm, collected and clinical.

I'd expect him to be of above-average intelligence and fully aware of what he's doing, prior to doing it.'

That was what Jack was afraid of.

Back in the MIR it took them less than ten minutes to fill everybody else in on the details, the information met with stony silence.

'Remember,' Pritchard told the assembled group, 'we are most likely looking for a white man in his thirties or forties, and he's probably got a job which holds regular hours through the day.'

DC Gerrard raised her hand. 'Why is that, sir?'

Pritchard replaced his glasses and stopped twirling his eyebrow, legs rocking on the spot. 'Two things. One, would you commit these crimes through the day, with a good chance of being caught, especially if you had a high level of intelligence? No, and the level of planning and execution involved, pardon the pun, suggests he has plenty of time around his work life. It may even be that he works part-time. This man is clever. My best guess is that he's a weekday worker, with a normal to busy social life and higher than average IQ. I would hazard a guess that he stalks his victims, then either kidnaps or talks them into being alone with him, before committing the murder. I know it's not ideal, but it's the best I've got for now.'

'And what about the second thing?' DI Russell asked.

Pritchard smiled. 'The law of averages, my dear. It's almost always a man in that demographic.'

The room nodded in collective approval, no doubt impressed with Pritchard's straight-to-the-point approach. Looking to the corner of the room, Jack saw that Edwards had slipped in unnoticed. The DSI glared at Jack, rolled his eyes, and left.

Yep, definitely old school.

Jack concurred. He'd made the connection, himself, when having first witnessed the grave. Disorganised killers more often than not killed out of some form of passion or mental instability. Organised killers were a much more sinister bunch. The Newcastle Knifer had been the former. He'd not gone to great lengths to cover his tracks, but they'd still made a hash of catching him. Judging by what he'd seen so far, they were dealing with somebody completely different now.

'None of this is good news to me, Pritchard,' Jack said.

'Oh, it gets better,' he replied. 'You want to hope he had a personal vendetta against them, otherwise it's clear to me that we'll be dealing with...'

He didn't need to say it. They all knew

CHAPTER 9

'Y ou came!' Watkins greeted him.

'It's a Friday, isn't it?' Jack said, pushing towards the bar as Watkins moved through the crowd.

Truth be told, he didn't much feel like doing anything. Back in his early twenties, he'd been one of the first to the bar. Nowadays, he preferred to drink in solitude.

'What'll it be, mate?' a young, spiky-haired barman asked.

'Becks.'

Looking about the bar for the rest of them, it seemed to Jack that Pilgrim Street was quite the place for young people with square-framed glasses and tweed jackets. The smell of aftershave and sweat clung to him as he attempted to wade through the sea of trendy folk, towards people he knew.

'Hello, stranger,' a familiar voice greeted him.

'DC Gerrard.'

The policewoman rolled her eyes. 'Really, guv?'

He rolled them back. 'Really.'

He followed the DC away from the bar, noting how different she looked out of uniform. She was wearing a black pencil skirt and a loose, red top. She'd tied her hair up and had put on some crimson lipstick. There was no denying it, Claire Gerrard was an extremely attractive woman. At one time, he might have convinced himself that he fancied her. He was surprised Watkins hadn't already made a play.

'There he is,' Watkins said, a little too loudly.

Jack pulled up a seat. 'Here I am,' he said.

'I need a good drink with all this Open Grave Murderer business.'

'Open Grave Murderer?' Jack asked.

Watkins turned to him. 'You should read the papers more; that's what they're calling him.'

Jack wasn't surprised. They loved a good nickname for their killers. 'Did Christensen not come out?'

Watkins snorted. 'You having a laugh? The Scandinavian Cyborg never comes out.'

'You should say that to his face,' he said.

Watkins coughed, sending a spray of blue WKD all over the table. 'You mad? He'd break my neck.'

'Can we please not talk about work,' Claire said. 'I want to have a good time tonight.'

Jack shrugged and took another sip of beer. In his experience, these social events often turned into off-the-record work meetings.

'Been anywhere nice on your afternoon off?' Watkins asked.

Jack shrugged. He'd spent the day poring over paperwork. 'Not really.'

'Oh, by the way,' Watkins said. 'You know Megan, right?'

Jack noticed the young woman sat next to Watkins, who seemed to not mind the fact that the DS had his hand on her knee. 'The FLO?'

'Yeah,' she said. 'Sorry we didn't get properly introduced before, you know...'

Jessica Lisbie's body flashed through his mind. He forced the image away and took another drink. So much for a night away from the job.

'Well, when I'm outside of work, I'm Jack,' he said, shaking her hand.

'Nice to officially meet you, *Jack*,' she giggled.

Claire brought his attention away from the happy couple. 'So, rumour has it you used to be quite the drinker.'

'Oh really?' he said, casting a cursory glance over to Watkins.

'Well,' she said. 'I've had a rotten end to the week with the Bulldog so I want to get drunk and have a good time. How does that sound?'

'That sounds fine to me,' Jack said. 'Except… Watkins and I are in work tomorrow so we won't be having a late one.'

Watkins pouted. 'Ah come on, Jack.'

Gerrard tutted. 'Well I'm not, so here's to me!' she said, sipping her red wine with an air of mock sophistication.

Jack downed the rest of his drink and stood to go back to the bar. 'Another drink?' he asked her.

'Yes, I'll come with you.'

'I see you've combed your hair,' Gerrard said once they were out of earshot.

'Well I can't have you having another go at my appearance.'

'You know,' she said, eyes resting on him. 'I have friends who are into the gay scene. I could introduce…'

He held his hand up. 'Thanks, but I'm not interested. I'm happy to comb my hair from time to time but I don't need relationship advice right now. I'm not ready for that.'

The barman served them their drinks and Jack made to head back.

'You still haven't shaved, though.'

'It's winter,' he told her. 'It keeps me warm.'

'It keeps you old.'

'Thanks, you are doing wonders for my self-esteem.'

'Well somebody needs to look out for you,' she said. 'You don't seem happy.'

He turned away from her. He'd never been one to discuss his feelings. That was part of the reason he and Rosie had broken up. Only a small part, of course. Ironically it was his being honest about his sexuality that had finally put paid to their affair. Gerrard was probably right but he had more important things to worry about than his love life.

'I'll be fine,' he told her.

'Well, just so you know, I'm on your side.'

'Are some people not, like?'

She grinned. 'Well the Bulldog certainly isn't.'

'No comment.'

As the night wore on, he found himself having an alright time. He even had a joke around with Watkins in between the sergeant necking on with his new lass – his words, not Jack's. When a couple of young PCs arrived, Jack felt it best to call it a night.

'Right, I'm off, early start tomorrow.'

'Okay everybody, off to World Headquarters.' Watkins ignored him, slamming his pint glass down in a drunken state.

'I once saw a man throw up on himself in there,' Claire said, then, turning back to Jack. 'You sure you don't want in?'

'Not for me,' he told her. 'I don't recover like I used to.' He leaned in towards Watkins. 'I'll see you in the morning, don't be hungover or I'll have to breathalyse you.'

The DS was seemingly having too much of a good time to listen to his warning.

He'd been watching them for some time now. Sitting across the bar within eyeshot was giving him a thrill. Sipping his gin and tonic to take the edge off, he saw his target, DCI Jack Lambert. The bulky officer leant over and whispered something to the ginger detective before grabbing his coat. It seemed he was leaving. He took one of the ice cubes into his mouth, rolled the cold ice around his gum before crunching down on it. Not once did his gaze leave him. Jack Lambert was the one who was heading up the investigation, according to the press. The great Jack Lambert – conqueror of the Newcastle Knifer. Even a killer that useless had managed to escape the law for the best part of two months. The furore surrounding the case had been borderline ridiculous. He smiled. His plans would bring things to a whole new level.

He finished the drink, barely registering the tang of the alcohol. Yes, Jack Lambert had caught his attention. Without him here, though, there was no point in hanging around. He'd already found what he was looking for.

CHAPTER 10

The next day Jack was sure he was coming down with something. He'd barely slept and felt the annual Newcastle cold coming on. The morning passed in a blur as he dosed up on an array of cheap medicines. First of all, he'd received a phone call from the hospital telling him that his father was showing promising signs, having regained some of his previous appetite. He'd thanked the nurse, felt guilty about going out the previous night and promised to visit early the following week.

He'd got over the gnawing in his stomach by fuelling up on Lucozade, poring over the double murder case files and thinking about what to do about Liam Reed. The lack of anything on either case was troubling him. With Jane Russell champing at the bit to get SIO status, he'd have to start getting some results soon. Christensen had chipped in during the morning, with Jack spending his time between the MIR and his own office. So far, he'd managed to avoid Edwards, but that wouldn't last forever.

The Nell Stevens issue wasn't even on his radar.

'Knock, knock.' A far too chirpy Pritchard entered the office, coffee in hand.

'I thought you were only coming in part-time,' Jack said, taking one for himself.

The psychologist shrugged and took a seat. 'You know me.'

He was right, Jack did know him. He also knew that his inability to let a case go had led to him practically having a heart attack just over a year ago.

It was as if Pritchard could read his mind. 'You're not my minder, Jack.'

'Of course not, I'm sorry.'

They settled into an uneasy silence as they continued their review of the case documentation. By the end, Jack found that the words had all blurred into one.

'We need the roommate,' Pritchard said.

He concurred. Surely she could offer something. So far, though, they'd been unable to track her down. The horrible thought that the killer had taken her as well momentarily ran through his mind. He dismissed the idea, for now.

'Sandra Beck,' Jack said, leafing through her profile. 'Moved down here from Edinburgh; has no local family.'

'That helps,' Pritchard quipped.

Jack was about to respond when Watkins came hurtling through the door, his face redder than usual.

'I'm here,' he spluttered.

'You're late,' he said.

'Only five minutes,' he replied. 'Plus, I brought us bacon butties.'

The DS was instantly forgiven. 'Sauce?'

'Brown.'

'Good man, pull up a seat.'

Watkins dished the food out and Jack hungrily chowed down on the sandwich. It was crispy, just how he liked it.

'Look, I'm glad I caught you in a good mood,' Watkins said.

The pork instantly soured in his mouth. 'What is it?'

Rather sheepishly, he pulled out a local tabloid, placing it across from Jack. He dumped the butty, looked down at the front page spread.

Open Grave Murderer Still on the Loose

'Are you kidding me?'

Pritchard chuckled. 'It is rather inventive.'

Yeah, the press had named the killer the 'Open Grave Murderer,' on account of the bodies having been in an open grave. Really inventive.

'This is Robson's lot,' Jack fumed.

They'd used an old image of Jack's from a couple of years ago as well. It wasn't his finest pose. No doubt Robson had fished it out to try and embarrass him. It didn't get much better as he read on.

The whole region shuddered at the horrific events of the double body discovery in Cleadon, South Shields, nearly two weeks ago. This paper can offer an official exclusive into the ongoing investigation. Fearing further attacks, the police are upping their numbers, clearly nervous at what could happen next. DCI Jack Lambert, known primarily for his role in the drawn-out saga of the Newcastle Knifer case, currently remains SIO. Lambert, formerly touted for the top, has a long road back after the calamitous events of just over a year ago, almost succumbing to local psychopath, Leonard Watson, in a knife attack. Worries remain about the mental state and competence of the detective after he let one of the most dangerous criminals in recent times slip through his fingers, leading to disastrous consequences. So far, police have not been able to secure any firm leads.

'What the hell!' he shouted, flinging the newspaper against the murder wall.

'What's the plan then?' Watkins asked.

Jack leaned back in his chair, massaging his temples. He could already feel another headache coming on. 'I don't know,' he admitted. 'But, whatever we do, we have to move quickly.' Glancing once more at the crumpled paper, he added, 'And I want to know who that damn mole is before I have to kill David bloody Robson!'

'Jack?' came a cold voice from the doorway. 'We have a situation.'

DI Russell didn't need to give further information before he knew. 'A body?'

'No,' she said, stony-faced. 'Two.'

The drive to the location was spent in sombre silence as Watkins navigated them out of the city centre. Jack was restless, tapping his fingers on the dashboard as they burst through the heavy traffic towards Gateshead. As if a second discovery wasn't enough, the fact that they had somebody leaking details to the press would lead to widespread panic once the words 'serial killer' were bandied about.

'Nearly there,' Watkins said as they passed over the green structure of the Tyne Bridge.

To their left, the Norman Foster-designed Sage building lay like a giant slug on the Quayside. It played host to a plethora of folk and pop music acts; Jack was more of a hard rock fan but had still found the time to go and visit the place. There was no denying it was impressive.

Veering left, they passed the Baltic campus of Gateshead College, heading along the country lane. The smell of horse manure hung heavy in the air as they parked up and waded through the muddy terrain, still wet from last night's rain. Clouds were gathering, threatening another downpour at any moment. The walk to the tent seemed to take forever as the hill grew steeper, each step growing more and more difficult as he approached. DI Russell had gone ahead with Gerrard, and they met up now, before suiting up outside the scene of the grave. The event passed in silence, as if they were attending the funeral of a friend.

'Through here, sir,' a tall, uniformed officer greeted them at the entrance.

They pulled on their white protective suits before heading over to where Rosie and a number of other workers were investigating the scene. It wasn't always general practice for Rosie to be there, but the serious nature of the crime had deemed it necessary. Behind him, Jane could be heard barking orders at anybody within earshot. As they moved forward, the unmistakable stench of death displaced the country air, a grim prelude to what he was about to witness.

'Rosie,' he greeted his former lover. 'Show me.'

She gave him a curt nod and motioned towards the centre of the tent. Her lack of eye contact told him she wasn't best pleased with his presence, but Rosie had always been a professional. In a situation like this, there was no one else he'd rather have there.

He tuned the rest of the world out as he approached the open grave. A cordon had been set up on the other side of the tent, indicating possible footprints. Jack noticed a distinct lack of action on that side, it would lead to less contamination. Anything in the way of a footprint or DNA would be a godsend right about now.

Watkins appeared by his side, his face staunch and expressionless. The two detectives moved forward, bringing the grave into view. Jack exhaled, a small shiver working its way up his spine, the familiarity of the scene all too similar to be marked off as coincidence.

'Looks identical,' Watkins said, hunching down.

It wasn't the image that was particularly disturbing to him. It was the smell. Nobody could train you to deal with the putrid stench of the dead. Jack had to concentrate to make sure he swallowed the acidic water that was working its way up his throat. He moved to the opposite side of the grave to try out a different angle. As before, both bodies had been stripped naked and placed into a ditch around six foot deep. He looked closer, could see the arm of the woman draped around the man's midriff, just like last time. The all-too-familiar bruising on the neck was prevalent and – judging by the smell and look of the bodies – the time of death was in line with what they'd previously seen.

'Jesus Christ,' DI Russell said, hunching down next to Watkins. 'You do know what this means, don't you?'

Jack met her gaze and nodded.

'It looks exactly the same as last time, Jack,' Rosie told him. 'Still, I don't want to pander to guessing games before I thoroughly investigate both bodies.'

He thought as much. Moving to his right, he looked at the footprints that had chewed up the earthy ground.

'Could be anybody's,' Watkins said.

'Could be his,' he replied.

'This guy is sick,' Watkins said. 'Digging up the graves so we would find them. Who does that?'

'You sure it's a he?' DI Russell asked.

'Oh, it's a he.' Pritchard stepped forward, speaking for the first time since they'd arrived. The group turned to him. 'Call it the benefit of experience,' he added.

Jack moved into action. 'Watkins, I want a team to start making enquiries nearby.'

'On which doors?'

He was right, the area was so sparsely populated that the chances of somebody having seen something, especially when it was so easy to slip in and out with the scenery, was very slim. Still, they had to try. 'Just do it.'

'Call me if you discover anything, Rosie... eh... Dr Lynnes,' he stuttered, stepping away from the scene.

Once he'd reached outside, he was glad to be back with the manure. As he approached the car, he began making mental notes of everything he needed to do. First port of call would be to get back to the station and update Edwards on the situation. He was looking forward to that.

The shrill ring of his mobile phone brought him out of his trance.

'Hello.'

'Jack, it's David Robson here...'

'Look, I can't be arsed to get into anything with you, right now, David. In case you hadn't noticed, I'm a police officer,' he said, sidling into the passenger's seat.

'That's just it,' he replied. 'After what you have just discovered, I can imagine you are pretty busy.'

Jack paused, hand gripping the device. 'If you are following me, Robson, I swear...'

'Relax,' he replied. 'Suffice to say, this is big news, wouldn't you agree?'

'How much do you know?'

'You've found two bodies in Gateshead. Identical situation to two weeks ago. If I didn't know any better, I'd say we have a...'

'Don't say it, Robson!'

'I don't need to, Jack. The paper will say it all tomorrow.'

'Don't you dare print—' The phone line went dead.

He let out a groan and dug his fingers into the seat.

'What's up with you?' Watkins asked, starting the engine.

'David bloody Robson just rang me. He knows.'

'What the hell?'

'Jesus, we'll be in a fire storm.'

'Now what?'

'I have to go and tell Edwards what's going on.'

'Glad I don't have to do that,' Watkins said.

'If I don't solve this thing soon you could be the one calling the shots before long.'

Jack saw Watkins gulp, bony knuckles gripping the steering wheel.

Pritchard lumbered into the backseat and pulled out a chewing gum. 'You do realise this could very well escalate now?'

Jack merely nodded. As they pulled away, he looked over the crime scene, seeing every colleague as a potential enemy. If they didn't close the information source down soon, Edwards would have no choice but to throw him off the case. As for the killer, unless they could track him down, whoever had committed the murders would have more surprises in store for them in the near future. They needed to refocus.

Lives depended on it.

CHAPTER 11

'I just can't believe it.'

Jack took a seat opposite Sandra Beck, who had the vacant look of somebody in shock. Watkins had just informed her of Jessica Lisbie's death. A neighbour had given them the call that someone had returned to the flat. It didn't take a genius to work out which housemate it was. It turned out Sandra didn't watch a lot of news. She'd been on a trip to Paris with her boyfriend; a last minute job, hence the lack of knowledge with regards to her whereabouts. University had seemingly tamed her Scottish accent, with only the odd word standing out as strange to his ears.

'I know this must have come as a big shock,' Jack said.

The diminutive redhead sniffed, bringing a neatly-manicured nail to her mouth. 'I was just speaking to her a few weeks ago. We've been sharing this flat for over a year now.'

It was a nice flat, too. Jack wondered who had decided on the decor. It had a fairly minimalistic feel, with the obligatory flat-screen TV mounted to the far wall and coffee table complete with family photos. He noted the photos were of Sandra's family, not Jessica's.

Although conscious of the need to tread carefully, Jack needed information. 'I'm sorry to have to question you like this, Sandra,' he said. 'But a killer is on the loose and we need to stop him.'

She took a deep breath, composing herself. 'What do you need?'

A suspect, he thought.

'Any information you might think useful to the investigation.' He fished out the mugshot of Travis Kane. 'Do you recognise this man?'

The young girl scrunched up her face. 'I... don't think so.'

He paused before continuing. 'This man was found alongside Jessica. Look again; is there any way Jessica may have known him?'

Watkins stopped scribbling, leaving the tick of the clock as the only sound in the room.

'Well, Jessica had recently started working at Blue Bamboo, in the city centre.'

That was news to Jack. 'I thought she worked in marketing.'

'She did,' Sandra replied.

'Then why work at a bar too? Did she have money issues?'

She shifted in her seat, her hands lightly tapping her thigh. 'Look, she didn't earn much but she had been having a hard time. I don't know if you've met her family but her dad is a grade-one nutjob. She was a really private person but anybody who knew her knew not to bring family up.'

Jack nodded. 'It had come to my attention.'

Sandra's face hardened. 'Yeah, well, because of him Jessica was kind of messed up, you know? She'd been drinking a lot and hadn't been coping well. I think she may have even sought help for her issues, I don't know. Anyway, she got the job there to take her mind off things in the evening. If she was at work, she couldn't get pissed, right? She wasn't big on hanging out with people, more of a lone wolf. But she was always looking for things to occupy her time. I could tell she was unhappy.' Her eyes began clouding over again.

They finished up speaking to Jessica Lisbie's flatmate and left her to mourn in peace. They might not have gotten the Travis Kane link that they were after, but they had received a piece of potentially important information. Nobody had alerted them to the fact that Jessica had been working at Blue Bamboo.

Jack fished his mobile out and rang through to the MIR. Christensen picked up on the third ring, his voice betraying no emotion as Jack filled him in on the details. He agreed to meet them at the bar.

Securing a link between the two victims would be the key they needed to unlock this mystery. Numerous potential scenarios were running through his mind. Had Jessica known Travis Kane through her job? Had they been lovers? Was it a crime of passion? If so, how did that explain the new discovery? Unfortunately for them, there were far more questions than answers at this point.

'How do you want to play it?' Watkins asked.

'I'll speak to the bar staff, see if I can get a rota or something,' he replied, checking his watch. It was early but hopefully somebody would be there.

'There might not be many people around at this time.'

'Doesn't matter,' Jack said. 'I want to get straight in on this, leave nothing to chance. We'll take a team down at a later time to scout the place out on an evening. If it's the venue that proves to be the commonality, we may need to go undercover at some point.'

'What do you make of the flatmate?'

Jack shrugged. 'She seemed genuine. Her eyes certainly lit up when she spoke about Jessica's dad. I guess she must have disclosed some stuff in the past. It might be worth speaking with the family again at some point. Also, I want Sandra's boyfriend checked, just to check her whereabouts and rule them out.'

They spent the rest of the journey in eager silence. Watkins pulled the car into a space and they crossed the road towards the bar. At the door, Christensen stood, bomber jacket open against the elements. The man was hard as nails. He'd been in the force for as long as Jack could remember but had never moved up the ladder. He couldn't help but wonder why. He was a damn fine policeman and everyone respected him. Originally from Denmark, he'd moved to Newcastle as a young boy and had picked up a unique melded Scandinavian-Geordie dialect. Given that he was almost as wide as he was tall, people didn't tend to mess with him. Stories had been circulating about his history for years now. For Christensen's part, he neither admitted nor denied them. He also had a habit of calling everybody boss, whether it be a superior officer or young subordinate.

Jack had never been to Blue Bamboo before, chart music wasn't his thing. Granite walls loomed over him as he looked the building up and down, a bleak welcome. During the day, pubs had a way of looking depressed as if punters' hangovers had stretched to their very foundations. A sign above the main entrance stood, unlighted, indicating they were closed. He'd take his chances inside. Jack pushed through a set of double doors, the unmistakable smell of cheap shots and teenage sweat hitting him like a kick to the gut.

A heavyset bouncer approached them as they made their way inside, multiple ringed fingers raised into the air as a warning. He was sporting a closely-shaved round head with a tattoo high up on his neck. A mammoth belly was straining against his black suit jacket, tie undone.

'Police,' Jack said, showing him his ID.

His eyes narrowed. 'The bar staff are through there,' he motioned, his voice thick with the mucus of excessive smoking.

'Don't go too far, my friend,' Jack said. 'We may want to speak to you shortly.'

They headed into the main bar area to be greeted by a huge empty space. Somewhere out back, bottles could be heard clanging, alongside the sound of excited chatter. Jack stepped up to the bar, his feet sticking to the floor.

'Anybody there?' Watkins called.

A small, pretty woman appeared in a side doorway, straining from the effort of lugging a crate of WKD into the bar.

'One second, fellas,' she said in a thick, Liverpudlian accent.

The barmaid dumped the crate on the floor before wiping her brow with the back of her hand. Jack ascertained that she must have been about five foot two and didn't look a day over twenty-one. Luminous pink bra straps were visible through her sheer-black T-shirt that read, 'Wanna Shot?'

'Hello, miss…?'

'Becky,' she said, her voice as small as her petite frame.

'Are you the only staff member on duty?'

'Other than Gruff,' she said. 'The bouncer.'

Gruff indeed, Jack thought. 'Christensen, would you mind going to have a word with our friendly neighbourhood bouncer, please?'

'No problem, boss,' he said, turning to leave.

'Becky, do you recognise this photo?' Watkins asked, holding up a mugshot of Jessica Lisbie.

'Yeah, it's Jessica,' she replied, her eyes darting down to the floor.

Jack took note. 'Are you aware of what has happened?'

She nodded. 'I've seen the paper.'

'How long had Jessica been working here for?'

'About three months,' she replied. 'Look, I can't give you much information, I'm afraid. Jessica kept to herself most of the time. She was weird.'

He noted Becky's disdainful attitude towards her former co-worker. 'And do you recognise this photo?'

The barmaid took the printout, her eyes scanning the image.

'I'm not sure. He just looks like every bloke who comes in here.'

Jack smiled. 'Was Jessica seeing anybody?'

She shrugged. Something in her body language told him she was holding something back.

'Becky, it's vitally important that you tell me anything you think you might know,' he continued. 'Was Jessica ever involved in any criminal activity that you know of?'

She snorted. 'No, Jessica was too innocent for anything like that.'

'How can you be sure if you only knew her through work and she was a somewhat private person?'

'Well... I... she just never came across that way.'

'Can you think of any reason as to why somebody would want to hurt Jessica?'

The girl paused. 'No.'

'Becky,' he said, locking her with his eyes. 'You do realise that if you are withholding something that eventually comes to light, you could be committing a crime and looking at serious jail time?'

That had the desired effect.

'Gary, who works here, had a thing for her. They'd flirted a bit, that's all. It didn't last long. She ended things not so long ago. But... Gary wouldn't harm anyone.'

Lies. 'Are you sure?'

'No... yes... of course he wouldn't.'

'Where is Gary now, Becky?' Watkins asked.

'He should be in tonight. But... he's been off for a couple of weeks. I don't know why. He barely speaks to me now.'

'But he used to?'

She sighed. 'Look, Gary and I used to have a thing going. Once Jess started, he wasn't interested any more. But, if you ask me, what goes around comes around.'

'Are you saying Jess got what was coming to her?' Watkins asked.

Welcome to the real Becky, Jack thought.

'No, of course not!' she spluttered.

'Becky,' Jack began, 'is there anything else you want to tell us now, while you have the chance?'

Her shoulders fell. 'Look, Gary... has a bit of a temper. Once or twice he...' she tailed off.

'He what?' Jack asked.

'Got a little heavy-handed is all, but he's okay really.'

The detectives finished up in the bar, ascertaining that Gary Dartford was a twenty-six-year-old barman with short, spiky blond hair and a slim build. After some gentle coercing, they'd been given an address by the Scouse barmaid.

'This could be big,' Watkins said.

Jack nodded. 'I'm going to go back to the station and get Gerrard to run a check on Gary Dartford, see if anything turns up.'

'You think the girl is involved?'

'My gut instinct tells me no,' Jack said. 'Still, we should keep her in mind, just in case. I want people interviewing all of the staff here. Right now, our priority is to locate Gary Dartford.'

'It still doesn't solve the issue of the other bodies,' the DS said.

Jack knew only too well. 'If we can establish a link, though, we could be close to solving this thing.'

Seconds later, Christensen appeared in the doorway.

'Anything?' Jack asked the DS.

He shook his head. 'Only started last week. He didn't much like being spoken to by the police so I made sure to waste some of his time.' He smiled.

Christensen rarely had a problem getting people to listen to him. Even if they were overweight bouncers called Gruff.

As they made their way back to the station, Jack couldn't help but feel a little optimistic that they might have secured a breakthrough. They'd keep a lid on it for now but, if Gary Dartford couldn't be located, they'd have to bring in the press. That's if they didn't already know. Looking to his two DSs, he dismissed the idea that one of them would be the mole. Why risk it all to talk to David Robson?

Once thing Jack did know was that Gary Dartford had a link to Jessica Lisbie and that he hadn't been turning up for work. They had to find out where he was. The words that he'd begun thinking in the bar were playing over and over in his mind, consuming his every thought, as they headed back to HQ.

We have a potential suspect.

CHAPTER 12

Now that they potentially had something to go on, the team moved into overdrive. Officers hurtled around the station, printouts, theories and coffee cups flying everywhere. Jane Russell was posted in the MIR, working with DC Gerrard to bring up some history on Gary Dartford, the barman and former lover of Jessica Lisbie. Christensen was giving orders out with his usual no-nonsense attitude. Jack sat, perched, overseeing them all as Pritchard drank a murky-green Cup-a-Soup.

Watkins had raised the question of whether or not the press should be brought in on it. Jack didn't think so. Get it wrong and the force would look even more ridiculous than it already did. There was no doubt a mugshot of Gary Dartford pasted across the local area would help them track him down, but what if he wasn't their man? They needed more to go on. Jack, however, kept coming back to the statistics: most people were killed by somebody they knew. Had Jessica been in a relationship with Travis Kane? It wasn't outside the realms of possibility that she could have been without others knowing. She wasn't close to her family and her housemate had been away. Perhaps Gary Dartford was the one person who did know about this and it sent him into a jealous rage.

'Good news,' Watkins said, looking up from a nearby computer screen.

Jack stood. 'What is it?'

The DS plonked himself down on a nearby desk. 'It seems Gary Dartford has previous.'

'Go on.'

'Spent a few months in jail for GBH. He's also had warnings over use of marijuana and a DUI.'

Jack exhaled. Just because somebody had a criminal record didn't mean that they had committed multiple murders. Still, he needed looking into.

'We also have an address.'

Jack knew the estate fairly well. Back when he was a bobby on the beat, he would spend many an hour trying to calm people down after an assault, burglary or family feud in the area. Most police couldn't wait to get out of that environment, but he had thrived in it.

They pulled up and left the car at a reasonable distance from the house. Jack had decided to take an unmarked vehicle, just in case. As they parked, another unmarked car fell in line behind them. Then a third car pulled in. All were awaiting Jack's orders. Watkins cradled a small radio, eyes darting across the street.

'You want to do the talking?' Watkins asked.

He nodded.

They left the car and began the short walk to Dartford's residence. To their left, a group of teenagers were hanging around on rusted BMX bikes, their hoodies pulled up tight around their heads. Jack couldn't help but feel a twinge of sympathy for them. What chance did they have? The best they could hope for was an opportunity to move away at some point before they ended up with a criminal record. Faces didn't seem to change as Jack's eyes roamed the streets. Most of the families here were in a perpetual cycle, locked into their own misery and despair. As if sensing an outsider, one of the young lads – no older than thirteen – turned to them and grabbed his crotch. *Nice touch*, Jack thought.

'If only I could pepper spray the little shit,' Watkins said.

'We have more important things to worry about right now, Watkins.'

The worm-eaten black, wooden door of number twenty-eight greeted them. It was a narrow house, just a tall thin doorway with one window to the right of it. A wooden board covered a large crack in the bottom corner of it. The lawn looked like it hadn't been cut in years, various thick weeds sprouting in all angles. Jack had to kick empty cans of Strongbow out of the way to get to the door.

He knocked three times.

There was a shuffle before it slipped open, a chain blocking their entry. A young face appeared in the narrow gap, tab in mouth, hair long and greasier than a doner kebab.

'The fuck do you want?' a broad Geordie accent greeted them, pitch rising at the end.

'Is Gary in?' Watkins asked.

'You can piss off. Always bothering my Gary, you lot,' she screeched, pulling her garish, pink dressing gown tight against her.

'Us lot?'

'Pigs. I can smell you from a mile off. What has he not done now?'

'We would just like to talk to him, miss?'

'Crystal. I'm his lass. He's not in.'

Jack moved his foot in between the door and the frame as she made to close it.

'What are you doing? I know my rights.'

'Crystal,' Watkins continued, 'we have reason to believe that Gary has been caught up in something very serious. If he is in the house, we need to know right now.'

The young woman began a throaty cough. 'I swear, he's not in,' she choked. 'Try the Black Bull down the road. He's usually in there at this time. If not, he'll be at a mate's house. I practically never see him now. If you do find him, tell him to get home.'

Jack glanced up at the various windows to the house. He couldn't see any movement. His gut instinct told him she was telling the truth. Still, given the serious nature of what Dartford might potentially have been involved in, he decided it was best to check anyway.

'If you let me in to have a look around I will be sure to pass on the message,' Jack said.

Gary Dartford's 'lass' took a long drag on her cigarette. 'Fine.'

Twenty minutes later and they'd found no sign of their suspect save for some old clothes, three dirty magazines and a small bag of weed. They stood outside, scanning up and down the street.

'Happy now?' Crystal spat.

'Not at all,' Jack replied. 'I'll be in touch about the drugs.'

They left the young woman to her swearing fit.

'Psycho,' Watkins muttered.

'Compared to most people around here that was pretty friendly.' He paused and looked up and down the street. 'Come on, let's go check this pub.'

The smell of stale beer hit them long before they entered the pub. The building stood at the top of the estate, a deep redbrick structure with what looked like prison bars on the windows. A large, black double door stood at the front, complete with a shoddily-painted wooden sign declaring, 'The Black Bull,' above it.

As they entered, the three or four patrons who were sitting in various places around the bar, fell silent. Jack suddenly felt like they were in some kind of Spaghetti Western film. A solitary barman stood talking to an elderly looking man with an eye patch, perched on one of the three stools that were placed by the bar. Unlike the bald patron he had a thick head of sheer white hair and a stained apron covering an enormous beer belly.

'What'll it be?' he barked, cigarette abuse lining his tone.

'I'm looking for someone,' Jack answered.

'Pigs,' he spat. 'I should have known. I don't give out information to non-paying customers.' He turned to face them.

'Fine,' Jack said. 'Two cokes.'

Whilst their host set about pouring their drinks, Jack looked around the various liqueurs on offer. An assortment of coloured bottles lined the back wall. He'd have loved a Honey Jack Daniel's right about now.

Watkins handed over the money. 'We're looking for a Mr Gary Dartford.'

'Aye,' he replied.

'Do you know where he is?'

'I might do.'

'Stop messing about,' Watkins snapped. 'Do you or don't you know where he is?'

The barman paused, placing a large hand on his bearded chin. 'No, sorry.'

'What a waste of time,' the DS fumed.

Jack would have been inclined to agree had it not been for the sound of the pub door opening at that very moment.

Before he could turn, the barman called out. 'Run!'

He spun round just as the back of a young man with a lot of hair gel headed in the other direction.

'Go!' Jack ordered.

'I'll be back for you!' Watkins called to the barman, before setting off in pursuit.

They fled the pub, cokes and change still on the bar.

'Suspect in pursuit, can be seen running south from the Black Bull pub,' Jack called over the radio.

'Will he be recognisable?' a crackled reply came.

'He'll be the one running from two policeman, blond hair, greased with gel, white sports shoes – yes, he'll be recognisable.' They rounded a right-hand turn, making up very little ground. 'I'll go this way, try and cut him off,' Jack told Watkins, turning right onto a housing estate.

The sound of the police sirens began blazing around him as he set off in pursuit. Knowing the area like he did, Jack would be surprised if anybody even batted an eyelid. It wasn't long before he could feel a stitch beginning to build up in his side. He cursed his lack of fitness, promising to himself that he'd cut out the tabs if he could just catch this one person. They had to avoid him going to ground at all costs.

He'd just begun to slow when the slender figure of Gary Dartford came running through a small cut between two fences, almost knocking him to the ground.

'Wait right—'

He was off again, sprinting away in the opposite direction. Looking back through the cut, Watkins appeared, panting. Jack turned and continued after the suspect.

Dartford was no more than twenty feet from him, but he couldn't seem to gain any ground. His stitch exploded into searing pain, but he forced it to the back of his mind. The assailant made a sharp left, pushing past two old ladies who were dragging small carts up the road. Jack followed suit, ignoring their foul-mouthed tirade. He then made another right and Jack pushed on harder, almost within touching distance now. He could hear Dartford's laboured breathing as the effort began to show.

Turning left into another cobbled cut, Jack reached out and grabbed a handful of white sports jacket. No use. It came off in a swift motion, almost knocking him to the ground in the process. He'd lost a few feet now. Tossing the jacket to the floor, he took off his own and pushed on, his shirt clinging to his body.

'I've not done nothing wrong,' a surprisingly youthful voice shouted from up ahead.

'Why are you running then?' Jack hollered.

'I know what you lot are like. Just fuck off and leave me alone!'

'I won't tell you—'

He was interrupted by loud crash. Unable to stop in time, Jack fell over the crumpled body of Gary Dartford, hitting the ground with a dull thud. Instantly, pain shot up through his right arm. The pram they'd run into lay off to their left, perched on the edge of the road. A young mother stood open-mouthed as the screams of a young child rose around them.

Clearing the stars in his vision, he grabbed the bony shoulder of his suspect, dragging him back to the ground as he attempted to scramble up. 'Will you just calm down, I only want to talk to you!'

The fist aimed at his head broke his speech, but Jack was equal to it, moving to the left to dodge the blow. Dartford shrieked, momentarily stifling the cries of the baby as his fist made contact with the concrete ground. He raised his arm back up, covered in blood and let out another yelp of pain.

'Police brutality!' he called out, tears forming in his eyes.

Jack took hold of him. 'Enough of this.'

Dartford began wriggling under his grasp and the other, less damaged fist came flying at him. Yet again Jack dodged it. Another cry rose up, this time, not from Gary Dartford.

'You punched me, you little shit!' Watkins whined, holding his hand to his nose as a sea of red exploded over his face.

The Blue Bamboo employee turned his attentions back to Jack, raising his one good hand up in a boxing stance.

Jack drew out his CS spray. 'Not today, sunshine.'

'My client has been clearly mistreated!' Casey Clifton, duty solicitor and grade-one asshole, bellowed, planting a fist down on the interview table for added effect.

Jack surveyed the chaos around him. To his left, Watkins sat, nose plugged up with bright red tissue paper. Sitting opposite him sulking, Gary Dartford had both of his hands resting on ice, his eyes resembling that of a heroin addict with a chronic case of hay fever. Clifton sat next to him, his pristine brown suit shimmering ever so slightly in the dim light of the interview room.

Typical of Clifton, Jack thought; *always flash*. The lawyer was sitting with a briefcase in front of him and an expensive-looking Rolex on his left wrist. His hair was the same colour as his client's, only natural. He had it perfectly combed over, much like a 1950s crooner. Stylish, square-rimmed glasses were perched low on his nose which gave him an air of faux-superiority over those who were around him. Jack wasn't buying it though.

Everyone on the force could vouch for their hatred of Casey Clifton. In fact, Jack was sure he hated him even more than David bloody Robson. He'd lost count of the amount of times the slimy solicitor had gotten a criminal off on a technicality. Just last year, he'd managed to get a well-known local druggie released from an assault charge. He'd attacked an off-duty police officer in a pub, breaking his jaw. Somehow, by the time Clifton had finished with him in court, it was believed that the policeman had not only instigated the assault but also had an alcohol problem. Although in his early thirties, he'd built up a fearsome reputation in the legal business. And the press loved him. None more so than Jack's arch nemesis and constant pain in the arse, David Robson. He wasn't the only duty solicitor who was used, but it certainly felt that way to Jack.

He leaned forward. The only sound to be heard was that of Gary Dartford's wheezing, and the churning of the recording equipment. 'Gary, you're here because—'

'I swear I never touched her!'

'Touched who?' Jack asked.

'Jessica.'

Clifton leaned in and began whispering in Dartford's ear before being shrugged off.

'I've got nothing to hide so what's it matter?'

Jack resisted the urge to smirk at Clifton the way he had to him over the years.

'If you're happy to speak about this, Gary, why don't we start at the beginning and you can tell me how you knew Jessica Lisbie.'

Dartford ran a swollen hand over his puffy eyes. 'Worked with her, didn't I?'

Out of the corner of his eye, he could see the cogs of Casey Clifton's mischievous brain turning over, waiting to pounce on any irregularity.

'Were you romantically involved with her?'

Dartford's fair-skinned face flashed red. 'Nar.'

'But you liked her, yes?'

'She was alright.'

'That's not what I've heard, Gary. In fact, I hear you were very fond of her.'

'Who the fuck told you that?' he snapped, his eyes meeting Jack's for the first time.

'That's a nasty temper you've got there. You should try to keep it in check. Do you often find yourself unable to contain your anger? Is that why you beat up your ex?'

Dartford's jaw dropped before Clifton tagged in. 'That's an outrageous slur. May I remind you that Mr Dartford is volunteering up this information and that there is no need to employ such a heavy-handed approach.'

'No need?' Watkins piped up. 'The suspect has a history of violence towards women. I'd say it's a fair point under the circumstances.'

Jack decided to push further, ignoring the weak attempt from Clifton to disrupt his line of questioning. 'You can't control your anger, can you?'

'Nar... I... it's in the past,' he spluttered. 'Look, we sort of had a bit of a flirt and that, but it never went any further as such.'

'And how do you know Travis Kane?' Jack asked.

Dartford frowned. 'I don't.'

'You could save us all a lot of trouble, Gary, by being honest.'

'Fuck knows, man,' he said, straightening. 'He may have been in the bar once or twice but I don't know the bloke, honestly.'

'Did Travis Kane and Jessica Lisbie have a romantic relationship?'

Dartford sighed. 'Look, the truth is, I fancied her. We went out a few times and it didn't work out. As for this bloke, I have no idea who he is.'

'Does Crystal know about Jessica?'

'Nar,' he snorted.

Jack noted the flash of fear in his eyes.

The faint sound of scribbling cut through his thought process as Casey Clifton began making notes on an expensive-looking moleskin notepad.

'Here's what I think, Gary. I think you were jealous of Travis Kane because he started hanging around the bar, chatting Jess up,' he stated.

'I've not done nowt!' he shouted, looking to his lawyer for help. The solicitor placed a hand on his shoulder.

'Let me guess,' Jack continued. 'You couldn't handle Jessica seeing somebody else, so you exacted your revenge on them both. How's my aim?'

'Purely circumstantial at best,' Clifton mumbled, allowing a small smirk. 'At worst, your aim is worse than your detective skills.'

Jack ground his teeth.

'I didn't do nothing!' Dartford repeated, covering his head in his hands.

Casey Clifton leaned forward, placing his notepad on the dimly-lit grey table. Jack glanced at it, to be met by what looked like a child's portrait of two police officers in clown hats.

'This line of questioning is over.'

They exited the interview room some twenty minutes later. All Jack could do was clench his fists behind his back, so as not to lamp Casey Clifton across his smug jaw. The press would love that one. 'Disgraced Police Officer Attacks Lawyer.'

'Let me go!' Dartford shouted as a uniformed officer guided him back to the cells.

'Unfortunately for you, Gary, you assaulted a police officer. In most societies, that is what we call a crime,' Jack informed him.

'Detectives.' Clifton motioned to them, straightening his jacket. 'You will be hearing from me in due course. My client has been maltreated and you can bet your gold-plated pensions that I will not let that stand.'

And with a wink, the lawyer was gone, gliding through reception.

'Shit,' Watkins sighed as they entered Jack's office.

'Shit indeed,' he replied, slumping into his seat.

'I hate that bloke.'

Jack blew out a long breath, raised a cheap cup of coffee to his lips. It surged down his throat, thick with the taste of artificial sugar.

'What do we do now?' Watkins asked.

'Make Dartford sweat. We've got him on a charge of assault. We have witnesses. Until then, we should see if there's any link to the other bodies.'

'Not likely, though, is it?'

After having met him, Jack thought it highly unlikely that Gary Dartford was capable of such an intricate crime. 'No, it's not. Still, if we don't chase it up and it turns out we were wrong, we'd be hung, drawn and quartered. Plus, given his link to Jessica Lisbie, there's always the possibility that he might inadvertently know something that could help us.'

Another headline flashed through his mind, causing him to shudder.

'So, check it out but look elsewhere?'

'Yes,' Jack replied. He gazed at the young sergeant, a depressing understanding passing between them.

Gary Dartford wasn't an intelligent, calculating man. He didn't fit the profile and he didn't seem to be lying. He wasn't their man.

CHAPTER 13

Jack had done his best to shy away from the news, but on his entry into work two days later the desk sergeant took great pleasure in waving the daily paper in front of his face. Casey Clifton's million-dollar smile was plastered on the front next to the headline:

Police Brutality.

It didn't get any better once he'd stolen away to read it. By the time he'd finished the short article, his mood had darkened to a shade usually unknown to him. The top and bottom of the story was that DCI Jack Lambert and associates had attacked poor Gary Dartford, forcing him to defend himself as they hadn't made clear who they were or why they were chasing him. Casey Clifton also alluded to the sense that the subsequent interview had been conducted in a shoddy manner, with his client unable to access medical care, despite being punched and sprayed with CS spray whilst unarmed. As if that wasn't enough, the name attributed to the story served to extend his fury, leading him to throw his coffee against the opposite wall.

David bloody Robson.

He grabbed his phone, fished through the contacts list.

'Hello.'

'I'm going to kill you!'

'Can I put that on the record?' Robson replied, snorting.

'No you bloody well can't. Listen here, if you really do want to help the public, stop printing this bollocks.'

'Come on, Jack, I'm only doing my job as a reporter.'

'Bullshit. You'll be getting nothing from me unless you clean up your act. And, before you ask, yes, that's a threat.'

Watkins came into the office, followed by Christensen. The look on their faces told him something serious had happened.

'I've got to go now,' he shouted the journalist down. 'Police business.'

'Wait, no... what's happ—'

The demeanour of his officers suggested something serious was going on. Christensen's usual posture seemed sagging, with Watkins tugging nervously at his collar, as he often seemed to do in stressful situations.

'What's happened?'

'A body's been discovered.'

The words hung in the air, weighing Jack's shoulders down. Bodies were discovered all the time. But, with the Open Grave case sending people into hysteria, the last thing they needed was something like this. At least it wasn't a double body discovery this time.

'Give me the details.'

Christensen stepped forward. 'Vague at the minute but the description matches that of McGuinness's former employee, Liam Reed.'

His relief was cut short.

They drove to the river in silence. Jack sat shotgun as Christensen manoeuvred around the busy city centre at an infuriatingly calm pace. Only the whites of the squat policeman's knuckles belied any underlying tenseness.

Wind blasted him in the face as they approached the police cordon. The sound of excited nervousness was all around him as a small crowd had gathered, not far from the bank of the River Tyne. A glance at his watch told him it was 2pm. A little early for the drinkers to be out, bar the stag and hen parties. Newcastle, and the Quayside in particular, was a hotspot for soon-to-be-married folk looking for a place to celebrate. He looked upwards; a swarm of seagulls were screeching, seemingly waiting for an opportune moment to swoop down for food. Jack suppressed a shudder at the thought of hungry birds pecking away at the dead body of Liam Reed.

'Detective,' a PC greeted him, motioning them through towards the tent.

He gave the officer a curt nod before heading down the embankment towards the edge of the river. Looking around, he took in the scene. The river itself was less like water and more of a deep green sludge. *Welcome to Newcastle*, he thought.

The smell of Rosie's familiar perfume greeted him before she did.

'What have we got?' he asked, suiting up.

'A dead body,' she replied, avoiding his gaze.

'Obviously,' he muttered.

'Sorry?'

'Nothing.'

He stepped past the pathologist to view the body. He wasn't in the mood for any more confrontations. The bloated remains of Liam Reed were laid out at the edge of the river. Having dealt with the Open Grave murders, he found the smell of this particular corpse mild by comparison.

Jack bent down to get a closer look at him. He was fully clothed, a pair of expensive but now ruined jeans clinging to his slender legs. He wore a dark grey Diesel T-shirt. A quick glance to his feet showed one shoe missing. It was the face that he looked to last, and for good reason. The small, dark features of what was obviously Liam Reed gazed up into space, his mouth twisted into a painful grimace. His eyes were open, suggesting he'd been awake when they'd tortured and killed him. Although conjecture to a point, the fact that he had three fingers missing from his left hand and two from the other seemed to rule out death by natural causes. Jack fished out the photo that Liam's partner Suzie had left with them. Yep, definitely him.

'McGuinness isn't going to be happy.' Watkins peered over his shoulder.

Jack nodded. 'Unless he did it.'

'Unlikely though,' Christensen chimed in.

He agreed. 'Yes, if McGuinness had done it, he wouldn't leave the evidence on his doorstep. If I had to guess, I'd say either Liam found himself in the wrong place at the wrong time, or it was a message to a certain aquatic shop owner. I'm willing to bet my prized Led Zeppelin records on Dorian McGuinness being involved in some way, though.'

The silence of the two officers confirmed their agreement.

'Who found the body?' Jack asked, straightening up.

'Me, sir.' A young man stepped forward from the back of the tent. 'I'm a PC, but off-duty today.'

'Fill me in.'

'I was just walking down the Quayside, with some friends, when I thought I noticed something in the water. I moved closer and saw it was a body.'

'Why were you walking down the Quayside?' Watkins asked.

The man's already small eyes narrowed further. 'My mate's stag do.'

'Alright,' Jack cut in. 'Watkins, I want you to make the call to Liam's fiancée, we'll need an official ID of the body. Rosie,' he said, turning to the flame-haired pathologist, 'we can get the body moved now. Keep me updated on anything you find.' He turned to his DS. 'Christensen, you come with me.'

Sporadic drops of rain had started to fall by the time they'd made the five-minute car journey to the centre of Dorian McGuinness's underground empire. Jack left Watkins to co-ordinate things back at the scene, having rung Edwards to inform him of what they'd found. He hadn't stayed on the phone long enough to listen to the DSI's inevitable rage.

'What's the plan?' Christensen asked as they stepped from the car, wincing as he put weight down on his leg.

'We'll just give him the news and see how he reacts.'

'Before next of kin?'

Jack shrugged. 'It's not like he'll go running to the press… besides, I want to look into the whites of his eyes when he denies any involvement.'

The warmth of the fish store came as a welcome relief from the wintery weather outside. At the end of the shop, a rough-looking bald customer was milling around by the till. Something told Jack he wasn't there for fish food. He sighed, removed his police badge and held it up. The man paused and rolled his eyes before making a heavy-footed exit.

'You scaring our customers away again?' Tank asked, shuffling behind the counter.

'Isn't that your job, Arnold?'

The man, who was known to be the main muscle behind McGuinness's business exploits, shrugged. 'Whatever.'

'I'm looking for Dorian,' Jack said.

'Why?'

'Do we have to do this every time?'

'Losing your temper, Lambert?'

'Is he here or not?'

Tank turned away from him, fiddling about with a small wooden shelf behind the counter. He paused to inspect a tub of fish food before turning back to the policemen.

'He might be.'

'Arnold, isn't it?' Christensen stepped forward.

Tank's eyes narrowed. 'What's it to you, pig?'

Christensen shrugged and stared him down. Jack could feel the tension rising and braced himself. Tank had never attacked a police officer as far as Jack was aware, but he knew he had it in him. The wild look about his eyes suggested he was about to make an exception today.

'What's all this about?' The sound of Dorian McGuinness's voice rose through the commotion.

Jack unclenched his fist as the crime lord sauntered through from the back with one of his other goons. The next ten seconds would determine whether or not this was going to get out of hand. Out of the corner of his eye, he saw the faint hint of a smirk from Tank. Christensen seemed unmoved. He could feel the sweat beginning to form on his brow as his heart rate increased. He didn't want to but, if forced, he was prepared to get his hands dirty.

Just like the old days.

'You should really be more careful of who you hire,' Jack said, his voice steady. 'Tank here has been most unhelpful.'

McGuinness turned on the thug. 'Surely not, Arnold? DCI Lambert and I are old associates. I've told you before that you should treat all guests, especially the police, with the utmost respect.'

Tank snorted.

'I'm sorry?' Dorian cut in, his voice taking on a more sinister tone. 'Is something funny?'

Tank started. 'No... not at all, boss.'

'Boss, that's right. Now be a good chap and fetch me a coffee with Barrel here.'

'You sure?' he asked, eyes dancing over Christensen.

McGuinness ignored him. Jack watched as the two men slumped from the shop, noting that Barrel's name was befitting of his appearance.

'Please, detectives, come through to the back and we can talk.'

Although Jack was glad of the time alone, he still felt uneasy in Dorian McGuinness's presence. Echoes of his past rebounded around the walls of his office every time he stepped into it. It wasn't a DVD he much fancied replaying.

'It's about Liam Reed,' he began. 'A body has just been discovered by the side of the River Tyne.'

McGuinness straightened up, his eyes narrowing behind his glasses. Looking to the table, Jack noticed his hands clench into fists before releasing. Once composed, he offered a strained smile.

'And you think it's Liam?'

Jack nodded. 'We're bringing his fiancée in for an ID as we speak. Early signs seem to indicate torture, although the body was probably dumped in the river after he was killed.'

He studied McGuinness's face. His cool exterior gave nothing away. Still, something in the glint of his eyes told him that he wasn't best pleased. Jack didn't think for one minute that it had been McGuinness's handiwork, but he still had to check. He knew fine well that he was walking a thin line with regards to giving away details of a sensitive murder of this kind. However, on balance, it was to serve the greater good.

Or so he told himself.

'I hope you are not accusing me of something, Detective.'

Christensen leaned in. 'Mr McGuinness...'

'Dorian.'

'Dorian, you knew Liam Reed, yes?'

'He used to work for me,' he replied, fishing out a Cuban cigar. 'We've been over this.'

'When did his employment end?'

McGuinness paused. Not a long pause, but a pause nonetheless. 'Well, he informed me of his intention to leave my employment in recent weeks. He was currently serving his notice when this... unfortunate event happened.'

'Can you think of any reason why somebody would want to hurt Mr Reed?'

McGuinness paused once more, a steady hand coming up to light his cigar. Three puffs later, it was in full flow, a thick smog clogging up the atmosphere.

'No idea. He was a nice enough man.'

'With all due respect, the man was tortured, having had some of his fingers removed.'

Jack noted the flash of fury across McGuinness's face.

'That's terrible.'

'Indeed, it is. That's why I need to know if you have any idea as to why anybody would do that. Did he have information that was valuable to someone? Is somebody trying to get to you?'

'An aquatics shop owner?'

Christensen paused, raised an eyebrow towards Jack.

'Look, Dorian,' Jack began. 'I'm not here to piss about. Hell, I won't even ask to inspect those boxes out there in your corridor. But please don't pull that bullshit on me. We both know what you're really running here.'

'Jack, Jack, Jack,' he chuckled. 'Let me begin by saying how much I abhor bad language. Secondly, you are free to search my premises if you can produce a warrant. Thirdly, you really do *not* have any idea what goes on here.'

He steeled himself, determined not to give an inch. 'Is somebody encroaching on your patch? I don't want warfare on my streets.'

'Your streets?'

'Figure of speech.'

'Look, Detective, I really have no idea what you're talking about,' he replied as Tank and Barrel entered, coffee in hand.

'Well, if you think of anything,' Jack said, leaving a card on the desk. 'Be sure to let me know. I'll be in touch.'

McGuinness seemingly ignored the veiled threat and took a drink of his coffee. 'Not enough sugar.'

'Sorry, boss,' Barrel said, taking the cup and leaving.

McGuinness turned back to them. 'Is that all? As you might imagine, I have some things to attend to.'

Jack turned around in the car to talk to Christensen. 'I thought it was going to kick off in there.'

The DS shrugged. 'I'd have fancied my chances with the goon.'

'I always thought you were unflappable.'

'Haven't you heard the stories?' Christensen said. 'Apparently I can kill a man with my little finger.'

Jack smiled. 'So you never lose your temper?'

'Not often.'

'What happens when you do?'

'Armageddon.'

Jack spent the remainder of the journey reflecting on what had just happened. McGuinness was hiding something, for sure. What that was, though, was anybody's guess. He'd definitely not been pleased to learn of Liam Reed's death. It was beginning to look more and more like Robson had been right. Somebody was making inroads into McGuinness's turf.

'Still,' Jack mused, 'we've moved things along somewhat.'

'Have we?' Christensen asked.

'Think about it. We've just told one of the North East's most notorious crime bosses that one of his employees has been brutally tortured and murdered. You can bet your last quid on McGuinness conducting his own investigation into what has happened. If somebody is encroaching on his business, he's bound to act.' He turned to face the Scandinavian officer. 'All we need to do is wait.'

And pray things didn't spiral out of control before they had a chance to put a stop to it.

CHAPTER 14

Jack had spent the majority of his day off scouring paperwork. He'd rung the station twice, both times being put through to Jane Russell, despite his protests. The DI seemed to be enjoying her newfound seniority, telling him in the most officious of terms that everything was in hand. Time off was a precious commodity in Northumbria's force, but Edwards had forced him to stay home and, in his words, *recharge the batteries*. Sure, he had the day booked in anyway, but was willing to cancel it to work on the case. The DSI had other ideas, though.

He spent some time pacing back and forth, thinking the case through, before sitting down to watch TV. Finally, in an effort to relieve the boredom, he'd rung Pritchard to come and keep him company. This was code word for 'fetch a takeaway.'

'Ah I've missed this, my old friend.' Pritchard stood in the doorway soaked, but with Chinese food in hand. 'Howay then, give me a hand.'

Jack smiled and invited him in, taking six ice-cool cans off the old man. Pritchard always did like a good drink.

'I remember when you'd sink at least double this,' Jack quipped.

Pritchard threw off his rain mac and patted his over-sized belly down. 'I've got to keep this nice and trim, or the missus will leave me.'

'How is Mary?'

The psychologist shrugged. 'Not too bad.'

Jack noted the silent words that flashed across his eyes, words that suggested: 'don't ask.' He didn't.

They settled down to their food, with Jack grabbing a few cans for himself before depositing some of the food in the fridge for later. The smell of black bean sauce permeated the room. He was grateful for the easy silences that often peppered their friendship. More often than not, the less they spoke, the more they really said.

It was some half an hour later when Pritchard finally broke the silence; by which time the sun had begun to set, casting a warm, orange glow over the living room. 'Anything on the case?'

Jack shook his head and put the side lamp on. 'Not a thing. It's only a matter of time before we get an ID on the bodies, though. The Bulldog is running things today. I've already had Watkins on the phone twice practically crying.'

'That Watkins is a bit soft, don't you think?'

'Don't underestimate him, he's got the makings of a fine policeman. Besides, he's already paid a visit to Dorian McGuinness with me so he's passed phase one of his fear management training.'

'Dorian McGuinness?' Pritchard whistled. 'You two still getting on well?'

'Not so much these days,' Jack said. 'Anyway, weren't we just talking about Watkins, not me?'

Pritchard took another drink. 'Touched a nerve?'

Jack ignored him and took a swig of his own. Bringing up his past running with the McGuinness crew wasn't something he was particularly fond of doing. 'We have a strong team,' he said in an attempt to swerve the conversation in a different direction.

Pritchard made to speak, before shaking his head, and taking another drink. 'You do. Claire Gerrard is tenacious.'

'I agree.'

'Let's just hope Watkins' feelings for her don't complicate matters in future.'

'Wait... what?' Jack spluttered, sending lager froth spraying on his carpet. 'What are you talking about? Watkins is seeing that FLO.'

Pritchard sighed, took off his glasses, and made a show of wiping them. 'Jack, you never were much good at reading people's emotions, including your own.'

'What's that supposed to mean?'

'Exactly what I said. I could have told you about your sexuality years ago if you'd only asked. It doesn't matter who Watkins is seeing, I'm telling you the lad is besotted with Gerrard.'

'Great, that's just what we need.'

'Ah it'll be okay,' Pritchard said. 'Workplace romances usually end well, don't they?'

Out of the corner of his eye, he watched the old man give a wry smile. In this light, he could be forgiven for thinking Pritchard was still ten years younger and on active duty, as opposed to semiretired and burned out.

'I can see you looking at me.' Pritchard turned to face him. 'I'm fine.'

'Really?' Jack asked. 'Frank, the pressure I put on you isn't fair. We should never have asked you to come out of retirement. Manchester could have sent somebody or...'

'Nonsense.' Pritchard waved him away. 'Nobody works a case like I do.'

Jack almost believed him.

'I just don't want to put too much on you.'

'That's a hell of a thing for you to say.' Pritchard leaned in, tears lining his eyes. 'After all we've been through.'

He backtracked. 'I'm sorry, Frank, I didn't mean any offence.'

Pritchard shrugged it off. Now it was his turn to change the subject. 'So, do you think Edwards is testing the waters with the Bulldog, to see if she's up to task?'

Of course he did. Edwards might be an old friend but, when it came to saving his own backside, Jack was simply collateral damage. Still, it wasn't something he went around saying.

'No idea.'

'Bullshit,' Pritchard laughed. 'And don't lie to me.'

It wasn't until their fifth beer that Jack's tongue loosened up enough to tell the full truth. Once Pritchard had started prying, he'd known it was only a matter of time before he opened up to him. He wasn't angry about it, though. Jack knew the psychologist only ever did it as a friend. In his years on the force, he could count on one hand the people he'd truly trusted. Pritchard was one of them.

'What's the story with Rosie then?'

Jack winced. It was like a plaster being ripped off a wound he'd thought almost healed.

'She hates my guts,' he said, honestly. 'And, to be honest, I don't blame her.'

Pritchard let out a belch, eliciting a belly laugh in the process. 'Why?'

'I thought I'd always known what I wanted, Frank,' he began. 'I've done some shady things in my past, but I don't regret them.' He met the psychologist's gaze head on. 'The stuff with McGuinness I... I don't know. Anyway, becoming a policeman was the answer, you know? I thought, if I can do right by others, it'll make up for my mistakes. I've hurt people, Frank, badly.' He flexed his fists, faint scarring lining his knuckles. 'But there came a point when I couldn't blame it on my upbringing any more. Sure, my dad was a bully, but I had to take responsibility for my own life.'

Jack noticed Pritchard finishing his beer, then he got up, grabbed a cold one for him, and waited until he pinged it open before continuing.

'I didn't have a criminal record, and I wasn't known to the police, so I managed to get in. Yeah, McGuinness wasn't happy but what could he do? Kill a policeman? I had the out I needed. Things went fine, I progressed up the ranks, eventually making DI. But those things never quite made up for the past demons. When the Newcastle Knifer case hit, it changed everything. I'd left Louise for Rosie. Nothing had particularly happened, but we both knew it was only a matter of time. I thought I was doing the right thing. Then that bastard started going around carving people up.' He spat the words out, remembering. 'Rosie had seen the effect the force was having on me and she wasn't happy in her job. After the Knifer case, I was running on empty – we all were. Remember?'

Through the dim light, Pritchard spoke. 'I remember.'

As the images passed between them, Jack waited a moment before continuing. 'I'd made DCI and, after it finished, I was on the sick, recuperating,' he said, feeling the sting of old wounds resurface. 'We talked about packing it in, moving to New Zealand, to start over. I'd never been but she has family out there. I knew it was all a lie though. I panicked, told her I had drafted my resignation letter and was going to put it in that day. When I got home from work, she'd thrown herself at me and told me she'd done the same and that we could finally get away from all the misery and hurt.' He paused, steadying himself before continuing. 'That's when I told her the truth.'

The images of that night were still seared on his memory. The feeling of her slap across his face, the tears, the shouting, all of it. That was the moment he knew he'd blown the best thing in his life.

'Then what?' Pritchard asked, cutting through his thoughts.

'I tried to explain, but she wouldn't listen. All she saw was the betrayal. I left the house and when I came home the next day, I found my things boxed up outside with a note. She told me she would never forgive me and that whilst we had to have some sort of professional relationship, we would never be friends.'

He'd kept the letter for months afterwards.

It seemed an age before Pritchard spoke again. 'Women, eh?'

'Yeah, something like that.'

'I'll be damned if that isn't the saddest story I ever heard.'

Jack nodded in agreement. 'I did love her, Frank. I still do. I just don't love her like that. I hate myself for what I put her through, but I couldn't go on living a lie. It was killing me. I realise now I was holding it in because of my family. My parents would have never understood. Now my mother is dead and my dad... well let's just say he won't be around forever.'

He left the part out where he'd stocked up on strong painkillers and vodka, staring at them for what seemed like hours before deciding against it.

It was near 9pm when Pritchard finally decided to leave. He'd mumbled something nonsensical before spending ten minutes putting his jacket on, stopping only to burp, before tipping his hat and stumbling to the taxi.

The last hour hadn't garnered much conversation between the two, with Jack spending the majority of his time stewing on an idea that had formed in his head. Convincing himself it was the right thing to do, he grabbed his jacket.

The walk was a fairly short one. The wind had picked up, causing his ears to sting. He huddled against the biting winter weather on the way to Rosie Lynne's detached house, pausing at the edge of her drive. It suddenly didn't feel like such a good idea when it registered with him just how many beers he'd had. He looked left to right, thinking about what to do. It was now or never. Or at least that's what he told himself. The conversation with Pritchard had brought up all manner of repressed feelings and memories. If he could just explain things to her, maybe she'd listen.

He rang the doorbell, the familiar ting of the wind chimes blowing in the gusty weather. This had been his home too, before it had happened. He found himself wondering whether it still looked the same inside. He hadn't been back since...

Convincing himself it was a bad idea, he turned to leave before the sound of jangling keys caused him to wait.

'Jack?' Rosie appeared in the doorway, glass of red wine in hand.
'I... erm...'

'Is everything okay?' she asked.

'Not really,' he said, unable to meet her gaze.

After a pause, she said, 'Come in.'

He followed her into his old home; the home they'd made together but which now felt foreign to him. The warmth of being indoors was tempered with the chill of the decor having been changed. He could still recall buying the teal wallpaper with her for the hallway, arguing over who would do a better job of papering. As he stood staring at the now red wall, he felt an intense sadness eating away at his insides.

'Sit,' she said, motioning to the settee.

'Thanks,' he replied, noting that she'd even seen fit to buy a new three-piece.

She took a seat far enough away to make the boundaries clear. 'So, what's happened? Is it the case?'

'The case?' he said. 'No.'

Rosie shifted, pulling her cardigan across her chest. 'So this is just some kind of social call?' Her tone darkened.

'It's not like that.'

She ignored him. 'What, and you thought that by coming here you could...' She trailed off, palms facing outward.

'I don't know what I thought,' he shouted, before composing himself. 'I wanted to come to tell you... to...'

'To tell me what, Jack?'

That I'm sorry. That I never meant to hurt you. That it's my fault, not yours.

'Nothing.' He stood to leave. 'This was a mistake.'

'So you're just going to run away again!'

He stopped. 'I didn't run away, I made a mistake. I was living a lie. But you seem to take great joy in making me pay for it every day of my life.'

She raised a hand to her cheek, as if slapped. 'Me! What about you? It was your choice, Jack, not mine.'

He growled. 'It wasn't a choice, Rosie. It's who I am, dammit.'

He stood to the spot, unable to move. Rosie was crying now, each sob a bitter reminder of the mistakes he'd made. He moved forward but she raised her hand. 'Get out!' she screeched.

'Rosie, I...'

'I said...'

The sound of the doorbell brought the argument to an abrupt end. She brushed past him and answered the door; a dark-featured bloke stepped through into the hallway. The protective arm he placed around her shoulder told Jack exactly who it was. Jack searched for some trace of anger in the man's eyes, finding himself struggling with his own, but he saw only surprise.

'Is everything okay?' the man asked. 'I forgot my key.'

'Yes, Alan,' Rosie said, stepping forward. 'Jack was just leaving.'

CHAPTER 15

The lapse of judgement from the previous night stuck with Jack throughout the morning, like the remnants of a bad dream clinging to reality. It was more the embarrassment of having put himself out there like that, something he didn't usually do, that seemed to hurt the most. In the cold light of day, suffering with a minor hangover, he realised how stupid an idea it had all been.

With his detective sergeants seemingly having gone AWOL, he took the opportunity to nurse his shattered dignity over multiple cups of black coffee. He'd decided to switch to Edwards' brand of brew after reading an article in the *Chronicle* about how milk was supposed to be bad for you. Today's newspaper sat before him, a smiling Liam Reed grinning up at him with his arm around his girlfriend, Suzie. He briefly scanned the obituary; 'family-orientated man, had a rough childhood but had turned his life around since he'd met Suzie – the love of his life.' Little did the *Chronicle*-reading public know he was a hired hand for Dorian McGuinness. It always amazed Jack how many people came out to praise some of the worst people in society once they'd passed on.

Still, Liam Reed didn't strike Jack as a particularly bad bloke. It wasn't like he was one to judge. He brought his mind back to the Open Grave murders as he folded over the paper. The killing of a gang member wasn't quite top of the force's agenda, compared to a serial killer with a penchant for the macabre. Still, despite that, he vowed to find out what had happened to Liam Reed. He owed Suzie at least that much.

'Alright, guv?' Watkins said, appearing in the doorway. 'Jesus, you look like shit.'

'Thanks,' he mumbled.

The DS took a seat. 'Anyway, I've got some news to cheer you up.'

Unless you have a time machine, I'm not interested, Jack thought. 'What is it?'

'We've got an ID on the two latest murders. When details of the discovery were released we were inundated with a whole host of calls. Obviously we had the usual crack jobs; there was this one guy...'

'Cut to the point, Watkins,' Jack interrupted.

'Sorry, nervous habit,' the DS replied. 'Anyway, we looked at the missing persons list and narrowed down the possibilities before bringing the families in to view the bodies. We got lucky.'

Jack winced at Watkins' unfortunate use of words. For the parents, they most definitely weren't lucky.

'Show me.'

Watkins tossed a grey folder onto the desk and Jack flicked it open, reading through the documents. Peter Rutherford, twenty-three, from Newcastle upon Tyne. For a moment, the smiling face of the dark, neat-featured, young man gave way to the gruesome image of his bloated corpse. Jack suppressed a shudder and read on. No known run-ins with the law but something told Jack he was no stranger to trouble. He had nothing with which to back up this opinion, it was simply a hunch. And more often than not his hunches proved correct. According to the details, Peter had been unemployed for six months, having previously worked for a cleaning company.

'Interesting,' Jack mused. 'He seems clean, pardon the pun.'

'As does the girl,' Watkins said.

He turned the page and read through the female victim's details. Amy Drummond, twenty-seven, originally from Sheffield but living in Newcastle for the past three years. Former business student who now worked at a local doctor's. Or 'had' worked, Jack corrected himself. Again, nothing to suggest she'd been involved with the law. She was strikingly beautiful, with piercing blue eyes. Jack noted the blonde hair, contrasting Jessica Lisbie who was brunette. So, the MO seemingly had nothing to do with physical appearance. It might have allowed him to rule out hair colour being a motivating factor, but it still didn't give them any further clues. All they could count on so far was that the killer was most likely from Newcastle, given the backgrounds of his victims and where they'd been found. He'd have to get Pritchard in again at some point. Chances were he was sleeping off a hangover at the moment.

He straightened. 'We need to speak to the families.'

Watkins nodded. 'The FLOs are with both of them now; I sorted it out.' The DS blushed as Jack raised an eyebrow. 'I... she's just...'

'I don't care who your girlfriend is, Watkins,' Jack told him, remembering what Pritchard had said the previous night. 'If it makes you a more efficient officer, I'm all for it,' he said, smiling. 'I say we start with Peter Rutherford's mother.'

Peter Rutherford's parents' house was pleasant enough, certainly compared to the housing estate they'd given chase to Gary Dartford in. Gone were the mattresses left in front gardens, replaced by expensive-looking ornaments and well-cropped hedges. The whole area screamed middle-class suburbia.

Jack rang the doorbell as a tiny set of wind chimes picked up next to them, small silver segments clinking together in syncopated beats.

'One second,' a faint voice called from inside.

Moments later, the door opened to reveal an attractive middle-aged woman. She smiled at them both, brilliant white teeth beaming out. Her red puffy eyes spoke of an intense sadness, though.

'Hello, Mrs Rutherford,' Jack said, 'I'm DCI Jack Lambert and this is DS Stephen Watkins. If it's okay, we'd like to speak to you about Peter?'

The woman bit a quivering lip and dabbed a small withered tissue at her eye. 'Of course, officers. Please, come in.'

Edith Rutherford sat them both down in the living room, disappearing momentarily to make a cup of tea. Taking the opportunity to inspect his surroundings, Jack noticed it was plainly decorated, but neat and tidy. A peach-coloured carpet complemented the darker-shaded wallpaper. Various family photos were dotted about the room, mainly placed on the mantelpiece of the faux-fire, opposite where they sat. A mixture of exotic-smelling spices wafted around the room causing his eyes to water.

'There we go,' Edith said, placing a small tray on the table in the centre of the room.

'We'd just like to ask you a few questions.'

Peter Rutherford's grieving mother stared out of the window. 'What? Oh... yes, of course.'

'Peter lived here, yes?'

'Yes, he does... did. He moved back in a year or two ago, once his father left and my health deteriorated.'

Jack motioned to Watkins, who began scribbling details down. Another father missing in action. Jack couldn't help but wonder what the cause of their breakup was. 'If you don't mind me asking, what is wrong with your health?'

'MS,' she said. 'It's been getting progressively worse for years. I had to give up work earlier this year.'

'Where did you work?'

'I worked at a local pharmacy.'

'And your husband?'

'Pardon?'

'What is his job?'

Edith Rutherford's face scrunched up at the mention of her former partner. The attractive woman who'd answered the door seemed to disappear before their eyes, replaced by a wife scorned. 'He's a doctor. He lives on the other side of the city now... with his new woman.'

So that was why. 'I see. And Peter?' Jack looked to his notes. 'Did he know an Amy Drummond, to your knowledge?'

She paused. 'If he did, he never mentioned her. He was always pretty open with me. We had a close relationship. I'm sure if he had been dating somebody, I would have known about it.'

Jack nodded. 'Do you know if he was in any kind of trouble?'

'No, Peter wasn't like that,' she answered a little too quickly.

It was an obvious lie.

Jack paused, watched her trying to hide her squirm. 'Edith, you do realise that any information we can get now may help lead us to finding out who did this to your son?'

'I... it was nothing, really. He had started smoking marijuana lately. I had no idea until he came to me one day. He was upset, crying. He told me he owed somebody money and he couldn't pay them. It was only about a thousand pounds, but he told me they'd already doubled the amount because he hadn't paid up and that they were beginning to make threats.'

'So what did you do about it?'

'I gave him the money, of course. He promised me it was just a one-off and that it would never happen again.'

'And when was this?'

'About three weeks ago.'

Alarm bells started ringing in Jack's head. *Drug dealer. Money owed.*

'Why didn't you mention this before?'

'Because it doesn't matter, does it?' She straightened up. 'He paid them back.'

Jack nodded. 'Do you mind if DS Watkins and I take a look at Peter's room?'

She shrugged, her face impassive. 'Go ahead.'

They were led to the top of the stairs, every few steps being greeted by a different, abstract piece of replica art on the wall. The spicy smell had been replaced by something different now. Something Jack instantly recognised.

'It's the first door on the left there.' She motioned to it. 'I've not touched anything.'

'Thank you,' he said. 'We won't be long.'

As soon as she left, Watkins turned to him. 'Jesus! Let's get some air in here.'

'Agreed.'

Jack marched over to the other side of the room, navigating his way through a sea of junk, and thrust the window open. He turned to Watkins, who was holding his nose between thumb and forefinger.

'He promised it was a one-off,' the DS imitated Peter's mother.

'From the smell in here, I'd say it was epidemic. Either she has no sense of smell, or she's got her head so far buried in the sand that she can't see what's right in front of her,' Jack said.

They set to work. In the centre of the room lay a queen-sized bed, complete with plain black bedding. Above the wooden headboard, a poster hung of Brandon Lee in *The Crow*. Jack had never seen the appeal; a vigilante taking the law into his own hands. To the left of the window, a small, cheap-looking wooden wardrobe stood. Jack moved over to it and threw the doors open. Considering the mess in his room, the contents of the wardrobe were unusually neat. Jack noticed how the array of band T-shirts and other casual clothes were hung up in colour order. Likely a mother's touch.

Watkins held up a set of soft porn mags. 'I wonder if Peter's mother knew about these?'

Jack shrugged. 'He was an adult.' He took the magazines from the DS. 'Albeit one with a distinct lack of taste.' He placed them down and turned back to the task at hand.

After about an hour of wading through various bits of dirty underwear, empty cigarette boxes and a bong with a Yoda head attached, Jack felt like his head was about to explode. Plus the fumes were making him sick.

'Right, come on, I need some fresh air,' he sighed, knees cracking as he got to his feet.

'Are you sure I can't trouble you for some curry? I make it especially for the local market,' Edith Rutherford asked as they trundled down the stairs.

Watkins beamed. 'Well, I am a bit hungry...'

'No, thank you, Mrs Rutherford,' Jack cut in.

They left Peter Rutherford's mother to mourn the loss of her son in peace.

'Now what?' Watkins asked.

Jack eyed him. 'Start with what we know. Let's find this drug dealer.'

'Please tell me you have good news.' Edwards turned to him, his huge body wobbling from the effort.

Jack looked around the people in attendance; Jane Russell, Watkins, Christensen, Gerrard and Edwards, all no doubt wondering why he'd called the impromptu meeting. The room itself was much plusher than what Jack was used to, on account of Edwards having sorted it. Tea and coffee were already prepared on entry, and the table they now sat round was complete with an overhead projector and office swivel chairs. One of the perks of being a DSI in the Northumbria force, he thought.

'It depends on your definition of good news.'

'For God's sake,' Edwards boomed, 'get on with it.'

He swallowed his irritation and turned to DI Russell. 'Jane, any luck today?'

The detective paused, took a sip of her black coffee and straightened out her suit jacket. 'No.'

'Same here.'

'Great,' Edwards said. 'So you called me out of an important meeting to tell me you've got bugger all to go on?'

'I think we have been barking up the wrong tree,' Jack cut in.

'What do you mean?' DI Russell peered over to him.

'I mean, we've been focused on what connects the victims.'

'Which is procedure,' Christensen said.

'Indeed. But DS Watkins and I paid a visit to Edith Rutherford's house today. We didn't find a lot, just some porn mags and empty tab boxes. However, we did find out that Peter recently owed money to a local drug dealer.'

'That doesn't necessarily mean anything,' Russell said.

'Alright,' Edwards sighed. 'So what tree should we be barking up?'

'So far, we've questioned families, friends and work colleagues – now, unless there's a cover-up of epic proportions going on, I think it's safe to say that the victims do not know each other.'

The room seemed to collectively groan at once. If they didn't know each other, the killer might prove even harder to find.

'Now,' he continued. 'Watkins and I will chase up the lead regarding the drug dealer. I've got someone pulling together all local known dealers as we speak. I would suggest, though, that we focus not on how the victims knew each other, but how the perpetrator knew them. It could be a place, event or, God forbid, completely random.'

'Please explain to me how this is good news, Jack?' Edwards asked, massaging his temples with a giant paw.

'It gives the investigation a new focus, which is sorely needed.'

'I agree,' Gerrard interjected. 'We've had nothing to go on so far. We've got nothing to lose by shifting our focus at this point.'

Watkins stood. 'So, what are my orders?'

'Get me that list of drug dealers – we've got a long week ahead. And, you better cancel any leave you had.'

'What? I'm meant to be taking my lass away on Friday.'

'Correction, *were* meant to. I need you here because, believe it or not, you can actually be quite useful.'

Watkins straightened up. 'Thank you, Jack.'

'Sometimes.'

'You can't take it back now,' he said, turning to leave.

'Oh, and, Watkins?'

'Yes?'

'That's DCI Lambert to you.'

The team sprang back into action, apart from Edwards, who had slumped off before the meeting adjourned. There was no doubt in Jack's mind that the team needed a new focus to the investigation. Hopefully this would be it. He was sure that the link was not that the victims knew each other, but that the killer knew them or where they were. Jack just hoped that they could find the crucial link before the Open Grave Murderer struck again.

CHAPTER 16

'How'd you manage to get the go-ahead from Edwards for this?'

'Edwards hates Dorian McGuinness. He practically jumped with glee when I suggested it,' Jack said.

'I didn't sign up for this when I joined the force,' Watkins yawned.

'Nobody is forcing you to sign up for anything,' Jack replied, adjusting the mirror on the unmarked car they were now sitting in.

'I was just kidding.'

He shrugged him off. Gone were the days when Jack had lived for a good eight-hour stakeout. They'd been sitting outside McGuinness Aquatics for over an hour now and the cold was beginning to give him a crick in his back. Still, to catch these boys out, they would have to make some sacrifices. Jack just hoped that this was as bad as it would get.

'What the hell is wrong with this thing?' Watkins said, jabbing the heater button.

'It's broke, only gives out cold air.'

'No wonder I'm freezing my nuts off. And to think, I could have been at home with my lass.'

'Pity for her.'

'Hey!'

He ignored the moaning DS and looked out of the window. Thick wisps of white air billowed out of people's mouths as they walked by. Not that there were many people around at this time. Another glance at his watch told him it was getting on for 7pm.

This could be a long night.

'Why can't criminals just go about their business through the day?'

'They do,' Jack sighed. 'But we'd be much more visible then and they aren't stupid. Dorian McGuinness makes sure he runs a well-oiled machine.'

Even if it wasn't well-oiled, they'd be dicing with danger if they staked them out through the day. Jack still bore the scars on his leg from a tussle with a local drug gang a few years back. The then DI had signed off on a 3pm stakeout at a warehouse down the A1. Needless to say, the shit hit the fan and they had been left short. Once the press got wind, the detective didn't last much longer, going on the sick for over a year before handing in his resignation.

Watkins began rustling about, fishing out a Greggs jam doughnut. Jack, not-so-subtly, brushed the sugar from his leg as he began munching on a makeshift packed lunch.

'Want one?' Watkins asked.

'No,' he said, ignoring the pleas from his stomach. He'd taken a long look in the mirror that morning and decided enough was enough. He needed to cut out the rubbish and lose some weight.

Was that movement? Jack's arm shot out, silencing his partner. His eyes scanned through the darkness, his vision slipping past the dim street lights that illuminated the cobbled side street.

Just a cat.

'Jesus, Jack, you scared the shit out of me,' Watkins said, spraying doughnut over the interior.

'Just keep your focus.'

'I prefer to stay relaxed.'

'I've noticed,' Jack said, eyeing his ginger companion as he slurped sugar from his fingers.

Watkins was right, Jack was edgy. He was sure McGuinness was up to something. He didn't know what, but he was sure as hell going to find out. If somebody was muscling in on his operation, Liam Reed's death had to be connected somehow. The lack of movement on the Open Grave case had given them an opportunity to check out what was going on with Newcastle's favourite crime lord. Friday nights were always 'business night' when Jack was on the books. Watkins had done a good job of pulling together the names of a number of local known drug dealers and they'd be pulling them in for questioning soon. Jack hoped they'd be able to shake something loose from one of them regarding Peter Rutherford. For now, though, McGuinness was his focus.

'There's Tank,' Watkins said, cutting through his thoughts.

The unmistakable hulk of McGuinness's right-hand man had come out of the shop, looking up and down the street.

Looks nervous, Jack thought.

'Get ready.'

Arnold 'Tank' Mohan moved from the front of the shop, his black bomber jacket and hat making him look like a stereotypical cartoon burglar. He stopped in the centre of the street, looking left and right once more. Jack's fist clenched as he looked over to their direction and paused. They paused too, wondering whether or not he had seen them. There was no reaction from Tank. He moved on. A second man appeared from the opposite side of the street. Jack couldn't make out his features in the shadows, but he looked slender and stood almost a foot taller than his companion.

'Want me to call backup?' Watkins whispered.

'Now who's on edge? No, we don't know what they're up to yet.'

They didn't have to wait long. A white transit van with heavily-rusted wheel arches parked up by the two men. Tank saw the vehicle and motioned to his silent partner. Moments later, they slipped out of view as the van moved in front of their position. Jack turned the ignition as both men hopped into the side of the van.

'Here we go.'

There were at least three men in the van. Jack hadn't managed to see the driver as he came past, but they had to assume they were outnumbered by one. At least.

He kept the car to a safe distance as the Transit weaved in and out of Newcastle's evening traffic. Whatever they were doing, they weren't taking much care with the speed limit. He resisted the urge to pull them over. Something bigger than going thirty-five in a thirty zone was occurring here. Still, he didn't call backup.

Drunk youths lined the streets, queuing up to sample the North East nightlife. Back when Jack was a young bobby, he'd venture to these parts of the city with Louise. Times had changed now, though. Looking at their attire, he couldn't believe how brave the women were, most of them wearing shorts that looked more like skimpy underwear. He changed his mind. Stupid, not brave.

Continuing their pursuit, they followed the van onto the dual carriageway. Old, pock-marked tarmac stood between them and their prey, causing the car to judder as its speed increased. They weren't hanging about. Jack could feel a spike in his adrenaline.

'Where are you off to?' Watkins mumbled.

They followed the van as it made its way further up the motorway, heading north towards Jedburgh. Jack hoped their trip wouldn't take them that far. Although he had fond memories of his grandparents taking him and his brother to their caravan up there, he had leftover lasagne waiting for him in the house once he got back.

Up ahead, the Transit made a left turn down a side junction. Jack slowed, allowing the distance to grow; with fewer cars on the road they'd be a lot more visible.

Every bone in his body seemed to jar as they followed the van into the dark woodland. Conscious of the danger of being seen, Jack cut the headlights, slowing to compensate for the night that now surrounded them. His instincts told him this was a bad idea, but they couldn't leave now.

'What's down here?' Watkins asked, bringing a hand up to wipe condensation from the windscreen.

'I don't know,' Jack replied. 'But I don't like it.'

A right turn in the road signalled the end of the mud track. From a fair way back, Jack could see the van's lights cut out after it parked up outside what looked like an abandoned factory. Trees lined the path on either side. The lack of lights in their environment added to the uncomfortable feeling Jack was now experiencing.

'Do we follow?'

Jack paused, then shook his head.

He pulled the car to the side of the road, keeping a safe distance from their new friends. Fumbling in his pocket, he brought out a stick of chewing gum and threw it into his mouth, the urge to light up a cigarette almost overwhelming.

Moments later, Tank exited the van, flashlight in tow. The tall stranger got out as well. Jack panicked, hoping Arnold wouldn't point the light in their direction. The last thing they needed was to be caught out. Something told him that these blokes wouldn't invite them in for tea and biscuits.

The mysterious other man was still bathed in shadows. From the front of the van, Jack saw the driver get out, followed by another passenger. He couldn't make out faces, but they looked male and they looked large.

No one else seemed to be around. Tank's flashlight bounced across the seemingly-abandoned building, never landing in one place. Whatever they were doing, they weren't going straight in. They seemed to be talking. Jack squinted, wishing he'd thought to bring binoculars. Watkins rubbed his arm across the windscreen, once again, and squinted into the distance.

'Can't see a bastard thing,' he moaned.

'They're just talking.'

Tank was pointing his light at different parts of the building, gesticulating rather vigorously. The building was massive, with Jack making out what looked like three storeys. Even from this distance, he could tell it was a dive. Most of the windows were boarded up, and those that weren't didn't seem to have any glass in them. It probably hadn't been used in years. Well, not legally anyway. Now it seemed that Dorian McGuinness had decided to bring it out of retirement. But for what? Drugs? Something worse?

They were moving now... but not towards the factory. Motioning in the opposite direction, the four men disappeared into the woods, sporadic beams of light breaking through the shrubbery.

'We following them?' Watkins asked.

Jack spat the already tasteless chewing gum into a tissue. 'Not unless you want your balls chopped off.'

'Well, what do you want to do then?'

'Nothing. We're leaving.'

'You aren't even going to call for backup?'

Jack waved him away. 'We struck lucky by finding this place. We need to take stock before we go running in. You never show all your cards at once,' he told the DS. 'I want to know what they're playing at before I go in all guns blazing. And I don't fancy getting my head smacked in right now. I know something bigger is going on here but if we play our hand we risk it unravelling before we catch them in the act. Besides, there's nothing to say it's linked to Liam Reed's death at this point.'

Watkins nodded in silent agreement.

They backed the car up and turned it around before switching the headlights back on. The car would leave tracks, but he didn't have time to worry about that now. Best to get away leaving a clue than be caught out.

One thing was for sure; McGuinness was up to something. The boys at the Aquatic store had moved the first pawn.

'Come on,' Jack said, heading back towards the city. 'I'll treat you to a McDonald's. In the meantime, pass me one of those doughnuts, will you?'

'Yes, sir.'

He manoeuvred across the lanes, using one hand to throw back what had to be the most sugary doughnut he'd ever tasted. The lasagne – and diet – could wait. Despite the sweet sensation, he couldn't shake the bitter taste in the back of his throat. McGuinness was up to something.

CHAPTER 17

'Alright, settle down!'

The noise shrivelled to a barely perceptible hum. One stern look later and the room fell silent. He'd been in a reasonable mood on the way into work, even stopping to inhale a bacon sandwich with extra sauce, until Edwards had gotten hold of him.

'Are we going to start actually solving some cases soon, DCI Lambert?' he'd shouted.

'We're working on a number of leads.'

'Oh, are we now?' he cut in. 'Because from where I'm sitting, it looks like fuck all is getting done. Perhaps you have too much on your plate?'

Jack bit his tongue and held his gaze firmly on the DSI.

Edwards cleared his throat. 'Where are we on the Open Grave Murderer?'

'We have officers speaking to the immediate family members of the second killings, as we speak. We thought we had a suspect but—'

'Yes, the barman. Worked out well, didn't it? And where are we on the Liam Reed murder?'

'It's clear Dorian McGuinness is involved in some way. The pieces haven't fallen into place – yet – but we are seeing some movement.'

The DSI looked almost disappointed. 'What about the stalker case?'

'Nell Stevens?'

'No, Simon Cowell. Of course, Nell Stevens!' he thundered.

'DS Watkins is taking the lead on that one.'

'I don't want Watkins taking the lead. That man couldn't find his arse with bog roll and a road map. The press are squeezing us on this and I want something sorted *soon*. If you can't do it, I'll find someone else who can.'

Jack stood up and leaned over the desk. 'Don't think just because we've known each other for years that I will sit here and have my professionalism questioned by you.' He jabbed a finger at the DSI. 'If you're not careful, somebody will eventually make a complaint about your attitude and you'll have nobody left to fight your corner.'

Edwards looked as if he was about to burst. 'Is that a threat?'

'Call it whatever you want, Logan,' he said, turning to leave. 'Oh, and don't ever speak about one of my team like that again.'

The image of DI Jane Russell, sitting in the front row, brought him back to the present. Having the Bulldog taking over his caseload was not something he was willing to entertain. They needed results quickly.

'Okay, let's get started,' he said.

He turned to the huge whiteboard he'd managed to commandeer, writing key notes down one side. It was a trick he'd learned from a cousin of his who was a lecturer. Apparently, it helped give focus to a discussion. The board itself was split into three different sections, with photos in the centre of each one; Liam Reed, the four Open Grave victims and Nell Stevens – fully clothed, much to the disappointment of Watkins.

'We can start with the Open Grave murders,' he said, pointing to the images. 'We have an ID on all four suspects. What we don't yet have is a connection between them. Find the connection, find the killer,' he said, pointing out the obvious. 'DC Gerrard, would you care to update the room on your progress.'

The young officer sprang into action. 'We have been following up leads on the second murders, speaking to family members and close friends. So far, we haven't got a link or known motive. We haven't finished our enquiries yet, but – unless something else comes up soon – we'll be at a loose end.'

Jack chewed it over. *Something else* meant more bodies. Something they couldn't afford.

'Thanks, Claire. I've been speaking to DI Russell and we both agree that finding a link between the victims knowing each other may be off the mark. Right now, I want to know what else might connect them, be it a place or event. I believe we need to consider how the killer knows them, not how they know each other.'

Jane Russell gave a curt nod.

'Now, on to Liam Reed.'

Jack and Watkins spent the next ten minutes updating the group on the key events in the case so far. With the advent of having found the abandoned factory, Jack thought it prudent to bring in the rest of the team. Of course, there was the possibility that it wasn't linked to Liam Reed's murder, but coincidences weren't something experience had taught him to ignore. Plus, whatever it was, he would bet his last penny on it being outside the law.

'Now, with regards to Nell Stevens...' Watkins began.

Jack took a seat, noting a faint wolf-whistle as he turned his back to the room. Watkins tugged at his collar, the familiar red flush appearing on his freckled face.

'We've had a potential development,' he continued. 'Builders, who were working on a conservatory for a local celeb across the road, noticed a bloke hanging about near her house, camera in hand, yesterday.'

'Regular paps?' DC Gerrard asked.

Watkins shrugged. 'Possibly, but I think we need to consider surveillance on the house, just in case.'

More overtime for Edwards to grumble about.

Jack watched the various officers slump from the room as he broke up the meeting. Morale was low, and he didn't blame them. He placed his palm against his forehead, sighed, and leaned back against the desk. The lack of progress on all of their cases was worrying. They needed to move fast. The problem was, he didn't know where to start.

'What's the next step then, boss?' Watkins asked.

Jack looked to the whiteboard, and stroked his stubbled chin, noting that it was now becoming more of a beard. 'We find that drug dealer Peter Rutherford owed money to.'

'You think it's related?'

'I don't know,' he replied. 'That's what I need to find out. I want a name by the end of the week.'

CHAPTER 18

A noise woke him. As he rolled over, he realised his mouth was like sandpaper. He tried to focus through the blur that was his tired state, sat up, and glanced at the digits on the clock by his bedside: 7.30am. He lay back down, his head thumping. Damn Watkins and his after-work drinks. Pulling the duvet over his head, he attempted to block out the light that was beginning to slither through the gap in his curtains. What had he been dreaming about? Most likely the Open Grave murders. They were torturing him on a near nightly basis now. Lately, people he knew had been appearing in the graves. First it was himself, then Louise, and even his daughter Shannon. If he'd been visiting a psychiatrist, they'd have had a field day with him. As it was, he'd only been advised to go and talk to somebody. Until that became an order, he would continue as he was. Suffering, but sane. At least that was his own opinion.

He tossed and turned, attempting to force himself back to sleep. He could feel himself drowsing, dropping back into his inner thoughts. He closed his eyes. Within seconds he felt himself falling into another slumber.

His eyes shot open as his phone buzzed.

'Shit!' he said to himself as he stared at the screen.

He thumbed the accept button and placed the handset to his ear.

'Where have you been?'

'In bed, it's not even eight in the morning,' he yawned. 'You sound stressed, Christensen.'

Jack paused, bracing himself for bad news. The fog that had clouded over him had receded. If Christensen was rattled, it must be bad.

'Is it another grave?'

'No, but if I were you I would get to the station before Edwards has a heart attack.'

'Details, Christensen.'

There was a pause on the line. 'It's Nell Stevens, she's had a break-in and she's freaking out at the station.'

So much for letting others take the lead. 'I'll be right there.'

He forced himself to shave, eager not to appear too dishevelled in front of the press. Forty-five minutes later, he arrived at work, stomach growling as he stepped through the media scrum into reception. Breakfast wasn't a luxury he could afford today.

'Dear me,' the desk sergeant greeted him. 'You been shaving yourself with a blunt knife?'

'I was in a hurry,' he snapped, looking away from her.

They managed to place Nell Stevens into a separate waiting area away from the press. Jack was on his way in to speak with her when Edwards caught him in the corridor.

'What are the details?' he asked.

'Apparently we received a phone call around five this morning. The... lover, reported the house broken into.'

'Lover?'

'Yes,' Edwards replied. 'He says they have been keeping a low profile about their relationship.'

Jack nodded.

'She'd spent the night at his place in the rough end of town and, when they went back to hers, they found the place smashed up.'

'Any leads?'

Edwards shrugged, palms outstretched in submission.

'Anyway, he's downstairs now drinking green tea,' he scoffed.

'I'll go speak to them,' Jack said.

'You do that, Detective.' The DSI eyed him. 'You do understand the ramifications of this? With no end in sight on the Open Grave murders and now this, we'll be lucky not to be shut down.'

'I understand.'

Jack confirmed the details of Nell Stevens' partner before beginning.

'Okay, Mr Armstrong, just tell us the chain of events from the start.'

The man sitting opposite Jack and Christensen inhaled a large breath and placed his hands on the table, as if steadying himself. His designer stubble and Marine-style haircut marked him out as a trendy, good-looking bloke. But the rings around his dark eyes highlighted a lack of sleep, perhaps a partying lifestyle.

'Nell came over to mine, as she usually does.'

'Is this every night?' Jack asked.

'Most nights. I sometimes stay with her at the weekend. She's pretty busy.'

Jack noticed the slight disdainful tone in his voice. *Busy being stalked in night clubs*, he thought.

'So what was the chain of events from her arriving at your house?'

Shaun Armstrong took a drink from the water Christensen had supplied, before continuing, 'She arrived just after eight, as usual. We put a film on...'

'What time?'

'About half an hour after she got there.'

'Then what?'

'Well we watched the film, obviously. Once it finished, we ordered some takeaway from a nearby Chinese and then sat talking.'

'What time did you order the food?'

'I don't know, about ten?'

Jack sensed irritation creeping into his voice.

'Please.' He gestured. 'Continue.'

'The food arrived maybe half an hour later and we ate it.'

Irritation gave way to sarcasm.

'After that, we just sort of hung out.' He flushed red. 'At around three in the morning, I drove her back to hers. The paps usually give up before then and nobody sees us. I drove to hers and when we arrived I noticed a mess in the living room, through the window.'

Jack paused, taking in all the details. He tapped a pen absentmindedly on the desk before proceeding further.

'Where was the point of entry?'

'Pardon?'

'Had the intruder gone in via the front or the back door?'

'The back door,' he replied. 'I opened the front door and we wandered through the house. It was clear somebody had broken in. The place was smashed up good and proper.'

'Was anything stolen?'

Armstrong shook his head. 'Not that I could see.'

'Do you know of anybody who would want to harm Miss Stevens?'

The young man snorted. 'Probably them damn paps. Or a crazy fan or something. Maybe that bloke from the bar the other week?'

'Thank you, Mr Armstrong, that will be all for now.'

Nell Stevens' lover stood up, pulling his Barbour jacket from the back of the chair. 'Just make sure you catch the bastard.'

Jack smiled. 'We're doing all we can, sir.'

He spent the next half an hour questioning a visibly upset Nell Stevens, who was sure somebody was out to murder her, before finally finding time to hide out in his office. He still couldn't quite reconcile the celebrity in the papers with the woman who had now visited the police station on multiple occasions. To him, she seemed a regular person; scared, yes, but nothing out of the ordinary. Hers wasn't a lifestyle that held any appeal for him.

'What do you think, then?' Christensen asked.

Jack placed his feet on his desk, which was becoming messier with every passing day. Taking a deep breath, he massaged his temples, trying to block out the tiredness that was almost overwhelming him.

What did he know? Nell Stevens had won a reality singing show and became an overnight celebrity. She was splashed all over the papers on an almost daily basis. Just the other week, however, she'd reported a potential stalking, having been bothered in a nightclub. She'd also been sent threatening and explicit mail. Now, all within a short time period, somebody had broken into her home and trashed the place, stealing nothing.

'We need to take a look at the house.'

'Now?' the DS asked.

'As much as I would like to sleep, Edwards has his foot up my arse on this one, so it looks like we'll have to. Besides, it'll take my mind off this Open Grave fiasco.'

'There's a team already going over the house for fingerprints but, given the size of the place, it may take a while.'

Jack nodded. 'Let's go.'

Darras Hall was a well-known area in the North East, home to a number of local celebrities and Newcastle United footballers, not that the latter deserved such dwellings given their current early season form. Pulling the patrol car into a space just down the street, he could see the technicians already at work, teeming around the property. They made for the driveway, Jack pulling his collar up to protect himself against the elements that were becoming ever colder. As they approached the giant structure he couldn't help but wonder if the powers that be would organise themselves on this kind of scale for Joe Public. Who was he kidding? If the victim was Joe Public, a DCI wouldn't even be aware of it.

'Can I help you?' A uniformed officer stopped them at the gate.

'Yes,' Jack replied, flashing his badge. 'You can move aside.'

'Sorry, sir,' he stammered. 'I'm new here.'

The detectives continued towards the front of the house. As they gazed up, at least a dozen windows stood facing them. The red brick structure loomed over them like an angry school teacher. On the roof, various solar panels sat, no doubt searching in vain for some semblance of sunshine. The garden seemed nicely kept. Jack made a mental note to check up on who the gardener was. A bit cliché, but it wasn't beyond the realms of possibility.

'Jack, good to see you, mate.' A tall technician approached, covered from head to toe in a white IB suit.

'Bill,' Jack greeted him. 'What can you tell me?'

Bill Ivey was an old hand in the force; reliable and straight talking. Before the Newcastle Knifer case, he'd often socialised with the man. Things were different now, though. They'd drifted, as if what had once held them together had been severed, like one of the Knifer's victims.

'Not a lot. I've got my team running over the house right now. It's huge, really huge.'

'It seems being a celebrity pays off.'

'Yeah,' he snorted. 'Until you get yourself a stalker.'

'If indeed she does.'

'You thinking along other lines?'

Jack shrugged. 'I'm always thinking along other lines.'

They continued their journey into the house, the smell of recently cut grass being replaced by an intense whiff of bleach. Jack scrunched his face up, his eyes watering against the onslaught.

'Potent,' Christensen muttered.

He noticed a large wooden staircase, to the right, heading straight up to the first floor. Down a long, grey-carpeted hallway an open door stood, looking into what must be the kitchen. He moved forward slightly and appeared around a doorway to the left, opening out into a huge living room complete with a smashed plasma TV and cracked wall mirror.

'Where should we start?' Christensen asked.

He paused. 'The boyfriend says the perp came in the back way. That's where we'll start.'

Two hours of painstaking searching later, they were still empty-handed. Bill had informed them of the lack of fingerprint evidence and, with no CCTV in the house, things were looking bleak. One thing was for sure, though. Whoever had broken in wasn't after money. They'd done a good job on the place. Photos, mirrors and TVs were all smashed, along with a number of clothes having been cut up. Everything pointed to a personal vendetta. Jack just hoped that he would able to find out who it was and stop them before things got out of hand.

CHAPTER 19

Interview 1: Michael Rogers AKA Mini-Snoop

'**N**o idea, blood, ya get me?'

Jack looked up from the documents that identified 'Michael Rogers' as a violent, drug dealing twenty-five-year-old pain in the arse.

'No, Michael, I don't get you,' he sighed.

Watkins leant forward in his chair, the springs screeching out in agony. 'So you're sure you've never heard of Peter Rutherford?'

'Well, only in the press, you know? That dude got sliced up good, so I read.'

'He wasn't sliced, Michael, he was... anyway, never mind that.'

The diminutive wannabe rapper tutted, bringing his tongue over his teeth for the hundredth time in the past twenty minutes. His fake gold rings clattered against the table as he drummed his hands to an invisible beat, gaunt features staring them down.

'This is very important; do you know of anyone in your... circle who might want to hurt Peter? I'm told he owed money to someone.'

'Not me, ya get me?'

Jack ground his teeth together, resisting the urge to grab the dealer by his tiny white vest and drag him across the table.

'Detectives.' Casey Clifton interrupted his doodling to lean into the scene. 'This is clearly going nowhere.'

'Interview terminated.'

Interview 2: Pauline Sketcher

Jack settled back into the plush interview room he'd managed to wangle for the morning. Although it was nicely furnished with a large oak table and a variety of office chairs, the lack of windows gave it a claustrophobic edge, and he had done away with his tie after finishing up with the rapper.

'And here we go again.' Watkins strode in, coffee in hand. 'I don't see why we couldn't just do this off the record, rent a room in a hotel, apply a little pressure.'

'Because I don't want the press getting a whiff of us not doing something by the book.'

'Fair enough.'

'Plus, it's quite amusing keeping Clifton here all day.'

As if on cue the smartly-dressed lawyer sauntered in, his client trailing behind him.

'Hello, Mrs Sketcher,' Watkins greeted their guest.

The huge thirty-year-old pulled the seat out opposite them, her skin-tight black leggings showing far too much of her leopard print G-string. Watkins seemed transfixed. She settled down, her V-neck top revealing enough cleavage to warrant a public indecency charge. Her greased-back hair looked like it had been glued to her head, massive gold earrings completing the profile.

'Here, it's miss now, right? The bastard left me.'

I wonder why? Jack thought.

'Do you know why we've asked you here?'

'Because pigs have nowt better to do,' she spat, a giant hand reaching into her garish pink bra to rearrange herself.

'Do you know who Peter Rutherford is?'

'I know lots of people.'

Judging by her extensive dealing history, she was probably right.

'Do you know him?'

'Can't remember.' She shrugged her shoulders. This was going to be a long day.

'Here is a picture of him,' Watkins said, holding out a mugshot for her to look at.

'He's the one in the press. I didn't do it.'

'We're not saying you did, Pauline.'

'Then why am I here?'

Jack didn't have to look over to know Casey Clifton was smiling.

'He owed money to a local drug dealer. We think it might lead somewhere.'

'Well I don't do that sort of thing, detectives.'

'Pauline, I know you deal in weed, coke and even a little heroin. For once, though, I'm not here to arrest you on that. I simply want to know if you knew Peter Rutherford or anybody who might want to hurt him.'

She shifted in her seat. 'I sold him a little weed a while back, alright? Is that a crime?'

'Yes.'

'Aye, well...'

'Did he owe you money?' Jack asked.

'No, not really.'

'We have a witness who says he was being threatened by a local drug dealer.'

'Well it wasn't me,' she screeched, spittle flying over the desk. 'Since our lad left, I've got no muscle anyway. What can I do?'

Something told Jack that she could handle herself just fine.

'So you have no idea as to who we might be looking for?'

She shifted again, and he saw something flash across her eyes.

'I don't do much dealing now. Comes through somebody else.'

'Who?'

'I don't want to say.'

Jack sighed. 'Pauline, if you can't cooperate I can always search your premises, see what you've got to hide.'

'That is out of order, Detective,' Clifton cut in.

He ignored the lawyer. 'Does this have something to do with Dorian McGuinness?'

She snorted. 'Nah, he's washed up now. Anybody who knows anything knows that.'

'Is that the word on the street?' Jack asked.

Fear flashed across her eyes. 'I... no... well it's not me saying it, okay? I never said that.'

'So somebody is muscling in on his territory, then?'

She shifted in her seat. 'Look, they call him the Captain, that's all I know.'

'The Captain?'

'Aye, man. Nobody knows his real name but he's a big deal and an even bigger dealer. Most stuff goes through him now. That's all I know, honest.'

'So—'

'I'm refusing to say anything else.'

Interview 3: Andy Owens

'Fuck off. I'm not saying a word.'

Interview 4: George Haddon

'You sure this is a drug dealer?' Watkins whispered.

Jack looked up from his notes at fifty-five-year-old George Haddon, complete with green tank top and park ranger shorts. His glasses sat far too low down on his nose, his face a sea of red, veins having exploded over his skin. He'd come quietly and was now sat smiling a toothless grin at them.

'This is the guy.'

He glanced down once more at his paperwork. George Haddon, drug dealer, knock-off watch distributor and owner of indecent images of children.

'I can assure you, detectives, that I have done nothing wrong. Those pictures were an accident,' he squeaked.

'You're not here about that, George.'

'I swear—'

'Alright,' Jack said, trying not to lose his temper. 'It's about a drug dealer.'

The man, sat before them, exhaled. 'So I deal a little weed from time to time, is that a crime?'

'Yes, George, it is.'

Three hours, four coffees and twelve interviews later, they'd finished for the day. Jack sat back in his chair, loosening his top button as evening began to set upon them.

'I could murder a pint after dealing with that lot,' Watkins sighed.

'I'm tempted to join you on that.'

'What you reckon then?'

Jack patted his pocket, searching for a cigarette. Old habits die hard.

'The Captain.'

'She could have been talking utter bullshit. Nobody else seemed to know anything about a Captain.'

He paused, stroked his chin and leaned forward. 'No, but that doesn't mean that they don't know anything. They were all nervous to some degree. Could be the situation. Could be because somebody is putting pressure on local dealers.'

'I suppose.'

'I want the word put out that we are looking for this Captain bloke. Let's see if our people on the ground can give us any information.'

'You do know who else might be able to give us some info?'

Jack dragged a palm across his aching forehead. 'Of course I do, but right now we're watching McGuinness to try find out what happened to Liam Reed. I don't want anything complicating that.'

'More important than the Open Grave murders?'

'No,' Jack admitted. 'But he deserves some justice, nevertheless.'

'Fair enough. I hope you know what you're doing.'

Jack had the exact same thought.

CHAPTER 20

It was just after 3am when he awoke. Heavy breathing suggested another bad dream had occurred, but he couldn't remember it. Darkness engulfed his bedroom, the faint sound of middle-of-the-night traffic just about audible. Shifting position, Jack lay on his side, closing his eyes.

That's when he heard it.

The intruder was seemingly at pains to move quietly, but Jack knew every creak within his house. And this creak was different. The short squeak of the living room door opening confirmed his suspicion.

He glanced to his phone, considered ringing the station, but the noise would give him away. Best to make them think he didn't know. Plus, he knew how to handle himself.

Footsteps. Growing louder. Making their way up the stairs. Jack stood slowly, pulled on his jeans, and weighed up his options. He could throw himself from the window or face the intruder.

As he edged closer to the door, one of the floorboards let out an ear-piercing creak. Jack paused, listening to the sounds from outside. There was a pause, as if they were trying to decide whether it was just a house noise or not. He could feel the sweat beginning to trickle down his forehead as he grabbed the cool door handle with a clammy hand.

Another creak.

They were close to the top of the stairs now. What if they were armed? What if there was more than one of them? His instincts were telling him that this was a bad idea. All he had was the element of surprise. Or so he hoped.

A heavier footstep planted down on the landing outside. He inhaled deeply, trying to slow his heart rate, and turned the doorknob.

'What the—'

After he threw himself onto the landing, he was instantly blinded by the light being flicked on. He hadn't managed to quite blink the stars away before a heavy fist smashed into the side of his head. His vision went red as pain exploded in his cheek.

'Argh,' he groaned, falling to his right.

So much for the advantage of surprise.

He grabbed the bannister as a black boot hurtled forward, catching him in the ribs. Judging by the agony he was now enduring, he was sure at least one was broken. Gasping, he looked up at his clown-masked assailant. It was definitely a man, clad all in black, leather gloves straining against huge hands. He looked like a gym type, one of those who spends all his time doing bench presses instead of sorting out their beer belly. The smell of fertiliser was overwhelming as he attempted to maintain his balance.

He spun to the left, missing the next kick by inches. The whistle of leathered air clipped his earlobe. He clenched his hand into a fist, aimed an uppercut between the bloke's legs.

The clown fell to one knee, his right hand moving down to shield himself. Left-handed – good to know. Jack pulled himself up, ignoring his screaming ribs, and landed a punch to the face. He wasn't one to pussyfoot around in a fight, but this bloke had a face of iron. He could feel his knuckles instantly swell.

The clown was recovering now, grasping at the bannister to pull himself up. Jack lunged for his arm and missed. He landed on the wooden railing, as another punch winged its way to his face. He fell onto his back, his new friend throwing himself on top of him, forearm across his throat.

So this was it. What a pitiful way to go. The stars were back, his vision blurring as the heavy arm crushed his windpipe. Although he was masked, Jack could tell he was smiling. Through the fog, he could feel himself moving from panic to drowsiness. Time seemed to slow as images of his family floated around his mind. He hadn't even had time to make it up with his father. Or Rosie.

Mustering up all the energy he could, he raised his arms towards the clown's eyes, forcing his thumbs into the darkened gaps. Within seconds, the bloke fell back, a guttural roar escaping his throat. Jack tried to force himself up, but fell back, seemingly paralysed. Across the way the intruder's left hand went to his boot and pulled.

The small flash of the blade brought Jack back to life. One giant effort later, he managed to scramble to his feet. The clown moved forward, but Jack was too fast. He lunged, grabbing him before hurtling to the right, sending them both over the bannister.

The clown grunted as they made impact, splintered wood landing around them like fallen leaves.

Out of the corner of his eye, Jack could see the knife lying at the bottom of his feet. He made a grab for it, before a heavy boot kicked it out of the way. The giant attacker steadied himself once more before picking the blade up.

'I was just gonna deliver a message,' he grunted. 'But now you've really pissed me off.'

Jack couldn't place the voice due to it being muffled by the mask; definitely local though. 'A message from who?'

The sound of approaching sirens grew to a crescendo. The clown snapped his head towards the door. Jack could almost see the cogs turning in his mind.

'Next time,' he growled.

'What message?' Jack shouted, feeling nausea rise up in his throat.

'Next time,' he repeated, before turning and making a limping exit.

The last thing he could remember before passing out was the shrill wailing of multiple police cars, followed by the screams of his next-door neighbour.

There was a vague sense of pain, clouded by a warm, fuzzy feeling blanketing his entire body. Voices cascaded around him in alarm, their pitch and tone slurring as if drunk. He blinked, his vision fading like an Etch a Sketch, before total darkness overcame him once more.

'Detective Lambert? Can you hear me?'

'Mmm?'

'You're in the hospital. You've suffered some injuries due to an attack. Don't be alarmed, everything will be okay.'

His head rolled, lips smacking in dehydration. Moments later, a straw arrived at his mouth.

'There, take small sips.'

Cool liquid coursed down his throat. He coughed, having taken in too much at once.

'Can you understand me?' the doctor asked, shining a light into his eyes.

'Y-yes,' Jack forced out, his voice barely a whisper.

'Let me through!' a familiar voice shouted from the distance.

Edwards appeared to his right alongside a red-faced nurse.

'It's okay,' the doctor sighed.

The stout woman gave a grunt before leaving, her shoes slapping against the linoleum flooring.

'If I didn't know any better, Doctor, I'd say I was high.'

The tall, stooped figure of his carer smiled, glasses perched on a long, crooked nose. He was dressed in green scrubs, a shower cap on his head.

'You're on a morphine drip,' he told him. 'It was either that or complete agony; you've got two cracked ribs and a swollen hand, not to mention some heavy bruising to that cheek of yours.'

'Doesn't sound too bad.'

'Just wait till you get home, my old boy. Then the fun will really begin. You were lucky,' he continued. 'We thought he'd crushed your larynx.'

'Swings and roundabouts,' Jack rasped.

'Yes... well, I'll leave you to it for now.' He turned to Edwards. 'I'll give you a few minutes, but we really need him to rest.'

Edwards pulled up a chair alongside him. 'What's this about, then?'

'I'm not sure,' Jack replied, his throat constricting.

'I don't like this one bit.'

Nor did he. 'I can't believe somebody broke into my house.'

'Who could it have been?'

'I don't know,' he lied.

'You'll have to vacate the premises until it blows over. I can't have my DCI getting murdered in his own home. You can come stay with me – it'll help keep the missus off my back.'

'I'll be fine,' Jack said, the thought of living with Edwards sending shivers through his battered body.

'Well you bloody well can't stay there! You'll need to rest up.'

As if to end the conversation, he closed his eyes and feigned sleep. After a few, quiet moments, he heard the DSI sigh, before making a tired exit. He'd be sure to get his rest. But, despite his weariness, the mystery of who had broken into his house refused to leave his mind. Sure, over the years, he'd built up his fair share of enemies, but this had a very particular set of fingerprints all over it. There was only one man who would be brash enough to hire a goon to send a 'message'. For years now, they'd had an understanding. Jack didn't pry too far, and Dorian McGuinness didn't push too far. Maybe McGuinness knew he'd been watching him. Maybe he was getting too close to the truth about Liam Reed. He flexed his fist and winced. Back in the day he'd been a pretty handy amateur boxer. As far as Jack was concerned now, the gloves were off.

CHAPTER 21

'Guv, seriously, if Edwards sees you he'll blow a fuse,' the desk sergeant pleaded.

He moved past the reception desk. 'Tough.'

In just three days Jack's boredom had reached heights that he didn't know existed. There were only so many times he could listen to Black Sabbath records and do his four mundane stretches as prescribed by the physio.

The desk sergeant ran after him. 'He's got you on two weeks' sick leave and says we aren't to let you in.'

'If anybody asks, just say I threatened you.'

His entire body was aching, and his neck had taken on a purple, Picasso-like hue, but he'd be damned if he was going to sit in the house watching dull TV quiz shows for six hours a day. As far as he was concerned, he had work to do.

'Jack?' Watkins squeaked, jumping out of his chair.

'Would you jump in my grave as quickly, Watkins?' Jack asked, wincing at his poor choice of words.

'I was... just... keeping it warm and that,' he spluttered.

Watkins had already made a mess of the entire surface, cartons of fast food and coffee cups strewn everywhere. The place stank.

'Well it's plenty warm now,' he said. 'Now clear this mess up. Honestly, I'm gone a matter of days and look what happens.'

Jack wiped his brow with his good hand, his other being currently mummified. To make matters worse, his headaches had now switched from regular to permanent. His body might be screaming out for bed, but his mind was firmly planted on work.

'The Bulldog has been on a rampage since Edwards put her in temporary charge.'

Jack wasn't surprised. 'Anything else?' he asked, his gaze falling on the whiteboard.

'Bugger all.'

'There must be something?'

'No further forward. We've been trying to contact Pritchard but he appears to have gone AWOL.'

How odd, he thought. If Pritchard was anything, it was reliable in a crisis.

A loud bang on the door interrupted their talk. Jack recognised the brand.

'Detective Lambert, my office, five minutes.'

He was there in three. He paused at the doorway, trying to make out his reflection in the frosted glass. It was no use. Taking a deep breath, he knocked and entered.

'Just what exactly do you think you're doing at work today?' the DSI asked, his giant body threatening to split his suit in half.

'I'm fine.'

'Jack,' he sighed. 'You were assaulted in your own home and spent three days in hospital.'

'Actually it was two,' he interrupted, casting his mind back to storming out of the hospital against the doctor's orders.

'Anyway, my point is, you look like shit.'

'It looks worse than it feels.'

Edwards shook his head, brought a biro to his mouth and began chewing on the lid. Jack couldn't help but notice the heavy bags underneath his eyes. It seemed he wasn't the only one having a rough time.

'I've tightened up security. There'll be somebody watching your house on a continual basis for the short term.'

Jack shifted, the pain in his hand flaring up. He winced, hoping Edwards hadn't noticed. 'It's not necessary.'

The DSI let out a guttural roar. 'Don't you think I know that? The bloke who did this would have to be stupid to go back there and try again. Still, I can't take the risk. So, while we are already down on staff, I'm going to have to spend more resources taking care of you.'

'I'm not going to just sit around doing nothing, guv.'

His boss's jaw tightened. 'Is that so?'

'Like you already said, we're short staffed. You need me.'

Edwards closed his eyes and pressed a thumb to his temple, a giant white welt appearing in the process. 'Okay, but if you die, it's your own fault. Also, you'll have to lighten your load.'

Jack made to speak.

'No, it's final,' Edwards barked, raising a hand. 'Now, this could be any number of people trying to exact revenge on you, but I don't believe in bullshit like that. You've got someone spooked.'

'I have a fair idea of who it might be.'

'McGuinness?'

An image of the abandoned factory flitted back into Jack's memory.

'Possibly.'

'Jane will fill in for you on the open grave case for a short time until you're in a more fit state. If you could bring her up to speed on any key details that she may not already have, that would be just dandy. Meanwhile, I want this Nell Stevens things sorted as a priority. Get digging into that for a week or so and then we shall see.'

Jack tensed. 'I'm not answering to Jane Russell.'

'Yes, but you do answer to me, so I suggest you get on with it before I change my mind and leave you pushing paper instead.'

'What about Liam Reed?'

Edwards glared at him. 'Until we can wrap our heads around who came after you, I want you nowhere near that case.'

It was pointless arguing.

He closed the door a little too firmly on the way out. He'd do as Edwards asked and would focus on Nell Stevens, but first he had to undertake one small task.

'Christensen, how do you fancy coming on a trip?' Jack approached the squat detective in the canteen.

The Boris Johnson-lookalike looked up, brown sauce dripping down his mouth from a half-eaten bacon butty. 'No problem, boss.'

He motioned for the DS to follow him and they exited the canteen, heading for the car park. Jack set a quick pace, keen to get out of the station.

'You look a little on edge, boss,' Christensen said.

'I'm fine,' Jack lied. 'But... needless to say, Christensen, this is...'

He eyed him. 'Off the record? Say no more.'

He motioned for Christensen to get in the passenger seat and started up the engine to his old Volvo. It reeked of stale food. He surveyed the empty coffee cups and fast food boxes strewn across the back seat.

They pulled out of the car park and began the short journey into Newcastle's city centre. The traffic started off okay but thickened into an annoyance by the time they went past Central Station, a variety of businessmen in cheap suits and university students carting masses of luggage around.

'If you don't mind my asking, guv,' Christensen asked, his eyes fixed on the road. 'Where exactly are we going?'

'I was attacked in my home the other day, Christensen.'

The DS nodded, eyes flitting to Jack's neck.

He shifted, pulling his collar up. 'I have a fair idea of who it was.'

'Who?'

'One of McGuinness's boys. He doesn't like to get his hands dirty but I've no doubt he will have passed the order on.'

'We paying a visit to the shop?' Christensen asked.

Jack shook his head and pulled the car into a side street. After parking up in between a battered Toyota and a gleaming Suzuki Swift, the two officers stepped out into the cold Newcastle air.

'No, not today.'

'Guv?'

Jack opened the boot and pulled out the steel pipe he'd brought with him, sunlight rebounding off its shiny surface.

'Can I trust you, Christensen? Because, if not, you can go now.'

The policeman straightened up and shrugged. 'No problem, guv. Way I see it, whatever goes down is self-defence. Whatever you need.'

Jack smiled. 'I was hoping you'd say that.'

They entered Friar Tuck's, a local underground hangout of the McGuinness crew. The first thing Jack noted was the stench of stale urine. The second thing he noticed was one of McGuinness's local goons. Behind the bar, the manager stood, leaning over to talk to a middle-aged woman with a blonde perm. He clocked them, eyes narrowing as they approached. He straightened up, gold rings clicking against the wooden bar. A large, V-neck shirt made him look like a darts player.

'What'll it be?' he asked them, his voice thick with mucus.

Jack got Christensen to order two cokes while he found a table at the back of the bar, ensuring he had his face to the room.

'See anybody?' Christensen said, sipping on his drink.

'Two o'clock.' Jack motioned. 'Don't look though, he hasn't noticed us.'

There were a handful of customers in the pub, most of whom were propping the bar up with their pints of ale and tabloid newspapers. Jack noticed Nell Stevens' million dollar smile on the front page of one.

'What do you want to do?'

Jack diverted his attention to the two men sitting by the window, pints in hand, laughing. The one with his back to their position was Henry Stafford, a relatively unknown local bouncer. However, having had multiple dealings with McGuinness and his boys, Jack knew him perfectly well. He also knew him as somebody who liked to get his hands dirty, for a price. He had a history of violence and drug peddling. He certainly had a little man complex, which had only seemed to grow stronger as he'd hit forty. Jack supped his drink, allowing himself a wry smile. Back in the day, Henry Stafford had had a George Michael hairdo but, once he came out as gay, Henry had wasted no time in shaving his own quiff off. The back of his cranium now revealed numerous battle scars. That wasn't what was catching Jack's attention, though.

He was much more interested in the fresh-looking cuts on the back of his trunk-like arms.

After two pints of coke and a packet of cheese and onion crisps for Jack, Henry finally got up to use the bathroom. He and his companion had polished off three pints in that time.

'Stay here,' Jack said. 'Keep an eye on Tweedle-dee.'

Christensen nodded.

Blinking away the stale smell of piss, Jack sidled up behind Henry, who was swaying in front of the urinal, whistling an old Thin Lizzy tune.

'Hello, Henry.'

'What the...'

The hired heavy made to turn but Jack was quicker, planting his head against the tiled wall. Blood smeared the surface, before he made a heavy fall to the floor.

'The fuck you want?' Stafford groaned.

Jack pounced, placing his right forearm across his throat, left hand bringing the pipe out so he could see it.

'Firstly, I want you to stop swearing, Henry.'

'Fuck you, pig!'

Jack applied further pressure to his neck as blood began pouring from a wound in the centre of Stafford's forehead. That drove the message home.

'You see this,' Jack said, turning his neck to reveal the deep purple bruising.

Stafford nodded.

'Someone broke into my house and saw fit to try and kick the shit out of me. You know anything about that?'

The bouncer shook his head.

Jack slammed the pipe on the floor next to his head. Stafford, whilst just about as hard as they came, flinched. 'Where'd you get those cuts on your arms?'

'None of your fucking business!'

Jack planted a fist down over his wound, eliciting a grunt. 'What did I say about swearing, Henry?'

'Alright,' he groaned. 'I was bouncing at the Bigg Market when a fight broke out,' he said, smiling. 'You should see the other guy.'

'Still working for McGuinness?'

'Here and there.'

Jack leaned in close, Stafford's stale breath hot on his face. 'I don't appreciate being lied to, Henry. Where were you on Friday night?'

'Bouncing.'

'Where?'

'Crown and Anchor.'

One of Newcastle's finest.

'You better not be lying to me.'

'You don't believe me, give them a ring.'

'I will. Now, you listen good, if I even get so much as a whiff of anybody coming anywhere near me or anybody close to me, I'm going to come for all of you. You got that?'

Stafford shrugged, his face a bloody mess. 'Seems to me you must have pissed somebody off real bad, Detective.'

'Is that why McGuinness sent somebody after me?'

Stafford laughed, spittle gurgling from his mouth. 'Now why would Dorian do that, Lambert? I thought you two were good friends. From what I hear, maybe more than that?'

Jack added a couple of extra pounds of pressure. 'And what exactly did you hear?'

'Fuck sake,' he gurgled. 'Nothing, alright!'

'Tell me, Henry... is somebody encroaching on McGuinness's patch?'

The bouncer grinned. 'I haven't got a clue what you're talking about.'

'What about Liam Reed?'

'What about him? He knew the business he was in.'

'And what exactly was that?'

Stafford laughed, wincing with the effort. 'Selling fish, aye?'

Jack straightened up, placed the pipe back into his jacket before wiping Henry's blood off his hand with a paper towel. 'Always with the smart answers.'

He zipped his coat back up and made for the exit, before Stafford's throaty laugh stopped him. 'What's so funny, Henry?'

'You pull a pipe out on me, you should finish the job. You just wait until Dorian hears about this. I'll be seeing you real soon, Lambert. '

Jack passed back through the bar, motioning for Christensen to follow him. Stafford's pal, seemingly oblivious to his disappearance, had moved to the bar and was chatting up the curly blonde.

'Any joy?' Christensen asked as they got back in the car.

Jack cranked the window open and took a deep breath. 'Not really. But sometimes you have to flush out a few rats before you find the nest.'

Christensen nodded; conversation over.

Jack knew he'd taken a big risk with what he'd just done. Best case scenario: he'd put the frighteners on whoever had come for him. Worst case scenario: Dorian McGuinness not taking too kindly to one of his henchmen being roughed up by Johnny Law. Either way, somebody was going to get hurt.

CHAPTER 22

A week later Jack had convinced Edwards to let him back to work. He'd heard nothing from McGuinness in the meantime and had enjoyed no luck with his enquiries into the Nell Stevens case, despite speaking with a number of close friends, including her agent. It was with this conundrum that he was wrestling when Robson's name popped up on his phone.

Jack accepted the call. 'What do you want?'

'You beat up one of McGuinness's boys?' David Robson's trembling voice hurtled down the receiver.

He held up a palm to indicate Watkins should wait outside before lowering his voice. 'How do you know that?'

'That's irrelevant. They think I've talked!'

'You have talked, David.'

'Yeah, but now I'm in the shit! You asked him specifically if somebody was muscling in on Dorian's patch.'

Jack sighed. 'Unless you start telling me exactly what's going on I can't help you.'

'It's too late for that,' Robson spat. 'They'll come for me now.'

'Some would call that karma. Anyway, that was nothing to do with the drugs stuff.'

There was a pause on the end of the line, followed by the noise of someone shuffling about.

'It's all connected, Jack. Or, at least, they think it is. You know it's my job to write those stories.'

'It's not your job to destroy the reputation of the police at every opportunity, Robson.'

The journalist lowered his voice. 'Look, if I go easy on you, make you look good in the press, will you watch out for me?'

'I'll think about it.'

He left the reporter in a nervy state and concentrated on the whiteboard in his office. Sure, Edwards had instructed him to take it easy but that didn't mean he couldn't keep up to speed. Pictures of the Open Grave victims lined the board: Travis Kane, removal man, thirty-one years old. Jessica Lisbie, twenty-six, worked in marketing. Peter Rutherford, an unemployed twenty-three year old. Amy Drummond, a twenty-seven-year-old receptionist. They still had no connection established between the victims.

The conversation he'd just had with Robson refused to leave his mind. It wasn't like his old nemesis to get so spooked. Maybe he really would have to keep an eye on the situation; not to mention on top of watching his own back. McGuinness would clearly know what had happened. What would his next move be?

He threw a pen at the board, picked up his canteen coffee and took a sip. Resisting the urge to gag, he left it on the desk and stood, running events over in his mind for the millionth time. Now that Robson was onside, that would be of help, but this was making national press. That, alongside Nell Stevens' stalker, was making the whole force look incompetent. If they weren't careful, the powers that be would call in somebody else to do their job.

Watkins appeared back in the doorway. 'You coming to the meeting?'

'What meeting?'

'The new PCC thing remember?' Watkins said.

The meeting was a gathering of the who's who of Newcastle's constabulary. Jack took a seat in the second row, right behind the considerable bulk of Edwards, who was positioned next to his superiors. All were clad in formal attire. To Edwards' left, Jane Russell sat – frowning – as Jack approached. She was no doubt fuming over his quick return to work.

'Right.' ACC Dalton stood, his voice bringing the room to attention. Anybody who was anybody knew not to mess with Dalton. He was getting on now, but was old school, didn't take any shit, and could just about destroy anybody with one of his renowned icy stares. 'This is Nadine Guthrie, the recently elected PCC.'

A tall, slender woman who looked about fifty stood up, straightening out her grey suit. She strode to the front and ran a veined hand through her wiry black hair before clearing her throat. Judging by her appearance, she didn't strike Jack as the type of person who took shit either.

'Good morning.' She smiled, baring a set of razor-sharp teeth. 'I am Nadine Guthrie, your new Police and Crime Commissioner.'

Jack frowned; he'd forgotten to cast his vote. Judging by the news, so too had about eighty per cent of the local population. He vaguely remembered receiving an email about it some months back. Sitting here right now, he couldn't help but feel it was a bigger deal than he'd given it credit for. She'd been elected in a by-election after the former PCC was found to have been on the fiddle. The way Edwards was now squirming in his seat told Jack that Guthrie was going to employ a completely different approach. She'd already fostered a tough reputation in the local community and now she was here to finally speak to them.

'Now I want you all to know,' she continued, moving about the stage, 'that nothing is really going to change round here.'

A collective breath was exhaled.

'I mean, yes, I will set the budgets...'

Groan.

'And, yes, I will be holding regular meetings with senior members of the force to discuss issues and pass on public grievances...'

Jack's grip tightened. Neighbourhood Watch would be loving this. The entire force would be on the beat, emptying out bottles of White Lightning all day.

'But... oh sorry, am I boring you, sir?'

'No... ma'am.' Watkins sat bolt upright, face reddening.

'What's your name?'

'DS Stephen Watkins.' He gulped.

PCC Guthrie nodded as if committing the name to memory. Jack suppressed a smile.

'Now, about these Open Grave murders...'

'Sorry, ma'am! ... Ma'am, don't hurt me.'

The teasing didn't stop until they were back in Jack's office. He did his best not to get involved but couldn't help laughing along as Watkins took his ribbing in poor humour.

'It's not funny – she shouldn't be speaking to me like that,' he moaned.

Jack pulled his face straight. 'Would you like to make a formal grievance?'

Silence.

He puffed out his cheeks and leaned back in his chair. After about half an hour of Guthrie basically accusing the force, and in particular leading officers, of not having any clue, she'd shooed everybody out, deciding to have a private meeting with Edwards and Dalton. That, in turn, meant that Edwards would be on the warpath at some point in the near future.

'Now what?'

'Well, the main thing is that I'm back at work,' Jack said, his arm instinctively reaching up to touch the fading bruises on his neck.

'Good,' Watkins said. 'The Bulldog has had my balls in a vice; usually I'd be up for a bit of that, but she's a bit rough.'

Jack winced, trying to wrestle the image of Watkins and Jane Russell from his mind.

'Could be worse, it could be Edwards.'

As if on cue, Jack heard the heavy footsteps of the DSI approaching his office. The walls were physically shaking by time the shadow appeared in the frosted glass of the doorway. Jack straightened up, pushing various bits of rubbish to the floor, as the handle began to turn.

'Lambert!' he thundered.

'Yes, sir?' Jack replied.

'Why are there no more leads on the Open Grave murders?'

'Erm... you told me to take a step back.'

Jack watched as the superior officer's face went beetroot-red, veins pulsing in his oversized neck.

'Yes... well... how are you now?'

'I feel fine.'

'Right, get back on it then,' he ordered.

Jack nodded, pleased to be given the green light to throw himself back into the case.

'And you!' Edwards turned on Watkins. 'Do something bloody useful, you're a DS for Christ's sake.'

'Hey!'

The door slammed before Watkins could make a case for himself. Another beasting from the boss. Standard.

'What crawled up his arse? Watkins mumbled.

Jack shrugged. Although, if he had to put money on it, he would bet that it had something to do with their friendly neighbourhood PCC. There was no doubt she was going to be a nightmare as time went on. Edwards wouldn't want anybody interfering in the general running of things, but he'd have a rude awakening on that one, Jack thought. Still, they didn't have time to dwell on it now. There was a killer to catch.

Before that, though, Jack had an appointment to keep.

'Thank you for meeting me here,' she said, eyes flitting around the café.

'That's no problem,' he replied. 'I could have come to your house, if that were easier?'

She shook her head, tears forming in her eyes. 'It doesn't feel like my home any more. I feel like an intruder and I'm scared of my shadow.'

Jack nodded. 'Have there been any more letters?'

Nell opened a Gucci purse and pulled out a small bundle of letters before passing them across the table. He paused as a stout woman waddled over to take their orders.

'I'll have a skinny flat white,' Nell said.

'Just a black coffee for me, thanks.'

Nell paused. 'I like it in here. I've been coming for years. Nobody treats me any differently because of who I am now.'

He briefly flicked through the bundle before placing it in his jacket to read later. 'It can't be easy.'

'You probably think I'm just some stupid, stuck-up wannabe celebrity.'

'Not at all, Miss Stevens,' Jack said. 'I've met celebrities, but you don't seem like them; you don't carry any airs and graces.'

'Please, call me Nell.'

'Okay, Nell,' he replied. 'I'm Jack.'

'Yes, I know,' she said. 'You seem to be in the papers more than I am.'

They paused while the waitress placed their drinks down in front of them. Jack emptied a sugar sachet into his and took a sip. He had to admit, it was good.

'Yes, I think the press has a different opinion of me compared to you,' he said.

She smiled. 'I don't know about that; haven't you seen what they've done with other celebrities? They build them up to make tearing them down all the more enjoyable. I'm just the latest in a long line of cannon fodder.'

He leaned forward. 'Forgive me for asking but why do you do it? I mean, you seem all too aware of the dangers the lifestyle brings. Does it even make you happy?'

She shrugged and took a deep breath. 'You don't understand; growing up, we had nothing. The fact I could sing a little and looked pretty in a dress was enough to give my mother hope that I could achieve something more. If anything, it was *her* dream for me to be a singer. I entered the show without any real hope of winning, I just did it to please her. Then this momentum built up and before I knew it I was on TV and being spoken about as a potential finalist. It was a whirlwind. They kept asking me, "do you have a sad story?" I felt like saying, "my life is the sad story, don't you get it?" I tried to fight back against the industry when they asked me to do magazine shoots and attend club openings. That stuff just isn't me. But, in the end, I learned to just smile and get on with it, just like I did with my mother. I'm sorry... you must think me such a spoilt brat.'

'Not at all,' he told her. 'I can relate. My father never wanted me to be a policeman. He worked down the pit and as far as he was concerned my joining the force was a betrayal. Truth be told, on some level, I probably did do it as a reaction against him and how strict he'd been when I was growing up. Nothing was ever good enough so, in the end, I deliberately went out of my way to annoy him and now he's very sick and it might be too late to go back and fix things.' He eyed her. 'I think, in many ways, what you have done is far braver than what I have done.'

She placed a hand on his arm. 'It's never too late to fix things.'

He shrugged, uncomfortable with her familiar gesture. 'I think on this occasion it is. The person I was before I joined the force was... not someone I was proud of. I had no direction in life and I was in danger of going down the wrong road. Hell, I was already half way there. The force gave me the focus I sorely needed. I'd have either been in jail or dead by now without it.'

She glanced at his bruises. 'Are you sure you won't end up there anyway?'

He smiled. 'Well, certainly not jail.'

Unless Stafford makes a complaint.

She laughed, her face lighting up and making her look younger than the worried woman who had sat before him when he'd first arrived. 'I just want a normal life now.'

'You can have it.'

She shook her head. 'It's too late.'

'It's never too late.'

She paused and met his gaze. 'I think on this occasion it is.'

He cleared his throat, keen to change the subject. How had he ended up telling this woman his life story? 'Could this person have been a jilted former lover of yours?'

'No,' she said firmly. 'I was in a relationship a long time ago, but he was killed on duty in Iraq.'

'I'm sorry,' Jack said.

'Thank you. Since then there has only been Shaun.'

'Does he have enemies?'

She shrugged. 'I doubt it.'

'How can you be sure?'

'I've dated him for some time now. He isn't the type. To be honest he only seems concerned with his own celebrity status. They offered him a place on *Celebrity Big Brother* and he's keen to do it, despite what I think.'

'Are you happy?' Jack asked solemnly.

'I...'

'I'm very sorry,' he told her. 'That was completely inappropriate.'

'No,' she said. 'It's fine. In all honesty, Jack, I don't know what happiness is any more.'

They fell into silence as he finished his drink. He stood to leave. 'Here is my card, Nell. If something comes up, give me a call. I promise I will keep looking into this. The difficulty we have is that, given your celebrity status, a crazed fan will be difficult to pin down. I'll do everything I can, though, believe that.'

'I do, thank you. Oh, and Jack?'

He turned to her. 'Yes?'

'You should allow yourself to be happy.'

'What makes you think I'm not?'

'Your eyes.'

CHAPTER 23

The gruesome granite structure of the Freeman Hospital stood before him. He stopped to neck an espresso in an attempt to calm the insects crawling inside his stomach, then made his way inside. Rain was hammering into the ground as he approached the entrance, the smell of cigarette smoke permeating the air from the newly-erected shelters outside. Various members of staff and patients stood, huddled together, puffing on the sticks that would one day kill at least one third of them.

He felt an unusual calmness. Though, an inability to cry was one of his many curses. The only time he'd ever allowed himself to shed tears was in private, at the death of his mother some ten years ago. Other than that, he couldn't recall ever even really being upset. Louise had called him Robocop.

It wasn't a compliment.

After striding through the entrance, he located the correct ward and rode the lift to the second floor. Seconds later, he entered the corridor, only to be stopped by a young nurse with a crooked nose and vomit-stained scrubs.

'I'm sorry, sir, but visiting hours aren't until two o'clock. You're much too early.'

'I'm here to see my father.'

'Like I said,' she sighed, irritation painted on her awkward features. 'You can wait.'

'Actually I can't,' he snapped. 'I've just received a phone call from my daughter informing me that he is gravely ill.'

He left the nurse to faff over her notes and entered the ward. He didn't even notice his father at first. Instead, his vision shifted to his daughter who was sitting by the bed crying. He wanted to go to her, but Louise already had a protective arm around her. It was only then that he noticed his brother, tanned and back from his travels, sitting on the opposite side of the room. An expensive magenta shirt covered his chiselled physique.

'I didn't know you were back, Carl,' he said.

His brother didn't look at him. 'You didn't ask.'

He placed a hand on his ex-wife's shoulder. She tensed at first, but then softened, taking his hand and giving it a squeeze.

'I'm sorry, Jack.'

He nodded, the silence stretching out.

'We'll give you two some time alone with him. Come on, Shannon.' Louise ushered their daughter from the room, puffy eyes blinking towards Jack.

He took a seat by his father and placed a hand on his arm. The doctors had sedated him. Part of him was glad – he'd only say the wrong thing and disappoint him if he were awake.

'Louise tells me you haven't been here much,' Carl stated.

Jack felt his jaw tighten. He whispered, as if his father might overhear them arguing. 'I've been here more than you.'

His brother snorted. 'Barely.'

He met his brother's stare, feeling the hostility rise. Carl had always been closer to his father than Jack was. It was their mother Jack had doted on.

'Are we going to sit here and argue at Dad's bedside?' he snapped.

Carl's shoulders drooped, tears forming in his eyes. 'No.'

'Good.'

'So I hear you're into blokes now?' his brother said.

'I always was, Carl. I just never admitted it to myself. Anything else you want to say?'

They sat in silence for nearly ten minutes before Louise and Shannon arrived back, Jeremy in tow. Jack's stomach lurched. He wasn't bothered about Louise moving on, it was the fear that Shannon would love her new father more than him. A pitiful jealousy, he thought. In some small way he guessed he was happy for them. The selfish part of him, which was a big part, hated the bloke's guts.

'Jeremy.' He nodded.

'I'm sorry about your dad, Jack,' he said, offering a clammy hand.

'Thanks,' Jack mumbled.

It was a family portrait painted to torture him. Jeremy's hand lay on Shannon's shoulder where his hand should have been. Everything about the room reminded him of his failures, tentacles grabbing at him and pulling him into an abyss of depression. Unless a donor could be found soon – the doctors had told him – his father would be dead within weeks. Jack felt powerless. Having always turned to work to avoid the pressures of his home life, he now found himself failing with both.

'Dad asked me to prepare all the details for the funeral,' Carl said.

That came as no surprise to Jack. 'He's not dead, yet.'

'Just in case,' Carl replied.

'That's fair enough. Look... I need to get back to the station.'

'Already?' Louise asked, her green eyes boring into him. 'For God's sake, Jack, it's your dad, can't they give you some time off?'

Time off was the last thing he needed right now. He stood to leave, nodding towards his brother.

'I can't stay, I have murderers to catch.'

'Right,' she said, through clamped teeth. 'Always the job, isn't it?'

Jack paused to plant a kiss on his daughter's head before turning to leave.

'I'll call you if anything changes.' Carl stopped him. 'Don't worry, you won't have to do anything.'

It wasn't the station Jack travelled to from the hospital.

After passing through the outskirts of Newcastle, he headed towards Gateshead. The drive passed in a blur, his ex-wife's accusing words swimming through his throbbing head. The worst thing was, he knew she was right. The only way he could cope with all of this drama was to throw himself into work. It had always been his way.

'Jack, I wasn't expecting to see you,' Pritchard said, beckoning him in.

It didn't take a genius to work out the man had been drinking. The smell of whisky was overwhelming. The old man hobbled through his meagre temporary living space and took a seat. Jack knew the walk well. Many a drunk had tried it when pulled over on the road.

'I've noticed you've not been around much recently,' he said, plonking himself down on the bed. 'You should just stay with me.'

The psychologist snorted, eyeing his bruises. 'And get beaten to a pulp? No thanks, the hotel is fine.'

Jack nodded. 'So, what's going on?'

Pritchard shrugged his shoulders, leaning over to pick up a tumbler. 'I've just been enjoying some time to myself.' Accusing eyes met Jack's. 'I don't work for that place any more. I don't have to answer to anybody.'

'I'm not here as a policeman, Pritchard, I'm here as a friend.'

Jack let the silence pass between them, motioning for his old comrade to pass him a drink.

'You not on duty?'

Jack shrugged. 'One won't hurt me. Plus, my father is dying so I think I need one.'

'Oh my God, I didn't know, I'm sorry,' Pritchard replied.

Jack waved him away, savouring the burning sensation of the whisky trickling down his throat. 'I'll be fine.'

Pritchard paused. 'She's ill, Jack.'

He nodded. Jack had come to know Pritchard's wife quite well over the years. She was always lovely to him, despite the pressures he'd put on her husband to help him track down killers.

'What is it?'

Pritchard drained his drink, coughed, and poured another one before continuing. 'Dementia.'

'I'm sorry, Frank,' he said. 'You should get back to her.'

The old man slammed his tumbler down on the table. 'She doesn't recognise me any more! She's in a home and I... I... had to get away.' He dropped his head into his hands. 'I'm a horrible person, Jack.'

He placed a hand on the man's shoulder. 'No you're not, Pritchard. We all do what we can to get by.'

Taking a deep breath, the profiler tried to compose himself. 'And what is it you do, Jack?'

'Usually the wrong thing.'

Pritchard continued drinking for the next half hour, whilst Jack switched to cloudy tap water. The station would no doubt be wondering where he was, but he couldn't bring himself to care.

After a while he said, 'I best be going then.'

'You know,' Pritchard said, clearing his throat, as people do when they haven't spoken for a while. 'Some people think profiling is a duff business.'

He sat back down. 'So I'm told.' *Edwards, for one.*

The psychologist swirled the dark liquid around his tumbler, glazed eyes watching the crushed ice swim around the surface. 'They think we just quote readily available facts, linking every murder to young, working class males.'

Jack shrugged. The numbers were there for all to see. 'You've been a real asset to me over the years, Frank.'

'Robson fucking Green has a lot to answer for.'

'I kind of liked that show.'

Pritchard smiled, ever so slightly. 'Me too.'

'You should be at home, Frank.'

The old man's shoulders slumped. 'I have to see this through, whatever happens.'

'You've got nothing left to prove.'

Pritchard eyed him. 'It's not about proving anything. This bastard is out there, murdering people. I'm not leaving until he's caught.'

'That seems to be easier said than done,' Jack sighed.

Pritchard nodded. 'The reality is, it'll be carelessness that gets him in the end.'

'What, and not the brilliance of Northumbria's finest?'

'Unlikely.'

'I'm starting to think some people are just born evil,' Jack said.

'Codswallop!' Pritchard shouted, leaning over. His hot, alcohol-fuelled breath blasted Jack's face. 'There's always a reason.'

'Well I'm all ears, Frank.'

The profiler necked the rest of his drink and replaced his glasses before continuing. 'The problem is, our guy is too bloody organised. He's planning his attacks out, thinking things through. He's not killing in a spur-of-the-moment blind rage. Don't get me wrong, he feels rage, but he lets it out at the opportune moment. Our man is a classic sociopath and I've no doubt he's getting his kicks from watching all the news coverage.'

Jack shifted on the bed. 'Well there's plenty to go on.'

'He's got one hell of an ego, our fella. Not only is he taking the clothes as a trophy, he's digging up graves for the world to see them.'

'It's a link we need.'

'No, it's the motive.'

'And what's that?'

Pritchard shrugged. 'Absent mother? Family breakup? Violent past? Take your pick, Jack.'

He allowed the words to sink in. They had nothing. It was clear he was going to strike again unless something came up. 'This guy is just picking up victims, binding them, then killing them.'

'It's hard to believe, isn't it?'

Jack paused. 'Yes... it is.' He stood, heart quickening. 'In fact, it's just about impossible to believe.'

'What is it?'

He turned to his old friend. 'How big would you say Travis Kane was?'

Pritchard shrugged. 'Fairly stocky. Why? Oh...'

'There's no way Travis Kane would willingly go with a strange bloke somewhere, only to be bound and killed. There was no sign on his body of a struggle.'

He could feel the excitement rising now; that familiar feeling a policeman gets when a new lead or line of thinking becomes apparent in a big case.

Pritchard stood, unsteady on his feet, before falling back into his chair. 'I'm okay, just a little tipsy.'

Jack watched him. Pritchard made a habit of immersing himself in a case to the point of becoming ill. In his later years, it was taking its toll on him.

'It's not that the victims knew each other.'

Pritchard nodded. 'Say it.'

'They knew him.'

CHAPTER 24

He thought about his family on the drive back to the station, vowing to himself that he would start making himself a bigger part of Shannon's life, whether she was receptive to it or not. He'd failed everyone else and he'd be damned if he was going to fail her as well.

The reception area was unusually quiet as he passed through, save for two drunks sitting shoulder to shoulder, asleep. He could smell them from across the room, wriggling his nose in disgust as he passed the sign-in desk.

'Guv,' the desk sergeant acknowledged him.

'Any interesting news?' he asked.

'Well, that DJ has been voted off on the telly,' she said, eyes lighting up.

'I mean with regards to the job we've been hired to do.'

'Oh.' She flushed red. 'Sorry... no.'

The team assembled in the murder investigation room, heat emanating from all of the buzzing computers, creating an artificial warmth that was a welcome respite from the harsh Newcastle winter. Watkins was standing, leaning over a desk, in discussion with a young female DC. Towards the other side of the office, Christensen was barking out orders to a small gathering of workers, distributing handouts, a stern look on his face. He appreciated the help from both of them, but he could see that their enthusiasm was waning. Christmas was approaching and there was no movement on anything. He couldn't blame them for feeling deflated.

'Right, everyone...' he shouted above the thrum of activity. 'Listen up. We have had not so much as a sniff with regards to any of our caseloads. I know you are feeling low, but now's the time to redouble our efforts.'

The faces in the room turned to him, most of them probably just feigning interest.

'Christensen, I want you working exclusively on the Open Grave murders.' He motioned to the gathered crew. 'I want us to operate on the assumption that the victims did not know each other but that they did know the killer.' He let the team chew over his observation. 'I will be meeting with Pritchard, in due course, to review our potential profiles. I want every witness, family member and pet re-questioned until something turns up. I also want any missing persons reported in the last few weeks to be chased up, best you can.'

DC Gerrard said, 'Pardon my asking, guv, but won't that take forever?'

'I can help you with that,' Watkins piped up, a little too quickly. 'I mean, if you need any help...'

'It might take forever but we need to do it,' he replied, ignoring the DS's blushes. 'If anybody on the missing list matches with one of our victims in terms of where they were last seen then we may be able to find the link. As for you Watkins, focus on Nell Stevens. Get door knocking in the area, let's check over any CCTV in nearby streets and see if we can get access to any film footage from the nightclub where Nell originally had trouble in. We cannot afford to slack off now, something will turn up. Watkins and Christensen, you are to report to me regularly, whether I am around or not.'

'And what about me?' Jane Russell asked, maintaining a stare as she chipped away at a long, painted fingernail.

Jack paused. 'You are to be involved in everything.'

That'll test your DCI credentials, he thought.

With that, he turned and left. Watkins caught up with him down the hallway. 'Nice speech, guv.' He lowered his voice. 'What about McGuinness and the factory?'

'Don't worry, I haven't forgotten,' Jack said. 'I just want to keep this on the down low, for now. I'm thinking that this may benefit from a more personal touch. Right now, though, we are stretched enough as it is, and the team need a firm structure to focus on.'

Watkins nodded. 'No problem.'

Pritchard arrived in his office some two hours later.

'I hope you didn't drive here.'

'Of course not,' Pritchard said. 'I took a taxi... after a short nap.'

They didn't have time to analyse Pritchard's current alcohol levels. Jack needed him now. As he sat behind his desk, he cast a glance over the man who had helped the police catch some of the most notorious criminals in the North East in the last twenty years. The only clue as to his previously inebriated state was a pair of bloodshot eyes.

'We're really in the shit with this one,' Jack said.

'Indeed,' he replied. 'Perhaps we should see the bodies again?'

Jack closed his eyes, his customary headache beginning to return.

'You okay?' Pritchard asked.

'Yeah, just tired.' He waved him away.

'You should get checked out,' he said.

Jack mumbled a response and fished around his desk for some paracetamol. He found a withered packet at the back of his bottom drawer, dry swallowed two of them then tuned back in. 'Shall we go?'

He called ahead and asked them to remove the bodies for inspection.

'This journey never gets any easier,' Jack said, as they headed towards the mortuary.

'What, looking at dead bodies or the lovely Miss Rosie Lynnes?'

'Very funny, Pritchard.'

'Actually, I find it quite peaceful,' Pritchard said.

The sound of their feet slapping against the cold, concrete floor echoed around them. The temperature seemed to drop as they approached the mortuary room. The blood in Jack's veins followed suit.

'Can we be quick about this?' Rosie greeted them as they approached. 'I have work to do.'

Jack avoided her gaze as they moved past her, the back of his head burning from her lethal stares. In the cold light of day, he felt a grade one fool for having thought it a good idea to randomly turn up at her house. Just one more to add to his long list of poor choices.

He stood back, having already seen the bodies and not wanting to throw up what he'd just eaten at the station. Pritchard got stuck in, fishing his glasses out, before placing them on and inserting a stick of chewing gum into his mouth. Rosie frowned.

'It helps me concentrate.'

She rolled her eyes before peeling back the sheets from the corpses of the four victims. Their lifeless bodies seemed to point accusingly towards Jack for not having caught their killer yet. He felt unable to tear his eyes away from the purple-blue complexion of Jessica Lisbie's corpse. The parents had requested its release for burial, but he felt it best to hold off for now.

For half an hour, Pritchard went over every inch of the four victims' bodies, asking numerous questions of Rosie, her methods, her analysis. By the end, Jack felt as though he'd been sitting in on a particularly useful, yet boring university lecture on the mechanics of body science. He undid one of his shirt buttons, the presence of death making him feel unusually clammy.

Pritchard spat his chewing gum into the palm of his sterile glove before peeling them off and placing them in the bin. Rosie followed suit, her gaze refusing to land on Jack.

'So, you're sure strangulation was the cause of death?' Pritchard asked for the thousandth time.

The pathologist fixed him with an icy stare. 'Based on my training, and years of experience, I would say so, yes.'

Pritchard nodded, seemingly lost in thought. 'But why no struggle?'

'I can't answer that, you would have to speak to toxicology.'

'We have,' Pritchard said. 'They've struggled to find anything so far.'

She shrugged. 'Doesn't mean there's nothing there.'

Jack's phone rang. He apologised, moved away from them, and answered.

'Christensen?' He listened as the detective told him the news. 'Shit.' He turned to his colleagues. 'We have to go, now.'

'Just up here,' Jack pointed.

The car skidded and wheeled away on the single-lane road as Jack navigated his way through Durham City Centre with Pritchard and Rosie in the back. In the distance behind them, he could just about make out the flashing lights of a marked vehicle that was tailing them to the murder scene. Durham wasn't in their jurisdiction, but due to the nature of the discovery it meant that they had no choice but to cross over.

'Do we have to go so fast?' Rosie shouted.

'Sorry,' he said, toning it down.

Pritchard sat, looking out at the area around them, snow lying heavy on the vast fields as they wound their way towards their destination. Jack was glad the psychologist had agreed to come with them.

He pulled up next to a muddied Vauxhall Astra. The three of them got out, huddling together up the hill towards the centre of the field. The killer was smart. Heavily wooded and always quiet, this was a well-chosen spot overlooking the Durham University Maiden Castle Sports Centre for his latest burial. Access wasn't easy on foot, particularly when dragging a body up, but it wasn't impossible.

Rosie jogged ahead, taking a lead role in the setting up of the white tent, which was in the process of being made. At the scene DI Jane Russell stood, flanked by Gerrard and Watkins, who was deep in conversation with another detective.

'Tomkins,' Jack greeted the Durham DI.

The lanky detective shook Jack's hand in a clammy embrace, his permanently drooping eyes giving him a constantly disinterested look. 'Jack. Nasty business this.'

'Indeed. Thanks for not putting up a fight on this one.'

'Are you kidding?' he said. 'We're snowed under right now; the way I see it, the Open Grave Murderer is your problem.'

Jack smiled. He'd known Oliver Tomkins for a long time. He was a dependable DI but had a reputation as someone who didn't go looking for work if he could at all help it.

'This is interesting,' Pritchard noted, drawing his attention away.

Jack motioned to Watkins who, shivering, pulled out a notepad and began jotting down the psychologist's ramblings.

'What?' Jack asked.

'Note the centre of the field. Our killer is arrogant. It's not necessarily that he wants to be caught, but he wants it to be known what he's up to. If he was a safety first kind of bloke, he'd stick close to the road; but the fact that he has ventured out this far suggests a confidence in what he is doing.'

'So the guy has serious issues,' Watkins mumbled.

'Of course,' Pritchard said. 'But he's also brilliant.'

If Jack didn't know any better, he'd say the old man was enjoying all of this.

'Jack.' The Bulldog nodded, ushering him over.

He moved off to the side to talk to the DI, noting the bags under her eyes and a pinched, pale texture to her face. Perhaps he wasn't the only one feeling the strain?

'What is it? Same as before?'

She nodded, snowflakes clinging on to her long eyelashes like tiny white leeches.

'I'm not even surprised now.'

He made to move but she stopped him, grabbing his arm in an almost painful vice.

'There's something else.'

'What?'

They marched over to the tent, which had finally been pitched up. Suiting up in their white overalls, they could have lain down and blended in to the field. Yellow police tape had been placed all around the scene, leaving a small gap for people to walk through to gain access to the tent.

'There.' She pointed, looking away.

Jack peered over into the ditch; it was the same MO as before. Two bodies, one male, one female, stripped and placed in a spooning position, in a six-foot deep ditch. Judging by the colour of the skin and acrid stench that was now threatening his nostrils, they had been dead for a number of days. That wasn't what had gotten Jack's attention, though. Nor was it the brutal nature in which the bodies had been dumped so unceremoniously into the ground. It wasn't even the fact that they had yet another set of bodies to contend with. It was because he had seen one of these people before.

There was no mistaking the spiked hairstyle of former suspect Gary Dartford.

CHAPTER 25

Edwards stood at the front of the incident room, his face impassive. The rest of the room, silent in anticipation, stared open-mouthed at what was unfolding.

'Details.'

Jack shook the remnants of snow and ice from his coat, his entire body beginning to ache from the long day he'd had.

'He's playing with us,' he said.

Edwards eyed him. 'How?'

'I was able to identify one of the bodies. It's Gary Dartford.'

The colour drained from Edwards' face, only to be replaced by a beetroot-red tinge. 'The suspect? Who knows?'

'Nobody, yet.'

The considerable bulk of the DSI stepped back, grabbing on to a chair for stability.

'Are you okay, guv?' he asked.

'I'm fine!' he snapped.

'The papers are going to find out sooner or later.'

'We'll have to hold a press conference,' Edwards said, pacing around the desk.

Jack ground his teeth. 'I'll sort it.'

Those in attendance sat in silence, no doubt nervous at the standoff that was now brewing. Edwards wanted to handle this one personally, but it was Jack's case. He'd be damned if he was going to be undermined in front of his team.

The DSI ignored him. 'Right, I want a press conference set up for one hour from now. Somebody get onto the officer and have them sort it out. If anybody needs me, I'll be in my office with Dalton's foot up my arse.'

He left the room in a stunned silence. Jack loosened his collar and turned to face them. The smell of stale sweat was permeating the air as the team moved into overdrive.

'It's fair to say that this is an escalation of events. From here on in, things could get a lot worse.'

'What do you need, guv?' Gerrard asked.

'I want a team out questioning not only Gary Dartford's family and friends, but anybody else he has been in contact with in recent times. We will have to hang tight on the second victim, but as soon as we have an ID, I want the same rules to apply.'

'Do we still follow the new theory?' Christensen asked.

He paused. Good question. He couldn't help but feel that focusing on Dartford would lead them to the others. 'No, not right now. Everybody, and I mean *everybody*, needs to throw everything into Gary Dartford.'

Jack surveyed the room. They might be light on potential leads, but the discovery of a new set of victims, mixed with the fact that he had deliberately targeted one of their original suspects, at least gave them something else to ponder. The killer's arrogance would be his downfall.

'Nice speech in there.' Watkins followed him outside.

'Thanks.'

Ten minutes later they were both sitting in Jack's office, Christensen having also joined them. Another mound of paperwork had washed up on his desk, various bits of post-it notes stuck around the room. Jack moved to the whiteboard and pinned up two pictures of Gary Dartford, one smiling and gelled, the other showing his naked, dead body.

'Where's Pritchard?'

'He's... not well right now,' Jack replied. 'I sent him home.'

Christensen merely nodded – excuse accepted without comment. After the bodies were discovered on the hill, Pritchard had taken a funny turn. Despite his protestations, Jack had managed to convince him to go back to his hotel and rest.

Jack mused. 'The MO has been similar all along – until now. Each set of victims includes a woman and a man, both in their twenties. Each time, he has killed them via strangulation in such a way that it has to be premeditated. The stripping of the victims along with placement of the bodies suggests, to me, that he has an issue with regards to relationships. But, I've no idea as to whether it's to do with men or women.'

'Would that be of importance?' Watkins asked.

'Well, it could help us narrow down his social movements.'

'It could be both,' Christensen interjected.

'Agreed. We've found no real link between any of the victims,' he said. 'I think we've been wasting our time on that one.'

'That's an awful lot of time,' Watkins said.

Jack nodded. And resources.

'It has to be social,' he continued. 'Maybe they all go to the same place. This is where he finds them. If we can find the place, we find the killer. Whether Dartford also fits into this, though, is debatable. It's clear he's changed his methods to target him. I think it's his first mistake.'

The three detectives entered a moment of silence as the facts settled into place. There was no doubt in Jack's mind that things had become personal.

'What an idiot, eh?' Watkins joked.

Jack laughed. 'In the end, they all are.'

He stood by the cars, watching. The wind was chewing at his face like an angry dog, but he didn't care – he couldn't feel it. All he saw was them. Glancing down at the paper, he saw *his* mugshot. The only one that mattered.

Detective Chief Inspector Jack Lambert.

He could see him moving about his office, gesticulating towards a square-looking blond policeman and a young Art Garfunkel lookalike. They were probably talking about him right now. He felt a jolt of electricity shoot up his leg. He shivered, licking his lips as the excitement began to build. They had to be talking about him. Surely they'd got the message?

He dug his nails into his leg, breaking the flesh as a smile began spreading over the detective's face. They were laughing. Kidnapping Gary Dartford had been a masterstroke. They had to know he was talking to them. Why, then, were they fucking laughing?

Maybe he'd not been clear enough. He was obviously talking to the wrong people. If he wanted their attention, he'd have to go through other means. A smile slowly spread across his face as the snow continued to fall about him.

Jack Lambert's car provided him with his own reflection. He saw his face, set in determination of what he must do. He'd make them listen.

Gary Dartford wasn't personal enough. Time to bring things forward.

CHAPTER 26

The media were already assembled as Jack followed Edwards into the lion's den. At the front, two reporters planted their miniature recording devices in the centre of the table, little red lights blinking at them almost in accusation.

Jack glanced to the front row and noticed David Robson's absence. At least that was one less thing to worry about.

'Good afternoon, ladies and gentlemen.' Edwards brought him out of his thoughts, straightening out his impeccable police uniform. 'I want to begin by saying we have some breaking news with regards to the Open Grave murders.'

Jack watched in silence as the DSI began the conference. His temper was still simmering from the conversation they'd had minutes ago, arguing over how to handle the press. His superior officer felt it best that he covered the key details, despite Jack's protestations that it would make him look weak as an SIO. Needless to say, Edwards had won out.

Without warning, a young, pimple-faced journalist stood. 'Sorry, but has this anything to do with the discovery of Gary Dartford's body?'

The entire pressroom erupted into chaos as everybody fired questions at the stunned DSI. Edwards looked like he'd swallowed an epileptic wasp.

It took ten minutes to escape the conference and, by the time they'd cleared the room, it looked as though a school fight had broken out. Jack turned, just in time to see Edwards stalking towards him.

'And just what the—'

'DSI Edwards, my office, now!' Dalton appeared in the doorway, his icy stare silencing the superintendent.

'This isn't over,' Edwards thundered, marching past.

Jack motioned for Watkins and Christensen to follow him back to his office.

'Jesus, what the hell was that about?' Watkins asked.

'Our mole strikes again,' Jack seethed.

'I've got the journalist,' Christensen said, checking his notepad. 'His name is Oliver Richards. He's currently sweating it out in a cell at the minute. Want to question him now?'

'No, let's make him think on his sins a little first. He's just found out he's potentially involved in a murder case. I'd say that warrants stewing over.'

Christensen nodded in agreement.

Jack paced around the floor, pausing to look out the window towards his car, which sat covered in snow. He turned, running his gaze over the two detectives sitting before him. Surely he didn't have to question their loyalty? Watkins could be daft, but he wasn't a law breaker. Plus, he was too afraid of Edwards to be so stupid.

As if reading his thoughts, Christensen spoke. 'You got any gut feeling on who it is?'

He shook his head. 'No.'

'Robson will be fuming that he missed out on the scoop,' Christensen noted.

Watkins laughed. 'Hey, maybe it was Edwards?'

'Why don't you ask him?' Jack said.

'Don't be daft!'

'No, I'm serious, I'm going to question Oliver with Christensen. I need you to stay here just in case Edwards comes back and needs a word.'

'But...'

'You can thank me later,' Jack said, motioning for the DS to follow him out.

'You're feeding him to Edwards?' Christensen asked, once they were out of earshot.

'No.' He waved him away. 'It's me who'll get it in the neck. Plus, Watkins isn't as soft as you think.'

They spent the next half hour questioning the journalist, whose face managed to fall between ghost-white and chicken korma yellow. By the time they'd finished, Jack wasn't sure if the hack would spend much longer in the newspaper industry. They turfed him out, warning him that they'd be watching, and he had to call them if he was contacted by anyone again.

According to Richards, he'd received an anonymous tip an hour or so before the press conference was scheduled to start. He didn't recognise the voice. The number had been withheld. The person offering the information had stated that this one was a gift but that, for money, more could be offered. At least they knew the motive, now.

'Any word from Edwards?' Jack asked Watkins, whom he found sulking in the canteen.

The DS took a sip of Fanta. 'No, but word on the grapevine is that Dalton is tearing him a new one upstairs. They reckon he could be sacked for this.'

Jack scoffed. That'd be highly unlikely. Edwards really *would* have to be the mole to lose his job over this one. His thoughts were cut short by the vibrating of his phone in his pocket. He took it out, checked the caller ID: David Robson. He forwarded the call. That bastard could get his scoop elsewhere. If word got out he'd been to secret meetings with the enemy, he'd be number one suspect in the mole case.

'Right, well I'm sorry to interrupt your lovely meal here, Watkins, but I'd say we have an important location to visit, don't you think?'

Gary Dartford, it turned out, spent his time between his girlfriend's place and a rented property near the city centre. Upon speaking to his hysterical other half, they'd been informed that he had been privately renting the place from his uncle, who wasn't really his uncle. The house itself was at the top of a high-rise complex, covered in various bits of graffiti and boarded up windows. It did, however, have the odd England flag pinned to the walls. Very patriotic, Jack thought.

Jack, Watkins and Pritchard, who had got a taxi from the hotel once they'd rung with the latest news, waded through the sea of food cartons and empty alcohol containers. It was a risk inviting Pritchard along, particularly given his strange turn earlier, but Jack wanted his expertise on the case. Besides, the psychologist informed him he'd been sleeping off the drink for the last few hours. Watkins had given the dishevelled old man a strange look upon meeting him but a quick stare from Jack had settled matters.

They reached the end of the corridor, only to be greeted by a broken-down lift.

Great.

'What floor is the flat on, again?' he asked.

'Thirteenth.'

Unlucky.

By the time they'd climbed the stairs, Jack felt like his insides were going to explode. However, he still put the others to shame. Pritchard's head was dripping in sweat as he heaved himself up, alcohol no doubt gushing from his pores.

'Come on,' Jack urged them.

Watkins hobbled next, holding his calf. 'Sporting injury.'

A teenager appeared in a nearby doorway, the hinges nearly snapping off as he slammed the door shut. He stopped, eyes narrowed, and surveyed the three of them. Hood up, scarf around his face, he looked like something out of a football hooligan documentary. Jack could smell cheap aftershave coming off him, too. Probably out for a date.

Deciding against confrontation, the lad passed them by and headed down the stairway.

'Nice chap,' Pritchard muttered.

'He couldn't be our guy, could he?' Jack ventured.

'Afraid not.'

Gary Dartford's flat, number 1324, stood at the end of the hallway flanked by a small, dirt-smudged window. On the door itself, somebody had been playing funny buggers, carving in a picture of a penis. Further down, a heart had been drawn with the inscription, 'L.W. 4 O.T. 4eva,' written on it.

They entered the flat, using the key they had managed to procure from his other residence, and took a look around. As they walked through the narrow hallway, the smell of garlic, bleach and fish threatened to slaughter Jack's insides. Pritchard, made of sterner stuff, simply wriggled his nose, then walked on.

At the end of the passageway, a dishevelled living room sat. On the far wall, a battered two-seater was placed, looking towards the opposite wall which housed a mounted flat screen TV. A large window was on the adjacent wall to the television, looking out over the city centre. Jack turned left at the end of the room and entered what must have been Dartford's bedroom. True to form, everything was a mess. One thing was certain, though, he liked his blonde women. Garish cream walls, riddled with damp, were plastered in various FHM magazine pull-outs and Playboy Bunny pictures. There were even a few of Nell Stevens in various stages of undress. Gary Dartford also seemed to be a big fan of David Beckham, given the ridiculous amounts of paraphernalia lying around. In the far corner, an open wardrobe stood, clothes tossed next to it on the floor.

'What do we think, Pritchard?'

The psychologist, who had been kicking his way through a maze of rubbish on the floor, turned, straightening out his cardigan. 'He was never our killer; just look at this place!'

Jack nodded, acutely aware that Dartford wasn't the killer, given that he had just turned up as a corpse. Still, it was nice of Pritchard to point out just how wide of the mark they'd been.

'I mean, anything I can use?'

The profiler wiped a hand across bloodshot eyes. Jack eyed him with concern, which was met with a fierce look from the old man.

'Well, I'd be surprised if we find anything of note here,' he said. 'But, I'd say we can expect a much higher level of involvement with us, from now on.'

'Meaning?' Watkins asked.

'The killer has turned personal. Killing this young man was a message. But it's also his first mistake. We can probably expect more indirect or perhaps even direct communication. We may start receiving letters, or he could go to the press with something. Worst case scenario? He may target one of us in some way. And I still maintain it's definitely a man.'

Jack nodded. 'All the more reason to focus our thinking on Dartford. This could be the break we need to shut this down.'

'And remember,' Pritchard continued. 'Our killer isn't thick. He probably has a skilled job and knows how to work a computer. I'd say that makes just about anybody a target. This won't be easy.'

Jack was afraid he'd say that.

'Come on, let's get this over with.'

They spent the next hour searching the house from top to bottom, finding nothing of any note save for some used condoms, empty beer cans and a pretty impressive porn collection, which Watkins seemed to mull over for longer than was necessary.

'Nothing,' Jack sighed. 'For God's sake!'

He aimed a kick at a nearby coffee table, knocking its contents to the floor. He turned to leave before something caught his eye. A red, flashing dot.

'Wait!'

He bent down, blowing dust off the small, black answer phone, before hitting the play button.

'Alreet, Gazza, Kyle here. Look, I'm sorry, man, but I'm gonna be a bit late tonight, aye? I'll catch you at the usual haunt though. Bring your pulling pants.'

Jack sat back and listened to the message twice more. Feeling his heart rate rise, he turned to Watkins.

'Sergeant, call the station, tell them we need to know who Kyle is.'

He listened to the message once more. Dartford's girlfriend hadn't seen him in weeks, due to an 'altercation' as she put it.

He'd gone AWOL from work and, upon speaking with his uncle who wasn't an uncle, they'd learned he hadn't seen him either. Perhaps Kyle had been the last person to know his whereabouts. For the first time since the case started, he allowed himself to feel some hope. The answer machine message was on the eighth of December. So far, nobody else had seen him after that date.

They had to find Kyle.

CHAPTER 27

They made it back to the station in record time. It was only when they got out that Jack noticed somebody had keyed the side of his door.

Nice.

'Christensen, get me Dartford's girlfriend, Crystal Walsh,' Jack delegated, blitzing into the incident room.

'She's already on her way, guv,' Gerrard interjected.

'Good. Let's get her set up in a room. Doesn't have to be uncomfortable, I just need to talk to her. She's not a suspect.'

'No problem, boss.'

Jack turned to face the rest of the room, their interest pricked. 'Listen up, I want everybody on the open grave murders to try and find out who 'Kyle' is. So far, we know he is a friend of Gary Dartford, and we have reason to believe he may be of importance to the case.'

'Do we have a surname, sir?' a PC asked.

'Oh yes, how silly of me to forget that.'

The policeman looked confused.

'No.'

The groans were audible as he left the room. He stopped only to place Watkins in charge of proceedings. Although he valued his life, he still felt he had to inform Edwards of what was going on, given the circumstances.

The superintendent had his forehead planted down onto the desk when Jack walked in. Paper, notepads and various bits of stationery had been thrown around the room.

'Sir?'

Slowly, the man raised his head. If Jack didn't know any better, he'd say he had been crying.

'I'm for the chop,' he said, staring out of the window.

Jack pulled up a seat. 'What?'

'Well, I haven't been given my marching orders yet but it was suggested that I take some leave after this case to... re-evaluate my life, so to speak.'

Jack sat motionless. He wasn't surprised. Edwards was working in the wrong era. 'I'm sorry, Logan.'

'Could be a promotion in it for you, if you play your cards right.'

He shook his head. 'Don't talk like that.'

'Like what?' he shouted.

'We're all on the same team here.'

Even if Edwards had been interfering in the case.

The DSI snorted. 'Tell that to Dickhead Dalton.'

Jack shifted in his seat, uncomfortable at the casual profanity levelled at one of the most dangerous and senior police officers in the local force. Edwards was tough, but the ACC was basically a robot, sent back from the future to torture Her Majesty's finest.

'I just thought I should tell you we may have a potential lead as to Gary Dartford's whereabouts before he disappeared.'

He ignored him, continuing, 'Mona hates me enough as it is; if I lose my job, she'll leave me, I just know it.'

'Sir?'

'I think she's been seeing somebody else for a while now.' He looked directly at Jack for the first time since he'd entered. 'Do you know how that makes me feel?'

'Sir, about the case...'

'Fuck the case!' He slammed a palm against the table, causing the room to quake. 'I have my suspicions as to who it is. It won't be long now.'

Jack didn't like the sound of that. The DSI reset his position to where he'd been prior to Jack coming in. Stunned, he stood, went to say something, and thought better of it. He paused in the doorway before leaving.

This was all he needed. All hell was breaking loose, they had a serial killer on the prowl and a gangland war that was threatening to get ugly. Meanwhile, one of the most senior officers in the Northumbria force was having a breakdown. Not to mention essentially threatening to kill somebody over his wife's supposed infidelity. Maybe Edwards taking a vacation wouldn't be such a bad idea. God knows he was tempted to do the same.

'I'm sorry to drag you in like this, Crystal,' Jack said, placing a cup of coffee in front of Gary Dartford's girlfriend. 'I know it's late.'

The woman stared at the lukewarm drink in front of her, took a whiff and sipped it. Jack mirrored her. Although the pink dressing gown was gone, she still looked much the same as last time they'd met. Only her bleached blonde hair had changed, having been scraped back into a greasy ponytail. She still had the bags under her eyes.

'What do you want?' she said, voice barely a whisper.

She'd spent the last hour screaming the station down, demanding answers. It seemed she had now worn herself out. She sat, shoulders hunched, nursing her cheap coffee.

'We know this must be difficult right now, but I need to ask you a couple of questions regarding Gary.'

'Am I a suspect?' she spat. 'Coz I want my fucking lawyer.'

'No, not at all.' Jack held his hands out. 'When we took a look around Gary's apartment, we found an answer machine message from a friend of his.'

'A woman?'

'Erm... no.'

She smiled. 'Good.'

Jack fiddled with the answer machine, placing it on the interview table before mashing the play button. Once again, the voice of Gary's mysterious friend Kyle warbled through the speaker. As the tape wore on, Crystal's eyes narrowed as she bit into her cheek.

'Do you know who that is?'

'Aye, it's Kyle,' she said, stating the obvious. 'I can't believe that. Gary told me he wasn't hanging with that piece of shit anymore.'

Bingo.

'Do you know his full name?'

'Yeah, but everyone calls him Lamaz.'

'His surname, please?'

'Walsh.'

'Walsh?'

'Yeah, he's my brother.'

Ten minutes later, Jack strode into the incident room. Watkins, who was standing over a rather attractive-looking female PC, was getting an eyeful of more than just computer screen. 'Sergeant, I want everybody and his dog tracking down Kyle Walsh, right now.'

'So she knew him then?' he said, moving away from the unsuspecting girl.

'You could say that. She's his sister.'

He filled him in on the details: twenty-two-year-old man, estranged from most of his family, fell out with Crystal a couple of years ago, but had been friendly with Gary Dartford for some time. Crystal thought him into all manner of trouble. She didn't know where he was living, only that he'd left home over a year ago and took up with, in her words, 'some slapper.'

'Shouldn't be too hard to find then,' Watkins said.

'I want his background checked and then I want him found. Send a patrol car to his parents' house, see what we can find out.'

'I'm on it.'

Jack paced up and down the incident room, turning events over in his mind. Gary had been due to meet Kyle for a night out at some point in recent history, he assumed. Where were they meant to be going? Who were they meant to be meeting? Was Gary Dartford intercepted whilst out, or did it happen beforehand? After? Would the dates even match up? Too many questions. It seemed a long shot that Crystal Walsh's brother was involved in his murder but, if he could provide them with enough information as to his whereabouts, they might be able to trace Dartford's steps and find a link between the victims.

This had to be the break they needed. They'd had too many misses so far. Something had to stick. During the Newcastle Knifer case, he'd had this exact same feeling, just before a major breakthrough. Unfortunately, it had also led to him getting stabbed.

'Sir,' a PC caught his attention. 'Kyle Walsh, twenty-two, male, last address named as his parents' house, works in a local gym, has previous for speeding, assault and drug dealing.'

'Not a bad record for someone so young,' Jack said. 'Watkins, on second thoughts, let's get ourselves to the parents' house. Christensen,' he said, turning to face the DS. 'Take Gerrard and check out the gym.'

Kyle Walsh's parents lived in a terraced house on the outskirts of the city. They'd called ahead and, after making their way up the neatly-lined pebbled path, Irene Walsh had invited them in and put the kettle on.

Jack sat, looking over the various pieces of art that were planted on the walls. The Walshes kept a tidy house, nothing out of place. Wood polish fumes hung heavy in the air as Irene floated about, humming a Carpenters' tune as she took their orders for coffee. Light cascaded in through their blinds, casting glows on their various ornaments. Even the air seemed devoid of dust. Mitchell Walsh sat opposite them, not paying them much attention as he perched his glasses on top of his balding head. He chose, instead, to continue with his crossword.

'I must apologise,' Irene said, placing a tea tray down before them. 'If I had known we were going to have guests, I would have tidied up a bit more.'

Jack shifted in his seat, hoping his feet didn't smell. While they hadn't been ordered to remove their shoes, the implication was there as soon as they'd entered the house. He took in his host, a weathered face that told of past hardship. Her hair was tastefully done, much different to her daughter's, but Crystal had inherited her mother's green eyes and high cheekbones. Other than that, Jack struggled to see any resemblance to what was sitting before him.

'Mrs Walsh,' he began, 'I know it's late so I thank you for agreeing to see me. If you don't mind my asking...'

'Why are my children so unruly?' she laughed, devoid of humour. 'Well...'

'It's okay,' she said. 'It all started when their father died.'

'Ah, I'm sorry.'

Jack cast a glance to the man who now lived here in his place. She waved him away. 'It happened a long time ago. It's been over ten years since he died but it hit Crystal and Kyle very hard. It was stomach cancer,' she said, staring out of the window. 'He was diagnosed and within six weeks he was gone.'

The widow took a sip of her tea before wiping her mouth lightly with a napkin, the faintest of tremors in her hand.

Jack flipped his notepad open. 'And how long have you and Mr Walsh been together?'

She placed a hand on her husband's knee; turned and offered a faint smile from his bulging face. It was the first movement he'd made since they arrived.

'I met Mitchell at a counselling group; you see, his wife passed away as well. We've been together for about eight years.'

'And how is your relationship with the children, sir?'

Mitchell snorted. 'Well they certainly don't treat me with any respect, despite my having adopted them.'

Irene's face hardened. 'They've never taken to Mitchell, even though they know he makes me happy. All they think is that he isn't their father. It's not like Alec was an angel.'

Jack raised an eyebrow and discreetly wrote 'abuse?' in his pad.

'When was the last time you saw Kyle?'

'Let me see,' she said. 'It must have been about six months ago now. He came round and demanded money, saying he was in some sort of trouble.'

'Did you give him any?'

She cast a glance to her husband before continuing. 'No.'

A lie.

'And nothing since then? No phone calls?'

'No, nothing.'

'Do you know where he's been staying?'

'No.'

'Do you know anything about his friends?'

'I know he was hanging around with that Gary Dartford.' She leaned forward. 'I know it's a terrible business, but he was a good boy until he started in with this other crowd. Gary was one of them.'

'Was he mixed up in anything he shouldn't have been?'

Mitchell Walsh stirred. 'Drugs, most probably.'

'Mitchell!' Irene scolded. 'You don't know that. Look,' she sighed. 'We can't know anything for sure since he cut himself off from us, but the people he'd begun hanging around with weren't the sort I would allow into my house, put it that way.'

No surprises there, Jack thought.

'Do you have any names?'

She shrugged. 'Only Gary.'

He nudged Watkins and made to leave.

'Oh, one last question, Mrs Walsh; do you know why Kyle and Crystal fell out?'

Irene Walsh's face remained impassive. 'Not a clue.'

'Interesting family,' Watkins stated once they were back in the car. 'Wonder what went so wrong with the kids?'

'I think they know why they fell out but don't want to tell us,' Jack said.

'Agreed. Doesn't necessarily mean anything though.'

He nodded. 'Indeed.'

Watkins stuck the car into gear and they pulled away, leaving Irene standing in the doorway watching them. Jack felt a twinge of sadness as her image shrank in the rear-view mirror. Estranged from both of her children, she seemed to be living a melancholy existence. Jack brushed the thought from his mind, and focused back on the task at hand. He was sure Kyle Walsh could help them track down where Gary Dartford had been, but finding him was proving more difficult than he'd hoped.

They needed him now.

CHAPTER 28

Three nights later Christmas arrived. Given his father's continued ill health he had nobody to visit, which was how he now found himself surrounded by a plethora of A4 folders, doing work rather than spending time with his family. Always being one to prefer his own company, he hadn't felt too sorry for himself.

Rather than sit around doing nothing he decided to throw himself into work. He leafed through the documents again. Who were they dealing with here? A serial killer for sure. Added to that, he was clever, and seemingly interested in pissing about with the police. There was still nothing to connect the victims save for perhaps a place they'd all visited. And then there was Gary Dartford. What were the chances he was picked up from the same location? Slim. Jack felt sure that Kyle Walsh might be able help them out with that one. Unfortunately, no one seemed to know where he was. Like so many people in and around this case, Kyle seemed to go AWOL right when they needed him most.

What they had found out, however, was the identity of the female victim found with Gary Dartford. He flicked to the relevant page. Twenty-nine-year-old Melissa Norman, classroom support worker. She lived alone, and her mother had died when she was twelve. The father had been traumatised when they'd told him, having reported her missing in the middle of December. Apparently, he hadn't seen or heard from her for a couple of weeks, which was unusual but not unusual enough to report at first. Work friends said they assumed she was ill initially and that she had often kept to herself.

Panic had started to take hold of the public. All missing persons cases were being double checked but a large number of worried friends and families were contacting the police on a daily basis for updates in case their loved one was a potential victim. They played the numbers game, deciding to prioritise recent missing people.

They were operating on a skeleton crew at the station and Jack had encouraged his officers to take some time off. Christensen was spending time with friends in the Lakes, whilst what Watkins was up to was anyone's guess. He'd managed to convince Pritchard to return to Scotland to see his wife. So it was just him and his Black Sabbath records now.

He was halfway through disc one of the greatest hits when his phone rang.

'Hi, Dad, Merry Christmas!' she shouted down the phone, the sound of music and numerous voices bleeding through from the background.

'Merry Christmas, sweetie,' he replied. 'What are you up to?'

'Well, Jeremy bought me a TV, so we've set that up and everybody is just messing around, playing games and stuff. Mum says to say thanks for the CDs.'

'No problem.'

'Well anyway, it was good to talk to you, I'll see you later okay? And Mum says hello.'

He wasn't sure about that one. 'Okay, bye, honey.'

Suddenly his solitude became oppressive. Sick of staring at murder victims, he threw the folders to the floor and massaged his temples.

Then his phone rang again.

'Watkins?'

He was met with background chatter and Take That tunes.

'Hello?' he tried again.

'Howay, just one kiss?' Watkins' drunken voice slurred.

'For God's sake,' Jack said, ending the call.

He sighed, picked up the Open Grave documents once more and began flicking through. There was something he was missing. *Until you solve the bugger, you're always missing the vital link*, he told himself, repeating a mantra he'd learned many moons ago.

The phone rang again.

'Watkins, honestly...'

'What did you do?' a panicked voice greeted him on the other end.

'Who is this?'

'It's Robson.'

Jack groaned inwardly.

'On Christmas, really?'

'Who did you talk to?'

He could hear shuffling on the line.

'I haven't got time for this—'

'You don't get it, do you? These people aren't fucking about. Whatever you've done, they know I've talked. I rang you days ago to say they're onto me but you didn't even pick up.'

'Who?'

A pause.

'If you're not going to tell me—'

'I've had my fucking windows put out. I know it's them. This is your fault.'

'David—'

It was too late; the journalist had hung up.

Somebody like David Robson would have a lot of enemies. Still, having your windows put out at Christmas wasn't your usual disgruntled reader.

'David bloody Robson,' he said out loud.

He tried ringing the journalist back on the same number but was sent straight to voicemail. Looking round the room, he felt a chill that wasn't just due to the Baltic weather. Since the break-in, it hadn't felt like home any more. He shuddered, getting that strange sensation people often experience when an intruder has been in their home. Since his altercation with the goon in the pub, Jack had been waiting for McGuinness to respond. There'd been nothing so far. Jack knew the gangster too well to think there'd be no comeback though. He'd shaken the tree, all he needed to do now was wait for the leaves to fall.

He considered reading the case notes again but couldn't stomach it. Instead, he passed the evening watching *It's A Wonderful Life* for the hundredth time until it was pitch black outside. He dragged himself to his feet, pulled the curtains closed and headed for bed, taking up a bottle of water for good measure. He lay down on top of his sheets, not even bothering to remove his clothes. The last thing he remembered before passing out was the faint wash of headlights moving across his bedroom wall.

Of course, if he'd taken the time to look out of the window, he might have noticed the car parked opposite the house.

The man smiled, turned his headlights on, and drove off slowly so as not to draw any attention to himself.

Not long now.

CHAPTER 29

J ack returned to work two days later. As he wandered into the station there was actually a spring in his step. No family problems here, just a series of unsolved crimes.

'Boss,' Christensen greeted him as he entered the MIR.

'Did you have a good Christmas, Christensen?' he asked.

The squat detective shrugged. 'Was okay.'

A number of party hats and banners had been erected around the room. Jack felt irritated that people were celebrating during such a tough time for the force, but stopped himself short of saying something. Everybody needs to let off steam once in a while.

'Let's talk,' Jack said.

Two minutes later, the detectives were sitting in his office gazing at a whiteboard littered with hidden riddles and marker smears. Jack slammed the case files onto the desk. Time to get to work.

Christensen raised his eyebrows. 'Been doing some light reading over the holidays?'

'I'm impressed, Christensen – was that an actual joke?'

The DS's face remained impassive. 'Almost.'

'Where's Watkins?'

'Out. There was a knifing near the Gate last night, so he's heading up a team over there.'

He nodded. Perhaps it was a sign of the times that a knifing didn't even register on his radar any more.

'Pritchard is off visiting family over the Christmas period,' he informed Christensen. 'He's available via phone but, until we get any other new information, there isn't really much need to drag him in. He is retired, after all.'

Christensen nodded.

Moments later a red-faced Watkins entered the room, shaking off a dusting of snow from his battered Parker jacket. He ran a hand through his ginger afro, spraying water everywhere.

'Could you not have done that outside?' Jack said.

'Sorry,' he mumbled.

'Is this knifing anything I need to worry about?'

'No.' He waved him away. 'Caught the bloke this morning. Drunken yob upset at how poorly Newcastle United are doing this season.'

'Have you seen the paper this morning?' Watkins asked.

The two detectives shook their heads.

He fished a copy of *The Sun* from his man bag and dumped it on the desk.

'Watkins, I'm really not interested in seeing another naked picture of Nell Stevens.'

'What? Oh, no, it's not that. Page five.'

Jack prised the pages apart.

'She's been getting more hassle?'

'Yeah.'

'Why hasn't she come to us?'

'Says she can't trust the police, that she came to us with what had happened, and it's still going on.'

Jack groaned. Great, now *The Sun* was up their backsides as well.

A knock at the door drew his attention away.

'Come in.'

A young PC entered, clipboard in hand. 'Hello, sir,' she said. 'We've had a call. A man matching Kyle Walsh's description has been spotted in Jarrow. A...' She rolled her eyes. 'Concerned neighbour sounded the alarm. Says there have been numerous parties going on there lately and that she thinks her neighbour is harbouring a fugitive.'

Jack felt his pulse quicken. He hadn't been to Jarrow in a while. The place had gotten a bad name in recent years. It was unfair, really. Ever since Thatcher had closed the pits and failed to offer people any alternative work, they'd been fighting a losing battle.

'Watkins… Christensen, I want both of you with me on this. We go in hard. This is just about the only lead we have right now and I don't want anything left to chance. If it is Kyle Walsh, I don't want him slipping through our fingers.'

Within minutes Jack and Watkins were in one car whilst Christensen followed close behind in a second. They'd alerted dispatch and arranged for two other plainclothes units to approach in unmarked vehicles. Glancing down at the address once more, Jack pointed to the right.

'I thought you liked to drive these days?' Watkins said, turning into the estate.

'Just not feeling great.'

'Headaches again?'

He shrugged. 'By the way, you rang me on Christmas. You should be more careful with your phone when you're drunk.'

'Did I? Sorry, things got a little wild I suppose; still, nothing you won't have been doing.' He winked.

Yeah, right. 'Just pull in here.'

The housing estate was heavily built up, unkempt gardens littered with broken toys and food cartons. Watkins manoeuvred the car into a space, and they waited, as Christensen pulled in behind them. Within a minute Jack saw the other two cars enter from the other side, pulling up just opposite the flat where Kyle Walsh was potentially being harboured.

Jack got on to the radio. 'Right, Christensen, I want you round the back with patrol one. Patrol two, you're with me, front door.'

He waited as the crackle of the radio gave way to affirmative responses. Taking this kind of manpower was going a bit overboard but he didn't want to take any risks. Besides, if anybody questioned him, he'd just say the old neighbour had told him they were armed.

They stepped out into the heavily pock-marked road. To their left, thirty-two Pariah Avenue stood, the downstairs flat blanketed in darkness, one window boarded up with balsawood and graffiti. As he approached the door he could already smell the marijuana. Although it was quiet, Jack sensed that there were people inside. Stepping forward, he gave the brass knocker a heavy *thud*.

A pause. Footsteps. Voices.

'Who the fuck is that?'

'Must be the dealer.'

'Nice one. Answer it then.'

Seconds later, Jack heard the latch move as the door opened. He was greeted by a spindly-looking man in his early twenties, complete with pasty complexion and the beginnings of a moustache.

'Aye?' he spat, eyes dancing over them suspiciously.

'Police,' Jack said, leg jamming into the doorway. 'I'm looking for Kyle Walsh.'

'Never heard of him.'

'We can either do this here, or down at the station. Either way, I will find him.' He leaned in close, so close that he could smell the man's harsh aftershave. 'But you could save yourself a lot of trouble by just letting us in now.'

The lad gulped and stepped back from the doorway.

Jack got on the radio. 'Christensen, we're inside. Come round the front.'

'Look, man, if this about the weed—'

'I don't give a shit about your drug habits, at least not today. This is about a murder case.'

'I didn't do nothing, I swear,' he panicked.

'Just tell me where he is.'

The young man paused, not for long, but his eyes moved just enough to the left to suggest Kyle Walsh was in the house.

'I can either turn this house upside down, looking for anything and everything, or you can give him up now.'

Christensen appeared in the doorway, his face flushed from the cold. 'Alright, boss?'

'We will be in about three seconds; what's your name, son?'

'Neil Haddon,' he replied, bringing a decimated nail up to his mouth. 'Ah, shit, I'm sorry, Kyle! He's in there.' He motioned to a door behind him.

'Watkins, see to it Mr Haddon doesn't go anywhere while we have a chat with Kyle.'

Jack motioned to Christensen, and the two men entered the living room. The pungent odour of marijuana laced the atmosphere as they stepped over various plastic cartons. In the far corner of the room, the unmistakable presence of Kyle Walsh sat, cross-legged, as if awaiting their arrival. All that was missing was the cat. He was seemingly enjoying the company of a tarted-up blonde who looked young enough to be in school. She was sitting with legs sprawled over him, her face nuzzled into his neck. It didn't look as though he'd been washed in days. As he sat in his stained wife-beater, Jack couldn't help but wonder what the appeal was.

'What's up?' he said, raising a joint to his mouth before inhaling deeply and blowing it into the girl's face.

'Christensen, please escort our lady friend here to the kitchen.'

The girl's head snapped back, eyes a blur. She was either coming off the back of a session, or she was just starting.

'Nah, man,' Kyle said, smirk on his face. 'She can stay.'

'Oh, I'm sorry, maybe I didn't make myself clear,' Jack said, focusing his stare on him. 'I'm Detective Chief Inspector Jack Lambert. I also happen to be in charge here, so how about you shut your mouth unless I ask you a direct question?'

Christensen helped the girl from the couch, her steps heavy as she made for the door. 'Come on,' he said. 'Let's get you some water.'

'Now,' Jack began. 'We can start.'

He took a seat opposite Kyle, across from a small coffee table that was stained with tobacco and various other substances. The owner didn't like to keep a clean house, it seemed.

'You going to arrest me for the weed, man?' He sniggered, taking another drag. 'Don't give a shit and neither should you. You got nothing better to do with your time, pig?'

Jack noted the slight tremor in his hand. 'Strangely enough, Kyle, no I haven't. However, I'll add it to the list.'

His eyes narrowed. 'What list?'

'I'm here about Gary Dartford.'

He rolled his eyes, taking another drag on his joint, sending plumes of smoke into the already thickened air. 'What's he done now?'

Jack stopped short. 'You're not too observant, are you?'

'Look, man—'

'Gary Dartford is dead.'

Jack searched his face for some semblance of previous knowledge, or guilt. Nothing, only shock.

'What the fuck?'

Jack took out his notepad and flicked it open to a blank page, removing a Parker pen from inside his jacket pocket. He paused, allowing Walsh to stew a little longer. His cocky demeanour paled somewhat.

'Are you seriously telling me you didn't know about his death?'

'No! Nothing. Jesus Christ.'

Christensen re-entered the room and took a seat next to Jack. 'Watkins is seeing to her.'

'When was the last time you saw him?'

'Weeks ago.'

'Specific date, please.'

'I can't remember.'

'What about the night of December eighth?'

'I... I can't remember.'

'That's strange,' Jack said. 'Because, I have a recording of your voice on Gary Dartford's answering machine, making arrangements to meet up that very night.'

The tension was almost visible above the smoke now.

'So,' Jack continued. 'I'll ask you one more time, when did you last see Gary Dartford?'

'I... I cancelled that night.'

'Why?'

Sweat was beginning to form on his brow now. 'Something came up.'

Jack removed a set of handcuffs from his belt and placed them on the table.

'What came up, Kyle?'

'I'm in a bit of trouble, is all,' he spluttered. 'Owe some people some money. They've been tailing me. That's why I've been hiding out here. I'd been threatened that day and was scared to go out. That's why I cancelled.'

Jack took in a deep breath before asking the next question, well aware that this was what they were really after.

'Where had you arranged to meet?'

'Dog and Parrot,' he said. 'We usually hit the same places up. From there, we head to Mr Lynch's, Blue Bamboo and Tiger Tiger, before a kebab. I can't believe he's dead. What happened?'

Jack scribbled the pub names down, aware that his heart was now racing. He wasn't sure whether it was adrenaline or the fumes.

'The Open Grave Murderer.'

'Fuck... wow, you don't think it's me, do you?'

His entire body was visibly shaking now.

'No, Kyle, I don't.'

Kyle Walsh exhaled a sigh of relief, resting his head on the back of the chair.

'Do you know what Gary did that night after you cancelled?'

'He told me he was going to go out. He was that type, always knew somebody. He'd go out alone and wouldn't think anything of it. Shit, I can't believe this has happened. What if I had been there?'

'We don't know what happened that particular night, only that you were the last person to have contact with him, as far as we know.'

'So now what?'

'Well,' Jack continued, taking the joint from Kyle and stubbing it out in a plastic Bob Marley ashtray. 'Now I am going to arrest you for the drugs.'

'Come on, man!'

Jack made to cuff him but stopped short, something popping into his mind.

'Just one more question.'

'Will you drop the drug shit if I answer?'

Jack considered it. 'It can't hurt your chances.'

'Fine.'

'Where do you get the weed from?'

Kyle squirmed in his seat, head shaking. 'Howay, man, you know I can't give shit like that away.'

Jack twirled the cuffs around in his hand. 'Then I'll have to assume it's you who's dealing it out.'

'No, wait! Ah, shit... look, I don't know his real name. Nobody ever sees him.'

Jack paused. 'A name.'

'Nobody knows, alright. We get it from all sorts of people. It's some new stuff that's on the market, really potent. Word is, the guy distributing it is called the Captain. Fucking stupid name if you ask me.'

He spent the remainder of the journey back to the station in silent contemplation, which wasn't easy given the stream of expletives emanating from the back of the car. Apparently, Kyle Walsh and his drug buddy Neil Haddon took exception to being arrested for breaking the law. On arrival, he escorted the two of them to the booking desk and left Watkins to see to the particulars. Jack had no doubt that Kyle wasn't the Open Grave Murderer, but it couldn't hurt to have him chew things over in custody.

'Well that was exciting,' Watkins said, plonking down in a seat opposite Jack's desk.

Christensen entered, closed the door, and followed suit.

'There's something we're missing here,' Jack said.

Watkins leaned forward, his eyebrows raised. 'Such as?'

'I can't shake the feeling that this 'Captain' person is bad news. Like proper bad news.'

'What makes you think that?' Christensen asked.

Jack stopped short, aware he was drumming on the desk. It was a nervous habit he'd picked up some years ago. 'This isn't the first time I've been made aware of this Captain fella. The name came up when we were questioning local drug dealers in relation to Peter Rutherford. Now I've got Kyle Walsh looking over his shoulder, getting hassle from local druggies. Turns out, his main supplier is this Captain bloke.'

'No such thing as coincidences,' Christensen said.

'Well, did Kyle say whether or not Gary Dartford was into the drugs too?'

Jack cleared his throat, embarrassed at having forgotten to ask. 'We'll have to check it out.'

'I'm on it,' Christensen said, rising.

Jack noticed his phone was vibrating. 'Watkins, go with him, two heads are better than one.'

He waited for both of them to leave the room before answering. 'Hello, Pritchard, enjoying retirement?'

'It's not so bad. I'm just in the pub, a few pints down, and I thought I would check up on how things are going.'

Jack filled him in on the details. 'Any ideas then?'

'Nothing.' The profiler coughed down the phone. 'However, I'd say that anybody who refers to themselves as 'Captain' must have one hell of a superiority complex.'

He smiled, thanked him, and ended the call. Jack turned to face the whiteboard. He could barely see what was in front of him, such was his tiredness. Still, he didn't need to look to know what was there. God knows he'd spent enough hours staring at the various fragments of the broken jigsaw. Each set of victims set out in pairs; first of all, Jessica Lisbie and Travis Kane. Next to them sat the images of Peter Rutherford and Amy Drummond. Perhaps most disturbing of all were the images of Gary Dartford and Melissa Norman. Details of the final female victim were sketchy, but DI Russell was working on it. Another victim seemingly socially isolated from those around her.

Surely it wasn't all linked to drugs?

Watkins and Christensen returned a few minutes later.

'What is it?'

'According to Kyle Walsh, Gary was in on the drugs as well.'

Jack let the news sink in. 'We are going to need a focus shift. I want a team looking into this new drug lord. Somebody must know something. Get a list together of all known drug offenders in the local area. I want door knocking, door breaking and all lines of questioning covered.'

'No problem, boss.'

'Watkins, look into the other victims. Any history of drug use whether it be themselves, their friends or family. I want answers as soon as possible.'

'On it.'

Both men left as quickly as they'd arrived. Jack glanced at his St Clare's Hospice calendar on the wall waiting to be opened. Maybe the New Year would bring a new set of results. God knows they needed it now more than ever.

He stood and faced the images of all the victims. Their eyes bore into him, demanding their own answers, their own justice. There was a link somewhere. Maybe it was a common location. Maybe it was a common enemy. Either way, Jack felt they were closer to an answer now than they had been this morning. He just hoped they could stop whoever it was before anything else happened.

Unless they were already too late.

CHAPTER 30

Jack sat nibbling at his thumbnail. The details of the phone call he'd just had with the *Newcastle Chronicle* editor were still swimming through his mind.

'What's up?' Watkins asked, balancing two cups of coffee as he waded into the room, a ginger snap perched between his lips.

'Just got off the phone with Craig Lisle.'

'What have we not done now?'

'Not us, David Robson.'

The DS grimaced as a glob of steaming hot cappuccino landed on his hand, before dropping the biscuit to the floor.

'Ten second rule,' he cried out before picking it up, dusting it off and taking a bite. 'What's he done?'

Jack shook his head. 'Nothing, that's the problem. He hasn't reported for work for a couple of days now and nobody can seem to reach him.'

'Maybe he's upped and done a runner?' Watkins said, cheerfully.

Jack sipped his coffee, taking a moment to recount the conversation he'd had with the journalist just days before. He'd told him that 'they' knew. Maybe he wasn't so full of shit after all.

'I don't think so.'

'How come?'

Jack knew he was treading on thin ice but had no other choice but to tell the detective. 'I had a private meeting with Robson a few weeks ago.'

'Jesus, Jack, did you take money from him?'

'Hardly,' he snapped. 'What do you take me for?'

An awkward silence ensued, the details of the hacking scandal still fresh in their minds. It wouldn't do to have a DCI to be seen to be taking bribes from a journalist. Especially one with the reputation of David bloody Robson.

'He asked to meet me, so I agreed. He gave me some info on Dorian McGuinness's group.'

'So we based an illicit stakeout on a tip off from a dodgy journo?'

It did sound bad when it was put like that. 'He was scared,' Jack continued. 'Said he may need something in return but never really said what. I'm thinking this is what he was talking about. Plus, we have Liam Reed to consider here as well.'

'So you think he was into something deep?'

Jack paused. 'I think he was tipped off and got in over his head. Who that tip came from, I have no idea.'

Watkins nodded.

He stood and began pacing, recanting the events in his mind, searching for a link. He always found he worked better on his feet. 'I think this theory has legs,' he said finally. 'The body of Liam Reed, Robson spooked, the abandoned factory, it all adds up to something big.'

'You thinking Reed was a rat?'

He shrugged. 'Maybe. It would make sense, wouldn't it? He wanted out. Maybe he knew what was going on and used it as leverage to broker his severance, only McGuinness couldn't just let him walk. Under torture, Reed tells them he told Robson who, in turn, turned to me to help out. And now this...'

'That's a pretty extravagant theory, Jack.'

Jack stopped pacing and glanced out of the window at the tightly-knitted clouds. 'Agreed. However, I'd bet my house on at least some of it being true.'

'It's not the biggest of houses,' Watson quipped.

He smiled. 'That's why I'm willing to bet it.'

Half an hour later they pulled up outside David Robson's luxury detached house in the Jesmond Dene area. According to official records, he lived alone. Watkins whistled as they headed up the paved garden path. Either Robson had won big on the stock market, or he was on the fiddle.

Jack knew which way he'd bet.

The house itself was a modern structure over three floors, with a clean white appearance and two bay windows on the ground floor. Above the blue double-breasted front door, a balcony hung, rocking chair perched outside yet another full-length window, the insides protected by a thick curtain. It looked like some kind of plantation house.

'Remind me to take up a journalism career once this is over,' Watkins said.

'I'll head round the back, you scout out the front and see if anything looks disturbed.'

He veered to the left, taking the opportunity to glance over at the neighbouring houses. Although not a huge garden, it was neatly kept with low cut grass and a thick hedge lining the perimeter. The nearest house stood some distance away. Already, Jack was thinking it unlikely that anybody had seen anything occur here.

As he headed round the side, he glanced up, one solitary window peering down at him. Probably a bathroom. The smell of fresh grass, and what he assumed to be turps, stung his nostrils like an out of date aftershave. So far so good.

The back garden looked much the same as the front. In fact, it was practically a mirror image. Jack hadn't thought of Robson as the neat and tidy type. Still, how much did he really know about the man anyway?

Glancing down, he checked for any fresh footprints. Nothing. There were ways of avoiding footprints, if you knew what to do.

The back of the house was equally impressive with a large patio door set off to the right. A kitchen window and back door stood on the other side. Jack moved over to the window and peered in. A giant wooden breakfast bar stood nearby with a copy of *The Sun* newspaper on the counter. Jack noticed the heavy colouring in of Nell Stevens' image. She'd had a rather ugly pair of glasses and some kind of strange hairdo drawn onto her. Other than the tabloid graffiti, there was seemingly not a hair out of place.

Just to be sure, he switched places with Watkins and checked over the front. Still he found nothing. Frowning, he pulled out the e-cigarette he'd gotten himself for Christmas and inhaled the nicotine. Not even close to a real hit. He sighed, and placed it back in the container.

'Not a hair out of place,' Watkins said.

Jack spent the best part of ten minutes hammering away at the door and peering in various windows before he was sure nobody was home. He stood back from the house and glanced up. Not even a curtain twitch. Unless Robson was dead inside, the house was most definitely empty.

'We are going to have to get a warrant and break in, just to be sure,' Jack said as they headed back to the car.

'You want to handle it?'

'No, I'll send some uniforms down; we have more important things to worry about.'

He'd barely made it inside the station before Gerrard cornered them in the corridor.

'Have you heard?' she asked.

'H-heard what?' Watkins stuttered, eyes unable to meet hers.

'Edwards arrived at work today then, after bollocking a couple of uniforms, keeled over.'

Jack exhaled. 'Is he alive?'

'Yeah, but he's in hospital now undergoing tests.' She paused, fiddling with a chewed biro. 'Anyway, just thought I'd let you know. Oh, and DI Russell has been placed in temporary charge.'

'You what?'

A glimmer of a smile. 'I thought you might enjoy that. Dalton has placed her in temporary charge for now.'

'Over Jack?' Watkins exclaimed.

'It's fine,' he interjected. 'I'm bad news right now. Plus, with Jane acting up, it allows me to continue as SIO on the Open Grave case.'

'Still...' Watkins muttered.

Only time would tell if the Bulldog let the power go to her head. Either way, Jack was determined not to take any shit from her.

'It makes sense,' he continued. 'Dalton knows I have my hands full.'

'Oh, and she wants to see you right away, guv,' Gerrard said.

And with that she was gone.

Jane Russell stood and greeted him stoically as he entered Edwards' room. 'Please, take a seat.'

She hadn't wasted much time in making herself at home in his office. Gone was the clutter, placed in a box in the corner of the room, an assortment of her own photos and paraphernalia placed in regimented fashion around her work space.

It was as if Edwards had already died.

'Jane.'

'And just where have you been for the last two hours?'

'Following up a lead.'

She raised a thinly-pencilled eyebrow. 'Care to elaborate?'

He shrugged, offended at the offhand way in which she was choosing to speak to him. 'Not really.'

'May I remind you that I am your superior officer...?'

'Jane, please don't play the hard ass with me,' he cut in. 'We both know that the station is completely understaffed at present and, despite your best efforts to prove otherwise, I haven't done anything wrong. So, what do you actually want?'

He watched as the acting DSI pursed her mouth into an ugly grimace. *Go on, say something else*, he silently urged her.

Instead of biting, she simply straightened out her jack and smiled – a fake smile, but a smile nonetheless. 'I am merely wondering what could be so important that you thought it wise to leave the Open Grave case understaffed. Could Watson not have done it?'

'Watkins,' he corrected her.

'Yes.' She waved him away.

Through gritted teeth, he brought her up to speed with the David Robson story, informing her of the phone call the hack had made to him in a panic, followed by the missing persons report filed by his editor that led to the search. He decided to omit the details about meeting him in a bar.

'Sounds riveting,' she said, once he was finished. 'In future, send one of your minions to sort it out. I want you here.'

'Look, Jane, I'm SIO on this case and I won't have you muscling in on my investigation, acting DSI or no acting DSI. If you insist on continuing with this approach, I will have no alternative but to file a report removing myself from the case due to outside interference.'

He saw the panic dance across her eyes. 'Yes... well... just make sure you keep your focus.'

'No problem, guv,' he said, emphasising the last part.

He left the office moments later, wound up and in need of a cigarette. Who did Russell think she was, ordering him around like some kind of lapdog? His only comfort was that she'd have to sit through meetings with PCC Nadine Guthrie on a regular basis. This was the thought he allowed himself to follow as he bumped into Watkins outside the incident room.

'Do you have a cigarette?' he enquired, brusquely.

'I thought you'd given up?'

Jack stared the DS down. 'Do you, or don't you?'

'No.'

'For God's sake!'

Watkins grinned. 'Just got word from uniform, no sign of any struggle in the house, or a body. Want to go down and check it out?'

Getting out of the station was tempting, but they really did have more important matters to attend to.

'No, I need an update on the Open Grave murders, including the potential drug link.'

Inside the MIR, they found an unusually dishevelled and somewhat wet DS Christensen waving a piece of paper around. The officers in attendance sat in silent intimidation. Jack had never seen the man exert any sort of dominance over anybody, and felt that perhaps Christensen allowed the rumours about his efficiency and temper to spread so that he didn't even have to try.

'Christensen,' he greeted him.

'Boss.'

'Any luck?'

The blond detective motioned them over to a table, cleared the contents and spread out a number of printed sheets. He paused, gazing over them, before continuing.

'We've looked into all of the victims' histories as best we can, re-questioning the relatives and close friends.'

Jack could tell by the look on his face that the drugs lead was a dead end and prepared himself for what would come next.

'So, anything come up?' Watkins asked.

'I'm afraid not. Apart from Gary Dartford and Peter Rutherford, there seems to be no drug link.'

'That doesn't mean there isn't one,' Watkins said. 'Just that their relatives didn't know about it. I know I wouldn't tell my parents if I had an addiction.'

The silence stretched as they lost themselves in thought. Although Watkins might be right, Jack felt there was no point in pursuing it. Still, this Captain bloke seemed to be popping up more and more. They'd have to keep an eye on him… if they could find out who the hell he was.

'So, we are back to square one,' Jack added, gloomily.

'Not necessarily,' said Christensen, stooping to gather the papers back up.

'Oh?'

'It may be nothing, but I thought I would check anyway.'

'What is it?'

'Well, I remember you saying about where Gary Dartford and Kyle Walsh were meant to be heading out to. I was going to check out the CCTV footage for the pubs, but you'd already sent a team in, so I thought I'd do some digging, see if any of the other victims could be linked to the location.'

'There's a link?'

'Possibly.'

'Go on,' Jack urged him.

Christensen continued. 'According to Amy Drummond's parents, they were unsure as to where she was going, but knew her to often visit Tiger Tiger.'

'And the others?'

'Nothing concrete but, according to a friend of Jessica Lisbie's, she often visited the Bigg Market and Quayside after work.'

Jack was sure the drugs link would get them nowhere, but finding a location might. The Open Grave Murderer had to find his victims somewhere. Where better than a nightclub he was familiar with filled with people who were intoxicated? He ran the list of pubs over in his mind a number of times before he realised that the two sergeants were looking at him.

'I need those CCTV images scrutinised. We'll need to split up, but I want an open line at all times. Anything looks suspicious, let me know.'

'Do you realise how much tape we are going to have to go through?' Watkins asked.

'Yes,' he replied. 'But, all we need is one of the victims, and we can work from there. Start with eighth of December, that's when Gary Dartford was last known to be out in a public setting. Perhaps the killer targets them in pairs somehow. If we find Gary, we can hopefully find Amy. If we find Amy, we may find the killer.'

Minutes later Jack stepped out into the crisp evening air, a red hue hanging low over the sky. His phone began to vibrate. An unknown caller. He cancelled the call, thrusting the phone back into his pocket seconds before it rang again.

'Look, I'm not interested,' he called down the line.

'I think you will be interested in this,' a familiar voice echoed down the line.

'Keira,' he greeted her. 'Please tell me you have good news?'

Keira Tilson was a fibre analyst. Not just any fibre analyst; one of the best Jack had come across. It was just his luck that she happened to work in Newcastle.

'I don't know about good, but I do have something,' she continued. 'I may have found some interesting fibres. I'll not bore you with the science behind it all, but suffice to say, we have a match between fibres on two of the victims.'

'You're right, I am interested.'

'Although I can't be one hundred per cent sure, I'd say we definitely have some kind of camouflage clothing involved here.'

'Meaning?' he asked.

'Army gear, perhaps,' she said. 'I know it's only a small detail, but it might help narrow down the suspect pool.'

The suspect pool of none.

'Great, thanks, Keira,' he said, ending the call.

Neat. Tidy. Army? Jack felt sure they were getting closer.

His phone vibrated again. Unknown caller again.

'Did you forget something, Keira?'

'Listen carefully,' a foreign voice began.

Jack felt ice running through his body.

'Who is this?'

'I make it a priority of mine to get to know people very well, especially when they are digging into my business.'

'What business?'

'You have captured my attention, Jack Lambert, and that is not a good thing.'

He strained his hearing. There was a muffled scraping noise in the background, as the stranger barked an order out.

'What do you want?'

'I propose we meet.'

'And why would I meet you?'

'Good question, my friend,' the voice went on. The accent sounded Eastern European, although he was well-spoken. 'Well, you don't have to but when you make it your business to pry into what I'm doing, I make it my business to pry into all aspects of your life. I could rattle off a list of all the important people in your world, Jack, starting with your daughter.'

Jack gritted his teeth. 'I understand.'

'Good. I'll be in touch in due course. In the meantime, I have someone here who wants to talk to you.'

There was a muffled discussion before somebody appeared back on the line.

'Jack, it's me – Robson.'

'Robson, what's going on?'

'They've got me holed up somewhere, you've got to help me, please.'

Jack felt his stomach tighten. Robson had been abducted after all; and, if Jack knew him like he thought he did, he'd have said whatever was necessary to save his own skin.

Including implicating Jack.

'Just stay calm,' he told him, despite his own nervous system doing otherwise.

'So, as you can see, we have ourselves a situation here,' the first voice returned. 'I will ring back with arrangements in one hour. Go to your house and wait there.'

The line went dead. Jack placed it back into his pocket and ran a weary hand across his forehead. Despite the cold weather, he began to sweat. They knew who his close family were and where he lived. They'd also kidnapped Robson. Protocol would tell him to inform his colleagues, but it wouldn't be the first time he'd ignored the rules. If he told anybody, he risked hurting others.

He was back at his house within twenty minutes. He ran up to the bathroom, splashed cold water on his face, and began pacing up and down the hallway. Unable to think clearly, he poured himself a whisky before thinking better of it and tossing it down the sink. Then he rang his daughter; she told him they were out of town on a family trip. Swallowing the hurt, he wished her well before trying Rosie's mobile. He got no answer, so he left a voicemail asking her to text him when she got the chance.

Then he made a call he'd promised himself he'd never do again.

'Jack, how good of you to get in touch,' Dorian said. 'On my private line no less. Are you looking to get back involved?'

'Save the pleasantries, is this your doing?'

A pause. When the voice replied, the tone was noticeably cooler. 'Remember who you're talking to, Detective.'

That was the McGuinness Jack knew.

'How about you tell me why I've just had some lackey on the phone threatening me?'

Another pause. 'I have no idea what you're talking about.'

'Oh, please, McGuinness,' Jack cut in. 'The bloke had my number, accused me of prying into his business and threatened my family. Is this because I roughed one of your goons up?'

'That was unfortunate, Jack. A small misdemeanour on your part, I'm sure. That is a conversation we can have another day.'

Jack didn't like the sound of that.

'Don't you ever think you can threaten my family, Dorian, or I swear to God—'

'I'm going to say this once,' McGuinness interjected, 'because we go back a long way. If you ever wrongly accuse me of threatening innocent people again, I'll be forced to revoke our little truce. Judging by the sounds of it, though, somebody isn't too pleased with you. We all have enemies, Jack, how long's your list?'

The phone went dead.

Jack was pacing across his living room with a coffee when his phone rang again. He polished off the espresso, answered the call.

'Ten minutes, the park across the road.'

Jack stood, methodically washed out his mug and grabbed his jacket. Glancing momentarily at the kitchen counter, he considered picking up a knife. What if he was caught? Bad idea. He checked for his phone and keys, he left the house and began the short walk across to Leazes Park. Being heavily wooded, it was perfect for an illicit meeting at this time in the evening.

He approached the gate and glanced round. The only movement seemed to come from what he assumed to be a couple, who were sat across the other side of the lake. He waited. Seconds later, his phone buzzed.

'The trees to your left.'

After gulping down the uneasy feeling that was threatening to paralyse him, he did as he was told. Every breeze and twig snap caused him to jerk around violently in search of his hidden pursuer. His pulse had quickened to what most doctors would label a health hazard and his breathing came in short, erratic bursts.

Whoever it was, they were upon him before he had a chance to react. Leaves and dirt scratched at his face like an angry child as he was manhandled down. A hood, which smelled of rust, was forced over his face, blinding him.

He fought against rough hands as he felt himself being bundled into a vehicle. A sharp kick to his head stopped him in his tracks and he submitted to whatever was going to happen. He needed to conserve energy for now. Seconds later, the sound of a side door sliding across could be heard. He knew it was useless to resist. No point in risking taking a beating now. That would no doubt come later.

He tried to follow the directions the van was taking. His mind took him back to the Sherlock Holmes film where the protagonist had been bundled into a cart, in similar circumstances, and managed to recount the exact direction they had taken. Unfortunately for him this wasn't fiction, and he wasn't Sherlock Holmes.

The drive seemed to take some time and Jack was aware of at least two different men in the back of the van alongside him, given away by their heavy breathing. That meant, including the driver, there were at least three assailants. The odds weren't great.

After what seemed like an age, he felt the terrain change to something far rougher as the van veered left. Within minutes they pulled to a stop, the engine dying. Seconds later, he heard the driver get out and the side door was pulled across. The heavies dragged him out and frogmarched him towards an unseen foe. He didn't have to fight against them, nor did he have to help them out. Making his body as heavy as possible, he heard them grunt from the effort. The cold was swiping at him now, making him wish he'd brought his gloves along for the ride. He attempted to move his hands as he walked, but it was no use; the bonds were too tight. He nearly tripped as they entered a building, the smell of off-meat and sewage greeting him as he did so. He felt his stomach tighten as they veered left, footsteps echoing against a hard surface.

They forced him onto a hard wooden chair and removed his blindfold, a brilliant, white light momentarily dazzling him. His head throbbed from stress, lack of sleep and the clip around the ears that he'd been given in the park. After a few heavy blinks, his eyes began to refocus. In front of him was a spotlight placed directly towards his seat. Although not quite a warehouse, the room that now held him was huge, with an expanse of boxes littered around. A high-beamed ceiling glared down at him, an assortment of boarded up and smashed windows completing the picture.

'Ah, Mr Lambert,' an Eastern European voice snaked out from the darkness.

'I've spoken to you already, haven't I?' he choked out, mouth dry.

'Yes, Detective, you have.'

'What is it you want?'

'Want? Why, we have *everything* that we want,' he continued, the voice moving closer now.

Jack noted the use of 'we'. 'So why bring me here?'

The scraping of boots to his right dragged his attention away. The heavies from the van, Jack assumed. Even through the damp atmosphere of the room, he could still make out the smell of Cool Water aftershave.

'You have been snooping, my friend, and that I cannot allow.'

Sweat was dripping from his brow onto his upper lip. There was no way they were going to let him live. He fought the urge to panic as best he could, straining to focus his mind.

'Look, I don't know what you think it is that you know but—'

A hand grabbed his shoulder in an iron grip, nails tearing flesh. Jack fought the urge to cry out.

'I hope you are not calling me a liar, Detective,' the voice arrived at his ear. 'Show him.'

One of the hired help stepped out from behind Jack and forced his chair around. There, directly opposite, was Robson, eyes wide and mouth duct-taped shut. Much like Jack, his hands had been bound and, judging by the redness of his face, somebody had been having their fun with him. Snot splayed from his nose with every breath as tears streamed down his bruised cheeks.

'Look,' Jack said, frantically trying to buy some time. 'Let him go, he knows nothing.'

'I can't stand liars. Let it not be said I am a hypocrite, though. I will be honest with you, Jack Lambert. I know that Mr Robson here has passed on information to you regarding our operation. I also know that—'

'I—'

A fist slammed against his jaw, out of nowhere, causing millions of small white stars to dance across his vision. He spat, red congealing on the floor as the taste of metal engulfed his mouth.

The voice continued, unperturbed, 'I also know that you have been following some of our movements. Indeed, it seems you have been to this very place at least once before.'

The abandoned factory? So, McGuinness *was* involved after all.

'How did you know?'

'Us foreigners are not as stupid as your tabloid newspapers would have you believe,' he snorted. 'I'm hardly going to run an operation from here without installing a camera now, am I?'

It hadn't even crossed Jack's mind to check for that. He'd been so consumed with following the van, he'd not even stopped to think. Now he'd put his and Watkins' life at risk. Not to mention those close to him.

'Oh, don't worry. I will catch up with your detective friend just as soon as we are done here. I hear he has a soft nature, isn't that right, Arnold?'

'Aye, that's one way of putting it.'

Jack snapped his head around as Mohan stepped forward, Cheshire cat grin on his face. It seemed Tank's brutal reputation might be about to be put to the test.

'Mr Mohan, why don't you show our guests what you have brought for them today?'

Tank dragged a small table in between the two hostages. In the centre lay a toolbox, which was opened, revealing an assortment of hammers, pliers and saws.... Jack was now face to face with McGuinness's right-hand man. A sly smile spread across his face as a gloved hand reached into the box to pull out a handsaw, eyes never leaving his.

'You're not seriously going to kill a policeman, are you?' he shouted, unable to contain the tremor in his voice.

Tank grinned. 'It's not my usual practice. But for you, I'm going to make an exception, like.'

Jack strained against his bonds but it was no use. He should have called backup. Playing the Lone Ranger very rarely worked. He'd found that out in spectacular fashion with the Newcastle Knifer. Now, Arnold 'Tank' Mohan was about to finish the job.

He needed time. 'So why kill Liam Reed? Because he wanted out? Because he was disloyal to McGuinness?'

Arnold snorted. 'Him? He was always wanting out,' he laughed. 'Liam knew the risks in this game. These things just happen.'

While the squat man spoke, Jack began working the bonds. It was slow going, but the tension was definitely loosening. 'Then why kill him?'

Tank raised a thick eyebrow. 'You really don't have a clue, do you? You're dumber than McGuinness gives you credit for.'

The cool way in which Tank was referring to his boss made Jack uneasy. Something was amiss. 'I don't understand—'

'You really aren't that good a policeman, then,' Tank interrupted him. 'Dorian is finished. I have a new partner now.'

So that was it. Tank had switched sides and betrayed the aquatic shop owner. Jack couldn't believe it. Mohan had never struck him as the devious type.

'So, what... Liam knew about the operation against McGuinness and you had to take him out?'

Mohan shrugged. 'Liam's death was nowt to do with me.'

Jack tried to remain cool and keep the conversation going. 'This boss of yours must be a powerful bloke.'

'Partner!' Tank shouted. Jack had obviously touched a nerve.

'Don't say his name,' the Eastern European voice hissed.

The thug bristled. 'Wasn't about to.'

'You sure it's your partner?' Jack asked. 'Sounds to me like you're still the hired help, Arnold.'

He was prepared for the fist that slammed into his face but it still hurt like hell. Blinking through the tears, he could feel his eye instantly begin to swell. Judging by the searing pain scratching down the side of his face, his jaw might well have been broken too. Still, the more he could keep them talking, the longer he had to think of a way out. He began using the back of his chair to saw away at his bonds, rope scraping against wood.

'Enough of this!' the European shouted from the shadows. 'Get on with it.'

Jack smirked, risking the wrath of his captor once more, but it seemed that his plan was having the desired effect. Tank turned, stuck out his barrelled chest and pointed a gloved hand into the darkness.

'Don't you fucking order me about!'

He could feel the bonds thinning, ever so slightly.

A click to Jack's right and, within a second, a black barrel was pointed at Tank's huge cranium. The heavy lowered his hand and shrugged, but Jack could see the sweat on his brow.

'Don't forget that you are a commodity that we can do without. There is nothing special about you, Mr Mohan, but I'll be sure to let your... partner know about your concerns regarding your role in this operation. I'm sure he would be most interested in your issues.'

'I didn't mean owt by it,' Tank's voice cracked. 'Look, inviting Liam in was a mistake, but it's taken care of now, right?'

'You advised us to use him. Perhaps you aren't as wise as you like to think.'

Jack continued gnawing at the ropes around his wrists. His hands were aching, but he forced himself to continue. It was his only chance.

Tank spluttered, clearing his throat. 'Aye... well, honest mistake, wasn't it?'

'My employer doesn't like mistakes; or those who make them.'

Nearly there.

'Alright, alright, point made.'

Tank turned back to his toolbox as Jack discreetly tried to loosen his bonds. Robson was sitting in silence, almost in a comatose state, unaware of the chaos going on around him.

'Now then.' Tank turned to Jack, saw in hand. 'Where to begin?'

The icy sting of blade hit his cheek as Tank, lightly at first, began to apply pressure on his swollen jaw. He tried to hold it in, but couldn't, a bloodcurdling scream erupting as metal met bone.

Tank's penchant for playing with his food would be his downfall. He turned, aiming the blade at Robson, whose eyes came to life just as Jack managed to loosen the bonds enough to free his hands. He stood, moving in before Mohan had a chance to react, aiming a palm into the throat of his captor before spinning to his right.

Mohan fell to the ground as a shot rang out. Dodging it, Jack moved into the darkness, throwing himself behind a row of boxes. *Stay low and move*, he told himself.

'You idiot!' the European shouted through the commotion. 'Find him! No loose ends.'

Jack took a moment to take in his surroundings. It was dark but he knew he was planted behind a giant, cloth-covered container.

He kept moving away from his original position, heading for the other side of the room in the hope of finding an exit.

Another shot rang out in the distance as a number of voices communicated excitedly. He moved on, adrenaline masking the pain in his face and wrists. He felt bad for Robson but, if he stayed, they'd both be dead. The best he could hope for was that they hadn't killed him already. He fished around in his pockets and placed his key between his fingers to use as a makeshift weapon.

'We will find you, Mr Lambert,' the European called.

Suddenly, the lights went up around him. He could hear the voices moving closer. He wondered how many there were, but didn't plan on sticking around long enough to find out. His vision was clouding as his jaw and eye continued to swell. If he ever made it out of here, he'd have to pay a visit to the nearest hospital.

'I can't see him!' a voice called out nearby.

Crouching, Jack moved around a set of cardboard boxes, key at the ready. The body of a heavyset man with unkempt black hair came into view. In his left hand a tiny black revolver hung loose. Jack snuck up behind him and forced the brass key into his throat, his other hand coming up to grab the gun.

'You even breathe loudly and I'll cut your neck,' he whispered.

He could feel the man nod in acknowledgment as he prised the gun from his hand. Checking his surroundings, he edged back towards the centre of the room, the pain of his jaw dulled by adrenaline. Now he had a plan.

'Nobody move!' he called out, dragging his hostage into view.

Tank spun to face him, eyes lighting up like a predator seeking its next kill. To his right stood whom Jack believed to be the orchestrator of the event. He was smartly dressed in a shirt and tie, hair slicked back, with just the right amount of designer stubble to tell Jack he gave a shit about the way he looked. His chiselled features remained unmoved, betraying no emotion. Just behind them stood two heavies, similar in build to Tank, but with more hair and better dress sense.

'And what is it you have to offer in this situation, Mr Lambert?' the European asked.

Jack motioned towards a terrified Robson. 'Let him go.'

'Anything else?'

His gaze landed on Tank, who was flexing his hands, itching to put them around his throat no doubt. He'd have to deal with him later.

'You let us both go,' he went on.

'And then what?'

A noise behind Jack caused him to snap his head around. Nothing there.

'Nervous?' Tank sneered.

Jack regained his composure. 'I'm going to ring this in. You'll have about ten minutes before you're picked up. What you decide to do in that time is up to you.'

'And what do I get in return?'

'A head start and the life of one of your partners,' Jack said, digging the butt of the gun into the bloke's back for good measure. 'We'll just call this a failed negotiation.'

It all happened too fast for Jack to register what was going on. The blow to the back of his head caused him to stumble. Releasing his hostage, he fell to the floor, faces blurring in and out of focus. Somewhere through the mash up of colours, he could sense men approaching him. A strong set of hands manhandled him to his feet before the bloke whom he'd held at gunpoint, just moments before, landed a heavy blow to his stomach. He retched, but stopped short of being sick.

'A noble plan, Detective,' the European sighed, before bringing his gun up and blasting Jack's former hostage through the eye socket. 'Everyone is expendable, though.'

Smoke was still rising as the gun turned to him. Jack closed his eyes, readying himself for what came next. They say people's lives flash before their eyes just before they die. If that was the case then Jack had lived an uneventful life.

A sudden crash from the back of the room seemed to catch everyone's attention. A shot rang out before the European hit the deck. Panicking, Jack nutted the man who was holding him before following suit and scrambling away behind a small container. He felt like he was in a scene from the Wild West as people threw themselves to the ground. Across the room Robson sat in stunned silence watching the carnage.

'Enough!' a voice called out.

A voice Jack recognised.

'Boss!' he heard Tank call out.

'You sure about that, Arnold?' Dorian McGuinness said, his tone flat.

'Detective Lambert, you can come out now,' McGuinness shouted.

Jack dragged himself up, the pain in his jaw throbbing away in syncopated rhythms.

'I swear, I had nothing to do with it,' Tank pleaded, flanked by two of McGuinness's other hired hands.

The mob boss stepped forward, no weapon in hand, but black leather gloves covering his sizeable fists. That was McGuinness's style; never get your own hands dirty if you could help it. Jack was surprised he was even here.

'You see that's what I like about you, Arnold, you're an ambitious man. I respect that. The problem is, you got greedy and got involved in something you didn't really understand. It's a shame because you had potential. Your biggest flaw was that you assumed I wouldn't find out.' He stepped forward. 'This is *my* city,' he spat, eyes landing on the now unarmed European.

The European's voice betrayed no emotion. 'My employer will be most interested to hear about this intrusion.'

McGuinness ignored the comment and turned to Jack. 'You should probably go now, Detective.'

He didn't have a choice. 'Robson too.'

The mob boss shrugged.

'And we don't have transport.'

Dorian McGuinness nodded, turning to face Tank.

'Here,' he snarled, tossing him a set of keys. 'White van. You know the one.'

'Oh and, Jack, I'll need your phone,' McGuinness said.

He paused before handing it over. 'You know I'll have to ring this in.'

'Of course.' Dorian smiled. 'I just need a few minutes to conclude my meeting here. I'll be seeing you soon, Detective.'

They'd barely made it outside before the screams started. Shuddering, Jack rammed the van into gear and sped up the dirt path. A cloud of dust sprayed up through the darkness onto the windscreen. Robson remained silent, eyes straight ahead. They needed hospital attention, straight away.

'Phone?' he called across to his passenger.

No answer.

'Robson. Do you have a phone?'

The journalist shook his head, dried blood planted in congealed splodges across his face. 'He took it.'

Within minutes they were at the Royal Infirmary. Jack dragged Robson out by his bloodstained shirt. An ambulance driver, dressed in pristine green, approached him to admonish him for parking illegally.

'I'm a policeman,' he informed him. 'Get him inside. Also, do you have a phone?'

The man stood, open-mouthed, and nodded.

Leaving Robson to get checked in, he rang straight through to the office.

'Jack, is that you?' Watkins picked up on the second ring.

'Yes.'

'Where have you been?'

'Never mind that,' he stopped him. 'Get down to the Royal Infirmary, I've found Robson.'

'Dead?'

'No, he'll be fine,' he said, picturing the journalist's severed finger. 'I'm a little bashed up, though. Come down here and pick me up. Oh, and send Christensen down to the factory off the A1. Tell him he'll need an armed team and to be careful. If Russell... queries it, tell her it's all out gang warfare and armed suspects may still be on site.'

Jack left Watkins to sort out the particulars. He knew it'd be a dead end, though. McGuinness would have cleared out by the time anybody arrived, leaving no trace of any action behind. He could drag him in for questioning, but he hadn't actually seen him do anything. As usual, McGuinness was going to slip through their fingers.

For now.

What bothered him most, though, was that he would now be in his debt. And McGuinness had a habit of calling those debts in.

He signed himself in and took a seat opposite a drunk couple who were arguing over a can of Tango. There was no sign of Robson. They must have deemed him a priority case. Severed limbs had that kind of effect on the NHS.

After around an hour he managed to get seen by an extremely short, bald doctor with a Scouse accent. Numerous tests later they were able to inform him that he was suffering from three cracked ribs, a fractured jaw and, quite possibly, a moderate to severe concussion. Despite their pleas for him to stay overnight, he allowed them to patch him up and ply him with strong painkillers before leaving the building. The Tango couple were still bickering as Watkins greeted him at the entrance.

'Wow.' He whistled. 'Quiet night?'

The drugs seemed to be kicking in. 'Not now,' he slurred.

'You look like an extra from a Rocky film.'

The journey back to the station passed in a blur. He'd barely made it through reception before Jane Russell was on him, waving a cardboard folder in his face.

'Just what the hell did you think you were playing at?' she shouted.

Jack noticed the young desk sergeant pretending to be busy filing paperwork.

'Do we have to do this now?' he asked.

'You're damn right we do...' She caught sight of his swollen jaw, eyes narrowing. 'What are you doing here in that state?'

Her gaze fell on Watkins, who instantly turned a shade of beetroot.

'Don't look at me, I was just following orders.'

'Orders indeed.' She shook her head. 'Well, as acting DSI, I'm ordering you to go home and take the rest of the week off.'

Jack tried to work out what day it actually was.

'I can drive him,' Watkins suggested.

'No, you clearly can't be trusted. You're holding the fort for him while he's off duty. I'll take him home.'

He was too out of sorts to argue with her, accepting the lift without comment. As she drove at high speed, Jack felt unable to truly grasp the surreal nature of being driven home by his career-nemesis.

'I don't want to see you back at the station any time soon.'

Through the fuzz of his brain, he felt himself mumble a reply.

'You think I'm not on your side but that's not the case at all,' she said, hands gripping the wheel. 'But you make things impossible. It's always about you, the great Jack Lambert. You're not a team player. At the end of the day you're more concerned with your own legend than doing things by the book.'

He barely registered her comments. The rest of the journey passed in silence, as he did his best not to fall asleep. He pulled himself from the car, ambled up the path to his house. Behind him, he could feel the Bulldog's glare burning into the back of his bruised head.

'Oh, and, Detective!' she called after him. 'When you return back to work, you can expect a call from professional standards.'

CHAPTER 31

On the seventh day of his recovery Jack felt like a kid at Christmas; only, instead of chocolate and presents, he had a job, unsolved murders and a trip to meet with an officer in professional standards to contend with. Still, anything was better than stewing in the house. Rosie had called once, to see if he was alright, but then disappeared off the radar again. He spent the rest of the week investigating the many bruises he'd been left with. Christensen had popped round with the Open Grave case files, but they were still no further forward. After two days of staring at essentially nothing, Jack – like everybody else on the force – was faced with an unsolved case that still had no link, suspect or motive. The press had given them a savaging, the only bright spark being that David Robson was out of commission.

Having said that, the camouflage fibres did give them something to go on. Christensen had ordered a team to look into criminals, who fit the profile, with an armed forces link. So far it had proved fruitless, though.

The New Year had passed without fanfare, save for the expected rise in crime figures. As Jack had sat nursing painkillers and coffee, he couldn't help wondering what Nadine Guthrie, PCC, would make of that.

So it was with a mixture of apathy and excitement that he bundled into work on the following Monday. As he walked past the desk sergeant he couldn't help but note the look of horror on her face. His bruises had taken on a yellowish hue and weren't pretty to look at.

'He returns.' Watkins beamed as he entered the MIR.

Jack managed a weak smile as the whole room turned to face him.

'Any update?'

The young sergeant's smile disappeared. 'Nothing.'

Jack nodded. Even though Russell had forbidden him from getting involved, he'd still managed to twist the odd update out of the DS during his time off, much to the nervousness of his youthful apprentice. Apparently, Jane Russell had threatened them all with castration if they so much as went near him during his 'sabbatical.' Jack had informed Watkins that his ex-wife still had his balls anyway.

'That's okay,' he said.

'And just what am I paying you all for?' Jane's voice thundered.

Jack turned to face his acting boss and put on his best fake smile. 'Jane.'

'Jack,' she said, curtly. 'I have a press conference scheduled for...' She caught his appearance. 'Never mind.'

'Just as well, boss,' he said, turning to leave. 'I have a meeting with professional standards.'

Minutes later he was standing outside the frosted-glass entrance to Larry Dawkins's office. Taking a moment to straighten his appearance, he stood up straight and knocked three times.

'Come in,' a deep, gravelly voice boomed from inside.

Jack entered.

'Ah, Mr Lambert, in trouble again I see. Can't say I'm surprised.'

For most members on the force being summoned to see Larry Dawkins, ex-county rugby player and renowned hard man, with his military haircut and immovable stubble, would be a trip to hell. Fortunately for Jack, he'd known Dawkins for a number of years, back in the day when they were both bouncers on the Quayside.

'Can't say I care,' he replied, peddling their usual rehearsed lines.

The fact that he'd visited professional standards four times in three years should probably worry him. As it was, he used the opportunity to catch up with his old mate.

The giant of a man held out a strong palm and shook his hand before beckoning him to sit in the chair opposite him. Jack tried not to wince at the sheer force Larry had placed on him. Gazing around the office, nothing had changed since his last visit here. That had been due to his 'poor' handling of the Newcastle Knifer case.

The officer still had an assortment of old rugby pictures nailed to the wall, alongside a painted portrait of his wife and two kids. In the corner of his room stood a bookcase, a number of true crime books and a collection of Jo Nesbo novels littered across it. The square space itself had no windows. Larry had informed him it was to make his guests feel at 'unease' and that he didn't mind the lack of view. According to him, 'Newcastle has very little to look at anyway for somebody who heralds from the beauty of Yorkshire.'

'Nice bruises,' he said. 'See the other guy?'

'Something like that,' Jack replied. 'Anyway, I've got murders to solve; you going to discipline me or what?'

He left the office an hour later. He passed a smirking Jane Russell on the way. He at least tried to look like a man who had just been given a tongue lashing. Truth was, he'd spent twenty minutes laughing about a drunken story Larry had been recanting. Still, if it kept the Bulldog off his back, he'd let her go on thinking his job was hanging by a thread. God help him if Larry ever left. He was the only thing keeping him from a disciplinary panel.

Christensen was waiting for him outside his office. 'Boss.'

Jack beckoned him inside. 'What is it?'

'We have a potential witness.'

Jack felt the hairs rise on his arms.

'Go on.'

The two men sat down, Jack fishing around in his drawer for a paracetamol. His desk felt alien to him, having been off for a week. It was also clear that Watkins had been using it as his own personal workspace.

'She's an A-level student at Gateshead College. A...' Christensen checked his notes. 'Miss Ruth Grabham.'

Giving up on the tablet, Jack motioned for Christensen to continue, knowing that the detective worked best when he was able to flow.

'Ruth states that she was witness to Gary Dartford on the suspected night of his... abduction.' As if reading Jack's mind, Christensen added, 'She says she didn't come forward before because she doesn't take much interest in the news and it was only when one of her friends pointed out a newspaper story, she twigged that he had approached her that night. As it was recently, she thought it best to report it.'

Suddenly, Jack's headache didn't seem so important.

'Is she here?'

Christensen shook his head. 'No, she offered to come in, but I thought it might be a better idea to go to her.'

He was inclined to agree – it was important to treat her as a witness and, for that, she had to feel as comfortable as possible when questioned. Her place would do fine.

'I assume we have the address?'

Christensen held up a printed sheet. 'All here, boss.'

Jack allowed Christensen to drive as he perused the notes they had on Ruth Grabham; no previous convictions and, to all intents and purposes, she seemed a perfectly normal A-level student. The only detail of note seemed to be that she had been adopted at a young age. Hopefully, Ruth could help them piece together where Gary Dartford had been on the night in question.

And the killer.

She lived in one of the new flats that had been erected opposite McDonald's in Gateshead. Gazing up at the apartment complex, Jack couldn't help but wonder how long the phase would last. They thought it a good idea to build flats in the 1960s, but the aesthetic appeal soon wore off. Still, as far as student digs went, these were pretty impressive.

Minutes later they were stood outside the main entrance, talking into a crackling intercom system.

'Hello?' a mouse-like voice greeted them.

'Hello, Miss Grabham? Northumbria police,' Christensen said.

'Hold on, I'll let you in. It's on the top floor.'

A trendy-looking man greeted them as they rang the bell to number fifty-eight. 'Alright.'

As they introduced themselves once more, the dark, neat-featured bloke stood aside, eyes never leaving them as they ventured into the living room. Closing the door after they'd entered, he followed them through like an irritating shadow.

'Hello, detectives,' a young woman greeted them, holding out a small hand.

Jack shook it and waited for her to motion to them to sit down, removing a notepad as he did so. The first thing Jack noticed was her striking beauty. She had piercing blue eyes that seemed to stare right through them; blonde hair framing a small-featured face, and a figure most women would pay good money for. It was no surprise that Gary Dartford had made a beeline for her. She had a look of Nell Stevens about her, truth be told.

Jack struggled to see the appeal though.

'Hello, miss, we appreciate you taking the time to see us.'

'What choice did she have?' her companion snorted.

Jack ignored him.

As if taking the hint, he left them to it, muttering to himself as he slammed the bedroom door.

'This is a nice apartment,' he noted, taking the opportunity to glance around at the many framed pictures that littered the place, alongside what he assumed to be a fake Rothko painting on the far wall. The leather settee on which he was now sitting certainly felt expensive. EMA had been abolished in recent years but the giant plasma screen TV in the corner of the room told a different story.

'My father rents it for me,' she said. 'He felt I was ready to move out and be independent. I think he just wanted the extra space, being the busy businessman that he is,' she added, her tone flat.

Jack nodded, deciding not to press further.

'Miss...'

'Please, call me Ruth,' she said, eyes dancing over his bruises.

'Skiing accident. Ruth, Detective Christensen and I are here as we believe you may have some very valuable information that we could use in our current investigation.'

The young girl nodded, her eyes flitting to the bedroom door.

'Is everything okay?' Jack asked.

'It's just Martin,' she replied. 'He's quite jealous.'

'Well, I don't think he needs to be jealous of somebody who is now deceased,' he said, voice devoid of humour.

'Yeah, I suppose so.'

'Ruth, what was the date of your night out in which you remember seeing Gary Dartford?'

'December eight.'

'You're sure?'

'Definitely, it was two days before my birthday.'

'Where did you see him?'

Her brow furrowed. 'I think it was in Mr Lynch's.'

'Towards Central Station?'

'Yes.'

'Approximately what time?'

'It must have been around 10.30pm.'

'How can you be sure?' he pressed, scribbling down her responses.

'We always follow the same route. It's my friend Sandra, she's anal about that stuff.'

Jack watched her as she talked, becoming aware for the first time just how young she was.

'Talk me through what happened?'

'I was walking back from the bar, with Sandra actually, when this bloke came up and asked if he could buy me a drink.'

'What did you say?'

'That I already had one, as well as a boyfriend.'

Again, her eyes moved to the bedroom door.

'And you are sure it was Gary Dartford?' he asked, fishing out a recent photo for her to look at.

'Yes, positive. I recognised him from his mugshot in the paper. Lots of hair gel.'

Jack smiled, replacing the photo. 'Then what happened?'

'Well... he persisted, so Sandra told him where to go. He left, tail between his legs.'

Jack nodded, finishing off his notes. 'Thank you.'

'I'm sorry I don't know anything else. Probably not much use, I imagine.'

'You've been more than helpful,' he replied then, handing her a business card, said, 'If you think of anything else, you can contact me directly via this number.'

He held her gaze for a couple of seconds then motioned to Christensen for them to leave. There was still no sign of life behind the bedroom door as they reached the hallway. Seconds later they were heading back down the landing, Jack already keying in the relevant numbers on his mobile.

'Hello, I want the CCTV from Mr Lynch's, near Central Station, December eighth from 10pm onwards. You have Gary Dartford's description; if he leaves, pick him up and follow the trail. Get me a copy of the tape from that night and send it to the station.'

He replaced his mobile as they made it outside.

'Useful witness, seems intelligent too,' Christensen remarked as they headed back in the patrol car. 'You think she's reliable?'

'I think she's remarkable,' Jack commented. 'Her memory is excellent but she's holding something back.'

The DS nodded in agreement.

'The boyfriend?'

'Grade one nut-job,' Jack said. 'That's why I gave her my card. I imagine she'll be in touch before the day is out if she can get shot of him.'

Rain began pitter-pattering on the windscreen, causing the automatic wipers to screech into action. Jack dragged open the glovebox and took out his e-cigarette, then took a few puffs.

'What's the next step then, boss?' Christensen asked.

He paused for thought. That's what he liked about Christensen. He only dealt in structure and details. Although his professionalism could be draining, it was what they all needed right now. Someday he'd no doubt rise in the ranks and make an excellent DI.

'Right now, the tape is all we have to go on. Drop me off at the station and then go question the staff at the bar to see what they know.'

He nodded.

The rest of the journey passed without talk, Christensen navigating the roads at an almost legal pace, before pulling in at the station. Jack packed his e-cigarette away and thanked him, moving to get out.

'Christensen?'

'Boss?'

'You had anything out of the ordinary occur lately?'

The DS lowered his eyebrows, perplexed. 'Like what?'

'Threats?'

The blond detective shook his head. 'Should I have?'

'Never mind,' Jack replied.

The car sped out of the car park, leaving him to ponder recent events. He had to assume that whoever had threatened him was now out of the picture. Dorian McGuinness had no doubt seen to that. Still, he couldn't shake the feeling that there would be more fallout from what had happened. At some point, he'd have to go back to the fish shop for a visit. Right now, though, he had to concentrate on the Open Grave murders. McGuinness and the gang could wait.

For now.

He'd barely made it back inside before the desk sergeant accosted him.

'DCI Lambert?'

'Yes?'

'Call just came through from dispatch, they have that tape you were after.'

'Brilliant, get a room set up for me and I'll be along shortly.'

Jack went looking for Watkins, without success. He was probably out following up a line of questioning. He was thankful for the time alone. After a quick drop-in to the MIR, he grabbed himself a cup of barely dissolved coffee from the canteen before bustling in to the cramped video room that had been hastily set up.

Sitting on a squeaky chair in front of him was a woman he didn't recognise, glasses perched low on her crooked nose. Her auburn hair was scraped back into a ponytail and long, green painted nails tapped away on a keyboard.

'Hello... where's Terry?'

The woman turned around and surveyed him. 'Oh, yes, the usual analyst. Heart attack last week. I've been brought in temporarily due to my knack for recognising faces and remembering things.' Seeing the look of horror on his face, she added. 'I'm told he'll live. I'm Penny.'

'Oh,' he forced out, taking a seat next to her.

Clearing her throat, she set about her work, bringing up the video image on the screen.

'I've been brought up to speed on the details,' she told him, matter-of-factly. 'If Gary Dartford was there, I'll find him.'

Jack had to admire her confidence, even if she was a little odd. 'Great.'

They spent the next half an hour laboriously going through the tapes in real time, the good, bad and ugly of Newcastle's nightlife flitting across the screen. Once or twice, he'd made an effort to point out a potential suspect, only to be swatted away by the tech's finely manicured hand. After a while he couldn't stand it any longer.

'I'm going to go and get another coffee, want anything?'

'No.'

Jack made to leave.

'Oh, and, Inspector?'

'Yes?'

'Take your time, I work better alone anyway.'

He somehow managed to make it back to his office, cup of coffee in hand, without being cornered for anything. Praising his good luck, he carefully shut his door and slumped into the battered office chair he'd grown so fond of over the years. The hot coffee served to warm his insides but he'd not put enough sugar in. He winced, placed the plastic cup on the desk and glanced at the whiteboard.

The faces of Jessica Lisbie, Travis Kane, Peter Rutherford, Amy Drummond, Melissa Norman and Gary Dartford stared out at him. They'd spent too long trying to focus on a link between the victims. Yes, they were linked by location, seemingly, but that was it. He realised now that he'd be asking questions of himself regarding this case until the day he finally retired.

Which might be sooner that he'd thought if things didn't pick up.

The priority now was to locate the Open Grave Murderer before he struck again. Mr Lynch's was the pub. He could feel it. As clichéd as it sounded, he simply had a hunch. More often than not, his hunches had steered him in the right direction. What concerned him, though, was the brazen killing of Gary Dartford. If the killer was willing to do that, where would he go next?

It wasn't as if they'd really made any progress regarding the gang warfare case either. Sure, he'd been kidnapped, tied up and assaulted, but what had they really achieved? In all probability at least two men were 'missing in action,' due to the actions of Dorian McGuinness. Jack knew what that would mean. He might push the boundaries every now and then, but he wasn't a bent copper. He refused to open up that can of worms.

By the time the team had arrived at the factory there was no trace of any action. Jack had thought as much. Still, he'd had to call it in. Something told him he wouldn't be seeing much of Tank from now on. This knowledge left him uneasy – he basically knew a man had been killed but had no way of proving it unless McGuinness slipped up.

And then there was the question of who was behind this rival gang. The Captain? Unfortunately for him, nobody seemed to know who he was and they had zero leads. With that and the Nell Stevens story currently destroying the image of Northumbria's finest, things were going downhill fast.

Jack's phone began vibrating just as Watkins ambled into the room. He motioned for him to sit down before taking the call.

'Hello?'

'It's me, Ruth.'

'Miss Grabham, hello,' Jack replied, almost adding that he'd been expecting her call.

'My boyfriend has gone to the shops, so I can't stay on long.'

She was scared of him. Jack couldn't help but picture his own daughter in the same situation at some point in the future. He ground his teeth at the thought. 'Was there something you remembered?'

'Well... it's about that night in the bar.'

'Yes?'

'I wasn't being entirely honest. Gary came on to me and I'd had a few drinks. I... may have... something may have happened.'

Jack's interest was piqued.

'Go on.'

'I left my mates, but told him we couldn't do anything in the pub. I got him to meet me round the back. We met there and, a few minutes later, I went back inside.'

'What time was this?'

'Probably about quarter to eleven-*ish*.'

'Okay,' Jack said. 'Hold on, did you both go back into the pub together?'

'God, no! Martin has spies everywhere,' she replied. 'I told him to wait a few minutes, then come back in. He wasn't impressed, but it was either that or Martin killing him.'

The irony that Gary had in fact been killed seemed lost on her. As for her fella's possible reaction, Jack wasn't surprised. 'Did you spot anybody watching you?'

'No, I don't think so, but it was dark.'

'Thank you.'

'I'm sorry I didn't tell you before; it's probably useless anyway.'

'No,' Jack cut in, 'you've been most helpful, Ruth. Listen, if there's anything else you remember, or you have any issues,' Jack added, boyfriend coming to mind, 'don't hesitate to contact us.'

After he'd ended the call, he filled Watkins in on the details, watching the DS's eyes light up as he laid it all out.

'So, we have a witness who was with Dartford on the night, who can testify that he was outside at around ten forty-five, where she left him before going back in? He had to have been followed.'

'Perhaps.'

Seconds later, a set of green fingernails appeared around the doorway.

'Got him.'

Success.

Jack and Watkins followed her to the control room, where a flickering screen had been paused. The time was stamped at 10.42pm.

'Where am I looking?' Watkins asked.

The woman sighed and jabbed the screen. 'Up there on the left.'

There was no doubting it. Unless somebody was going around with the exact same ridiculous hairstyle, Gary Dartford had been in Mr Lynch's on eighth December between 10pm and 11pm.

'Fast forward it, slowly,' he instructed her. 'I want to watch his movements.'

She turned to a second screen.

'I'm running these simultaneously, just in case he moves between camera angles.'

They stood in silence as the images played out in front of them. At first, he stood stock still, then – moments later – moved out of view before appearing on the second screen. Jack leaned forward, eyes scanning the monitor.

The video tech manoeuvred different frames around, going forwards and backwards between segments in time. Jack could feel sweat prickling down his back as they all watched in eager silence.

'If you see here.' She pointed a slim hand at the screen. 'He's at the side of the bar nearest to the toilets.'

The assembled party watched as the image juddered across the screen. Right on cue, Dartford approached what looked to be Ruth Grabham; almost unrecognisable with her hair done up and a layer of make-up that a plasterer would be impressed with. Penny allowed the video to run in real time, the seemingly endless number of bodies on the screen blurring into one large fuzz as Jack focused in on the couple in question. They talked for around two minutes with Ruth pausing to wave a few of her friends away at one point. Leaning in close to him, Ruth alternated between fidgeting with her hair and taking sips of her cocktail through a small, black straw.

Moments later Ruth motioned to the main entrance and he nodded, his hand lingering on her arm before turning to leave. They all followed as Dartford's image exited the club.

'Want me to rewind?' Penny asked, her voice cutting through the tension.

'No, not yet,' Jack replied.

He watched Ruth in the second screen as she made her excuses to what looked like three of her girlfriends, before following Dartford out of the pub.

'Wait!' he commanded.

The video played out, with at least twelve different people leaving through the very same door, before a rather dishevelled-looking Ruth Grabham reappeared, straightening out her skirt. The video played for another ten minutes.

Gary Dartford didn't return.

'Interesting,' Watkins said.

'So,' Jack said, beginning to pace. 'We know that Gary Dartford was alive and in public at ten forty-two on the eighth of December. We also know that Ruth Grabham's story checks out. At ten forty-eight Gary leaves the club, where he is followed by Ruth. At ten fifty-five the girl re-enters alone and, from there, we've lost him.'

'Maybe it's someone from the bar?' Watkins suggested.

'I reckon it was,' Penny interjected. They looked to her. 'Just a gut feeling.'

'I counted twelve people leaving the premises during that time,' he said.

'Me too,' said the DS.

'If we are to assume that Dartford was abducted during this time, and that's a big assumption, then chances are it was one of those twelve people who did it, given that he was deliberately targeted. I mean, what are the chances that the killer wasn't watching him?'

The room nodded in agreement as Christensen appeared in the doorway.

'Rewind the tape.'

CHAPTER 32

The nights were growing darker now, allowing him to go about his business with ease. Not that he needed any help. Everything was playing into his hands. As if it wasn't already easy enough, he now had a bigger window in which to work.

The press called them 'victims.' Their fear had caused each of them to plead for their lives, turning to pathetic sobs when they realised there was no chance. That was when the bargaining began.

It wasn't a negotiation.

Of course, he nodded his head, feigning concern while listening to them. But he was only playing along, needing them to believe they had a chance so that the truth would hit them harder.

The muffled cries from below broke through his thoughts. Bitch. She'd get what was coming to her. Just like the others. She'd been a real nuisance but then he knew she would be. He had half a mind to kill her here and now. She was no good to him dead, though. She needed her partner. He already knew who *he* needed. Gary Dartford had been a stroke of genius, but that would be just a prelude to what was coming.

He thumped his foot down on the wooden flooring. Seconds later, the cries turned to sobs. He smiled, feeling his pulse quicken. Too easy. He opened up his toolbox, took out an electric saw and screwdriver. They were just for show, though. He couldn't be dealing with mess. He checked his watch. Twelve hours since he'd locked her up. That left him with another twelve hours to complete the job.

The floorboards creaked as he made for the basement door. He fumbled for the handle, excitement causing him to perspire. He allowed himself heavy footsteps, twelve in total, each one placed with a more emphasised thud. By the time he reached the bottom she was pleading again, cowering away in the corner.

He'd hoped for more from her.

'Please,' she cried, hair matted to her head.

He gazed down upon her leg, bruised and raw. Hurting her hadn't been part of the plan. He just couldn't help himself.

He plugged the saw in, turned it on, the shrieking of the instrument matched by the screams of his prisoner as he slowly approached her. It would be easy to cut her throat, but that wasn't neat enough. He had to be neat.

He flicked the saw back off and laughed at her terror. Shuddering at the impact of her fear, he sank to one knee to catch his breath.

She reached a trembling hand towards him. 'Just let me go,' she pleaded.

'Don't touch me!' he shouted, slapping her across the face.

He stumbled backwards as she raised her palm up to her grazed cheek. The tears had started again.

'Look what you made me do!' he screamed.

Suddenly overcome with sickness, he turned on his heels and ran up the staircase, slamming the door behind him. How could she do that? They never touched him, not once they were locked up. It was against the rules. What a mess! *Stupid, stupid man*, he scolded himself. *This is what you get when you aren't tidy.*

He jammed his eyes shut, counted to ten and grabbed his jacket from the bannister. Twelve hours was too long to wait.

CHAPTER 33

A red-faced Pritchard bustled through the incident room. 'Details?'

Jack spun around to face the semiretired psychologist, noting a sallowness to his face as if he hadn't slept properly in a while.

'Are you okay?' he asked.

'Yes, yes,' Pritchard said, waving him away. 'What do we have?'

Jack spent ten minutes filling him in on the details. By the time he'd finished, the silence was palpable.

'Show me the tape.'

Five minutes later they were back in the video room, the image of hundreds of Newcastle revellers plastered across the screen. Seas of barely-dressed women and highly-groomed men caroused, unaware of the carnage that would follow.

'There!' Jack snapped, pausing the tape.

'What am I looking at?' Pritchard asked, lifting up his glasses to peer at the screen.

'Observe.' Jack rewound the tape. 'Here we have Gary Dartford approaching Ruth Grabham...'

Jack, Watkins and Pritchard all watched the video in silence as Gary made his move on the young woman. The difference this time was that they were not focused on the couple in the centre of the screen but the top left, by the edge of the bar.

'I see him,' Pritchard said.

They all watched as revellers manoeuvred in and around the bar, the one exception being the tall, slender, dark-featured man, in the top left corner. His eyes didn't move.

'Keep watching.'

Moments later, Gary exited the bar, followed by Ruth stumbling in her high heels. All the while, at the bar, the man's eyes never left them. Once they had disappeared, he finished his drink, placed the glass carefully onto the bar and walked out.

Jack felt Pritchard massaging his temples, before replacing his glasses around his neck. Watkins sat, stony faced, staring at the images playing out before him.

'I know it's a long shot...' Jack began.

'I wouldn't say so,' Pritchard interrupted, his gaze landing on him.

Jack motioned for him to continue.

'Look at the precision of the murders – not a hair out of place, yes?' He began pacing. 'Now that tells me that perhaps he is just meticulous, but it may also be a signal as to the type of person he is. For example, maybe neatness is a *thing* for him. He *has* to be tidy. This man fits the bill in that sense. Look at his clothes and the way he keeps on straightening his shirt out. He doesn't look like he's on the pull. So, who is he trying to impress? Only himself.'

Watkins rewound the tape so that they could all watch again. Sure enough, almost subconsciously, their suspect repeatedly straightened out his shirt.

'You're right,' Jack said.

'He's not aware of anybody else. In fact, I'd go further and say he's not even interested in the couple. Only one of them.'

'Dartford,' Watkins said.

'Indeed. Now he's taking risks, going after somebody who was a suspect at one point. But, that's what he wants. He's not getting sloppy, he's just getting cocky. And he's sending a message.'

'Who to?' Watkins asked.

'To the police, perhaps even a specific policeman,' he replied.

Jack could feel an uncomfortable heat clawing away at him.

'Look at the way he's carrying himself,' he went on, taking command of the tape. 'Straight as a dart. Jack, if I had to ask you to guess what kind of profession this man came from, what would your best guess be?'

'Armed forces,' he said.

'Exactly.' Pritchard clapped his hands together. 'Neat, tidy, straight posture and trained to kill... it has all the hallmarks.'

'That fits in with what the fibre analyst said, as well.'

'So what's the motivation?' Watkins asked.

'I'm unsure at this point but what I can say is that he is picking off his victims one at a time. This means that there is no particular link between them, making it harder. I assume you have somebody else looking at earlier tapes.'

'Christensen is doing it as we speak,' Jack informed the psychologist. 'If he turns up on there we can be pretty sure it's him.'

'Of that I have no doubt,' Pritchard said. 'I think the pub holds some kind of meaning for him.'

Jack stood up, straightening out his back. He felt his phone vibrate, but ignored it, imploring Pritchard to go on.

'Sentimental?' he asked.

'I would say so. It will be a pattern. He goes there to pick up his victims. Look at him, he's a good-looking chap. He probably has no problems picking up a woman. He then goes back and gets a man at a different time, which means he has a location to hide them in. Somewhere either remote or soundproofed enough so that he won't be discovered.'

Jack sighed. There were plenty of remote locations in the North East. Just as one door opened, another stream of corridors lay out before them. 'I'm not so sure, Frank. If he was following Dartford specifically then it could well be the case that this bar was simply where he found him.'

Pritchard nodded. 'Perhaps. However, why pick that particular moment, just as he was leaving with somebody else, to follow him? It's the bar, I'm sure of it.'

'Maybe it's where he met his partner or former partner,' Watkins mused.

'So, you think he goes there because it reminds him of his wife?' Jack asked.

'It's all guesswork,' Pritchard said, taking a seat.

'You okay?'

'I'm fine,' he puffed. 'Just not used to the excitement any more.'

'If you need a break...'

'No!' he shot back. 'We need to catch this bastard. Look, I'm telling you; ex-military, scorned by a former lover, returns to the scene of where they met, and picks up his victims. That should be enough to get started, yes?'

Jack nodded, taking in every detail. 'Easy, eh?'

Pritchard offered a pained smile.

'What's the plan?' Watkins asked.

Jack began pacing. 'Speak to Christensen, fill him in on the details. Meanwhile, get a copy of some older tapes and get the analyst to look through them. I want to know whether the bar is a coincidence or whether it's his hunting ground. Meanwhile, we're going to take a picture of this bloke to every bloody base in and around Newcastle to see if he really is military.'

'Every base?' Watkins asked, eyebrows raised.

Jack smiled. 'Better put in some overtime requests. I'll let Jane know afterwards.'

CHAPTER 34

Jack managed to make it out of the station without the Bulldog cottoning on to what he was up to. It had taken some half an hour for the plan to be drawn up as there were a surprising number of potential military bases across the Tyne and Wear area. With a mixture of marked and unmarked cars, the team set out to cover the entire immediate area. He was under no illusions about the scale of their task, but that's why he'd assembled just about every spare bobby the Northumbria force could spare.

He pulled onto Rhodes Street, beginning with the Northumbria Army Cadet Force. Veered right, through the gate, then approached a reception area. Jack flashed his ID and was waved through to a small car park that was littered with a variety of vehicles and motorbikes. This was a youth army organisation.

He signalled for the PC to pull in. 'You wait here,' he told him.

He'd ordered Christensen to stay with the analyst while sending Watkins out to another nearby base. Striding across the car park, he passed a group of three curious-looking cadets who returned his smile with stern glances.

As he approached the barracks, he was greeted by an extremely tall sergeant major with an old-school silver moustache that seemed to constantly twitch. Fighting the urge to salute, Jack held out his hand.

'DCI Jack Lambert, thank you for seeing me.'

'No problem,' the man replied, crushing Jack's hand in a vice-like grip. 'Name's Taylor. Robert Taylor.'

'Hello, Mr Taylor,' Jack said. 'How long have you worked here?' he asked, following Taylor into a small office space near the entrance.

'Twenty years,' the man replied, sitting down on a comfy-looking chair by a whirring computer.

Without being asked, Jack took a seat opposite and took the opportunity to take in his surroundings. Much like his own office, the place was cascading with paperwork. However, unlike his office, this was kept extremely tidy. A small window sat behind Taylor, the afternoon sun glaring in on them, causing Jack to have to reposition himself to the side. Taylor watched him with interest, eyes never leaving his face. Jack pulled at his collar, conscious of his unkempt appearance.

'As you may have heard, we have a serial killer on the loose,' Jack informed him. 'And we have reason to believe he may have a military background.'

Taylor's face twitched again, his features remaining impassive. 'That so?'

Jack got the impression this was a man who was used to getting his own way. He also got the impression that he would be impervious to questioning, torture, and would be handy in a street fight. It was the scarred knuckles that gave him away.

'Yes,' he replied, meeting the sergeant major's gaze. 'Can you tell me if you know this man?'

Jack handed him a colour print of the image from Mr Lynch's. They'd managed to zoom in on the suspect, his features only slightly blurred. Jack had circled the image in bright yellow pen.

'No,' Taylor replied, without hesitation.

'Are you sure?'

His eyes narrowed. 'I've been here longer than anybody else, Detective. I know every man who has come in and out of this organisation. Never, in all of my service, have I seen this gentleman.'

Jack stood, signalling the end of their conversation.

'Thank you for your time,' he said. 'If you think of anything else, please don't hesitate to call me.' He placed his contact details on the desk beside him.

Taylor didn't move.

They were no further forward. Jack checked the map again. So far, they'd covered the Cadet Force, naval establishments and the Queen's Own Yeomanry. He could feel his energy levels sagging, the initial hope at finding their man long since evaporated. Even the PC had given up on talking to him.

They were heading back through Newcastle City Centre, rush hour traffic beginning to form, when his phone rang again.

'Any news, Watkins?'

'I'm at the Royal Marine Reserves, you might want to get down here.'

They were by the Quayside within minutes, flashing lights aiding them as they sped towards the riverside area. It wasn't far from where Jack had once completed a charity zip wire. People had called him brave but, the way he saw it, spending twenty seconds on a wire was infinitely better than having to run for twenty-six miles to raise a couple of hundred quid for a good cause.

Leaving the PC to park up, Jack got out of the car and worked his way through a throng of people out walking dogs. He found Watkins not far from the water's edge.

'He's in here,' Watkins motioned.

Jack made his way through a set of double doors, the unmistakable whiff of boot polish lathering the atmosphere up. To his left, another PC was perched, cup of tea in hand.

'He's just in here, guv,' the policeman said, dipping a large, chocolate cookie into his mug.

Jack found himself in an office similar to the one he'd sat in talking to Robert Taylor just an hour or so ago, the only difference being the sheer size of the place. A mixture of army and admin staff moved about, papers flying, phones ringing and voices booming.

A uniformed army officer stood nearby. 'Detective Lambert? I'm Philip Baines.'

Jack shook the man's hand.

'Thank you for seeing me, Mr Baines.'

'Please, call me Philip.'

The man motioned for Jack to follow him out of the office, heading along a narrow corridor lined with portraits of former servicemen. Towards the back of the corridor sat a small cafeteria. Upon entering, a table housing two Marines stood to attention, raising their arms in stiff salute.

'At ease, gentlemen,' Baines said, indicating for Jack to sit at a nearby table.

'I understand you may have some key information for me,' he said, cutting straight to the point.

The stocky sergeant removed his beret, revealing a thatch of pepper-grey hair. His eyes looked tired but alert, freshly shaved stubble indicating a lifelong battle with razors that he was never going to win. Fumbling in his pocket, Jack placed the CCTV image on the desk in front of him and waited.

'Yes,' Baines replied, shoulders drooping slightly. 'His name is Ian Kellerman – he was a former Marine here.'

Jack could feel excitement nipping at his spine.

'Did you know him well?' he asked.

The officer nodded. 'He was a good bloke,' he said. 'Once upon a time.'

'What happened?'

'Ian was always good at his job. A stand-up soldier… an asset to any company. He'd spent time in Iraq, doing two stints before coming home for good.'

A short-haired woman, wearing a polka dot apron, approached with the offer of hot drinks.

'No, thank you,' Jack said.

The sergeant nodded without comment, their conversation on pause whilst the woman poured black coffee into a chipped mug.

'I'm afraid Ian was never the same after the first time he came back from duty. Here, or at home.'

Jack let those words sink in before continuing. 'At home?'

Baines moved his hand towards his neck, scratching away as his eyes left Jack's for the first time since they'd sat down.

'I…'

'Philip,' Jack leaned in. 'I'm not here to judge you and, unless you've broken the law, I'm not here to arrest you either. We have reason to believe Ian Kellerman is a key cog in an ongoing investigation. Anything you can tell me would be of great benefit.'

'I had an affair with his wife, Emma,' he blurted out. 'It started when he was on active duty, second time round. I'd known them both for quite a while – through the army obviously – though once he returned to the Middle East, Emma and I became close.'

Jack removed his jacket before continuing. 'Go on.'

'She confided in me that he'd changed, was prone to violent outbursts. He never hit her, but he would smash the house up, emotionally bully her and so on. I don't know how it happened, but it did.' He sighed, puffing out his cheeks.

'Did he find out about you two?'

Baines nodded. 'He came home one day and found us together.'

'What happened then?'

'Nothing.' He shrugged. 'He walked in on us, clocked me, turned on his heels and left. I never saw him again.'

'And Emma?'

'She broke down, told me it was over, and that I should leave. That's the last I saw of her. I heard she'd moved to another part of Newcastle but I'm not sure where.'

Jack surveyed the man. He was in no doubt that Baines was telling the truth. His eyes betrayed somebody still emotionally sore about what had happened. He must have really cared for her.

Minutes later Jack was standing outside the barracks shaking the hand of the man who had just given them a name for their suspect. Baines generously had one of the admin team photocopy details from Ian Kellerman's file. They stared at the mugshot, sunken eyes and dark slim features; there was no doubt it was the same bloke from the bar.

Jack made to leave before Baines called out to him.

'Is he in serious trouble?'

Jack paused. 'Potentially, yes.'

The man slumped against the wall. 'If you see Emma, tell her I wish her all the best.'

Jack strode into the MIR as soon as he arrived back at the station.

'Listen up, everyone,' he bellowed.

The room came to a standstill.

'We have a suspect.'

A collective intake of breath occurred, what was left of the sporadic clicking of computer mice fading to expectant silence. Moving across to the centre of the room, Jack held up the folder Baines had given him. The team gathered closer to the image of the man who had potentially been responsible for six deaths.

'Ian Kellerman.'

Jack allowed it to sink in before placing the folder on the desk and fixing the room with a determined stare.

'This man is now our priority. I want to know if he has previous, no matter how minor it is. If this bloke has sniffed out of turn, I want to know about it. I also want a current address for both him and his former wife, Emma Kellerman.'

Jack paced over to the whiteboard and placed the mugshot in the centre. A fraction of a second passed before the team burst into life.

CHAPTER 35

It turned out that Emma Kellerman was residing just along the River Tyne, on the Quayside. Jack couldn't help but note the irony that she and her former lover were situated a mere stone's throw from each other. Before they'd left, he'd managed to persuade Jane Russell that Philip Baines needed to be watched, as he was potentially at risk. After a debrief with Pritchard they both agreed that the ultimate goal had to be Baines and his ex-wife. Everything else was a prelude to the main act. Jack just hoped they had enough time to insert their own twist.

Watkins pulled in round the back of the swanky new flats, lining up alongside a pink Mini Cooper with a chessboard-like design on the roof. Early evening was setting in now, bringing a chill that chewed away at Jack's face.

They made their way to the front and pressed the silver buzzer. Seconds later, a voice crackled through.

'Hello?'

'Mrs Kellerman, it's DCI Jack Lambert, I called before.'

'Okay, I'll buzz you in.'

'Why is it that everybody we interview seems to live at the top of a block of flats?' Watkins moaned.

A small, solitary window was casting a dim glow over the narrow hallway as they reached flat number eleven. Watkins knocked three times and stood back.

After a few seconds a woman appeared. 'Hello, detectives,' she said.

The first thing Jack noticed was how striking she was, with brilliant blue eyes and a trim figure, complete with pencil skirt and red blouse. She smiled but Jack sensed an unease in her demeanour.

Emma Kellerman led them in to a tidy living room area and offered them a seat on a cream leather settee. On the opposite wall a large mirror hung, mantelpiece underneath laden with various trinkets and photos. At first glance, there was no sign of Kellerman ever having been a part of her life. By the bay window a large glass coffee table sat, various photography magazines piled high underneath it.

As if reading his thoughts, Emma said, 'I'm a photographer. Well, alongside my office job. It's what I really want to do. Once my marriage broke down, I decided to try something new, so I enrolled at Newcastle College in an evening class. Would you like a drink?'

He noted the crack in her voice as she mentioned the failed marriage.

'No thank you,' Jack said, eager to get down to business.

She took a seat opposite them, straightening out her skirt in the process.

'Is this about Ian?'

Jack nodded. 'Yes.'

The woman took a deep breath before continuing. 'What's happened?'

Jack unfolded his arms, an attempt to create a friendly atmosphere, but it wouldn't help with what he was about to tell her. 'I'm afraid your husband—'

'Ex-husband,' she cut in. 'It might not be official yet but it's how I refer to him. I go by Lonsdale now.'

'Yes, your *ex*-husband is a potential suspect in a serious murder investigation.'

Emma sat back as if physically struck by his words. She brought a hand up to her brow and ran it across, tears filling her eyes. 'Are you sure?'

'I'm afraid so and, right now, you are our best chance of finding him. We've been to his last known address but he's currently not there.'

'But... I haven't seen him for months,' she said.

Jack could feel hope dwindling. 'Do you remember exactly when you last saw him?'

Emma paused, considering. 'It must have been June last year. He phoned ahead to pick up some belongings I had kept.'

'Were you in when he arrived?'

'Yes, but he didn't speak. I tried to explain, tell him what had happened to... to make me want to leave him.'

'We've already spoken to Philip Baines,' Jack told her.

She slumped back into her chair, nodding. 'I... I didn't plan any of it,' she said, her voice barely a whisper.

'Ms Lonsdale, we aren't here to judge, we simply wish to find Ian as quickly as possible.'

She cleared her throat and took a large breath before continuing. 'Phil and I had been seeing each other for some months when Ian found out. When he saw us, it was as if something in him snapped and he refused to speak to me again. He didn't even seem angry, just resigned. The day he came back to collect his things he sent a text – letting me know – before turning up and ignored me. He hadn't been the same since his army service, that was when he really changed,' she added, bitterly.

Jack nodded. He'd read countless stories about ex-servicemen who, having seen the horrors of war, returned and were unable to find peace at home. Some withdrew into themselves, some lost their minds, and others turned to crime. God knows he'd seen his own fair share of horrors on the job, the Open Grave case undoubtedly one of the worst.

'So, other than that, are you positive you have had no contact from your ex-husband?'

She paused, searched her mind.

'No,' she began, 'but, I have been receiving some strange phone calls.'

'In what way?' Watkins asked.

'Well, late at night, or early morning – always when it's inappropriate to ring somebody unless it's an emergency. There's nobody on the line, but I swear I can hear breathing. After a few seconds, they hang up.'

'And the number?' Jack asked.

'Withheld. The calls started around six weeks ago, but they've been getting more frequent lately. Oh my God, do you think it's him?'

'I'm not sure,' he lied. 'Just out of curiosity, does the bar Mr Lynch's mean anything to you or your husband?'

She shook her head while wiping tears from her eyes.

'Yes, she said they'd been getting more frequent lately,' Jack shouted down the phone. 'You have a terrible connection.'

'The connection is fine,' Pritchard said. 'It's *your* phone.'

'So, what do you think?' he asked the psychologist as Watkins took a left turn at speed, causing Jack to fall into him. 'Careful.... no, not you, Watkins.'

'I'd bet my pension on the fact it's him,' Pritchard went on. 'She's the ultimate trophy for him.'

'Does that mean...'

'Yes, Philip Baines is the partner he will seek for her.'

Jack ended the call and dialled straight through to the station to emphasise the need for round-the-clock surveillance for both Emma Lonsdale and Philip Baines. Russell wouldn't be happy, but he had no time for that now. Jack had told Emma that they might have to step up security for her. She'd taken it all rather well, Jack thought – her composure only faltering when she'd asked if Philip Baines was okay. Jack, not quite knowing what to say, said he seemed fine and that he'd asked after her. She'd nodded, wiping another tear away, before seeing them out.

'It won't be long now,' Watkins said, pulling into the station.

'Potentially,' Jack said. 'We still don't know where he is though.'

There was still no word from Kellerman's address. For now, they had to play a waiting game. After filling the team in on their progress, Jack and Watkins met up with a flustered-looking Christensen back in his office. With the tension in the MIR reaching fever pitch, Jack welcomed the peace and quiet of his own workspace. He sat and took a swig of water before diving in.

'Water?' Watkins asked.

'I'm trying it out,' Jack told him. 'What's the latest, Christensen?'

'No luck so far. It's like searching for a matchstick in a jungle.'

Jack nodded. 'Is the bar being helpful?'

'Had to have a difficult phone call with the doorman,' Christensen said. 'Still, it was nothing I couldn't handle.'

Jack smiled. 'I'm sure it's not. Threaten him with obstruction of justice?'

'Something like that,' he replied, smiling.

Seeing as the Danish detective had stood by and allowed Jack to assault a man in a bar toilet, he was sure he could let him off. 'We have to assume he specifically targeted Dartford to send a message. As of right now, we can't be sure the bar has any other relevance. It's time we leaked Kellerman's picture to the press. I also want teams out questioning his family, friends, ex-lovers and any other colleagues who might know something.'

Both detectives left just as a thumping headache landed on him. He felt like he hadn't slept in weeks. The bruising on his face had turned an awful yellow colour, making him look like a character from the Simpsons. If it wasn't for the fact that they had to catch Kellerman before he killed again he'd have probably taken more time off.

He noted the earlier missed call from a withheld number on his phone. He then scrolled through his contacts list, his finger finally resting over Rosie's number out of habit. He stood, pocketed the phone, and headed for the MIR. They had work to do. Watkins was right.

Not long now.

CHAPTER 36

J ack pushed the tape in with a steady hand, pausing to check the recording was working. Other than that, the only audible sound was that of the clock ticking away on the far wall. Watkins sat to his left, directly opposite Casey Clifton. There were no smarmy smiles or jokey quips this time. Because opposite Jack was the man who they were sure had murdered six innocent people.

Ian Kellerman.

Finding him hadn't taken too long in the end. Just minutes after Jack's meeting with the detective sergeants, a call had been made to the station alerting them to Kellerman's presence at his home address. He'd come quietly, without fanfare. In the end they hadn't even needed to leak his photo to the press.

Pritchard was sure he was their man. He fitted the profile; intelligent, male, mid-thirties, military background and – more importantly – had potential motive for harbouring grudges against couples.

Once the preliminaries were over, he began one of the most eagerly anticipated interviews the force had ever had. 'Mr Kellerman, are you aware of why you are here?'

Kellerman's dark eyes flitted up to Jack's. 'Why don't you tell me?'

A prick. He wasn't the first. 'Mr Kellerman, where were you on the eighth of December of last year?'

The suspect paused, as if recollecting his thoughts. 'I don't know off the top of my head.'

'Were you on a night out, perhaps?'

'I might have been.'

'You make a habit of going out alone?' Watkins asked.

Kellerman paused once more, turning deliberately towards the DS. 'Are you the good cop or the bad cop?'

Jack leaned forward, invading the man's personal space. 'We're both bad cops. Answer the question.'

'Sometimes,' he said. 'Sometimes I go out with friends.'

'What about that night?' Jack asked.

Again, he shrugged. 'No idea.'

'Can you confirm whether or not you were in Mr Lynch's on December eighth?'

Still, the eyes didn't leave Jack's. 'I cannot.'

Watkins opened the envelope, revealing an image of Kellerman in Mr Lynch's on the given date. 'Can you, Mr Kellerman, confirm that this is you in Mr Lynch's on the aforementioned date? For the benefit of the tape, I am now handing Ian Kellerman a photograph pulled from CCTV footage we found in the bar.'

The ex-army man glanced at the picture. 'It looks like me.'

Jack took over the questioning once more. 'Mr Kellerman, how do you know Gary Dartford?'

'I don't.'

'Why then, do we have footage of you watching Gary Dartford and Ruth Grabham, in Mr Lynch's, which then shows you following them both out of the bar?'

To emphasise his point, Jack pulled out the rest of the images, which clearly showed the suspect mirroring their exit.

'You're wasting my time,' he said, pushing the pictures back across the table.

'A life sentence for murder gives us plenty of time, Ian.'

The man rolled his eyes. 'You're barking up the wrong tree.'

Jack made a show of straightening out the photos, before replacing them in the envelope. He allowed the silence to stretch between them, all the while searching Kellerman's eyes for some signal of guilt. They didn't show much of anything.

'If you like, I can show you a video of you watching them before following them out, see if that jogs your memory?'

He might have been playing it cool, but Jack could see the sweat beginning to form on Kellerman's brow. 'Nervous, Ian?'

'Should I be?' he replied.

He went on the attack. 'Is that where you go to stalk your victims?'

Kellerman snorted. 'Is this a joke?'

Jack continued. 'Why do you do it, Ian? Is it to get back at your wife?'

That lit up the suspect's eyes.

'What are you talking about?'

'We know about the affair, Ian. We also know about the emotional hell you put her through before she left you,' he said, leaning in once more. 'And we know about the strange phone calls. The affair must have made you really mad.'

'What the fuck would you know?' he shouted, fist cracking against the table.

Casey Clifton leaned over and whispered into his client's ear.

Jack ignored the solicitor's intervention. 'You picked the others at random, didn't you? But when it came to Dartford, you had to get personal.'

Clifton raised a hand. 'Detective, I think this has gone too far—'

'I'm just getting started,' Jack cut in, before turning back to the suspect. 'Unless you give me a reason for tailing Gary Dartford, I'm going to throw you in a cell and let you stew overnight. We can pick this up again tomorrow.'

Kellerman shook his head. 'I didn't murder anyone.'

'Who's the ultimate trophy then? Your wife? Philip Baines?'

'Just shut up!' he spat.

They'd obviously touched a nerve. From the corner of his eye, Jack could see the lawyer squirming in his seat. 'Yeah, that sounds about right.'

Ian Kellerman's shoulders dropped. 'It's not what you think. I didn't know this Gary bloke you're on about.'

'Then—'

'It's Ruth, alright!' he shouted, placing his head into calloused hands. 'I'm her father.'

'What?'

'She doesn't know me, and her mother died when she was just a baby. I found her a while back. It wasn't Gary I was watching, it was her. Although,' he snorted, 'I had a good mind to slap that cocky bastard for the way he was behaving around her.'

Alarm bells started ringing in Jack's head. Thinking back to the details they held on Ruth Grabham, he remembered reading that she had been adopted at a young age.

'Can you prove any of this?' Watkins cut in.

Kellerman held out his palms. 'How about a paternity test?'

Jack leaned in and whispered into Watkins' ear.

'Interview terminated.'

CHAPTER 37

'Jesus,' Watkins exclaimed. 'I wasn't expecting that.'

Jack watched as Ian Kellerman left the interview room. Casey Clifton paused in the doorway, made to leave, then turned.

'Detectives,' he said. 'I sincerely hope the next time you drag a suspect in he proves to be the right man.'

With that, the arrogant solicitor turned on his expensive heels and left.

'I want you to call Ruth Grabham and find out what she knows about her estranged father. I'm going to speak with Emma Lonsdale again and see what she knows,' Jack said.

Watkins nodded and left him to it. Minutes later, Jack was in his office, having had a short but sharp phone conversation with Ian Kellerman's ex-wife. She'd confirmed his story about having a daughter who had been adopted when she was a young child. She assumed her to be around eighteen now, but she'd never met her. How could they have gotten it so wrong?

Pritchard entered the office. 'I don't understand it,' he said, shaking his head. 'He fit the profile. It doesn't make any sense...'

Jack raised his hand as Watkins followed him in. 'He's not our man, Frank. What's the latest?'

Watkins slumped into the seat opposite his desk. 'Ruth doesn't know much about her dad save for the fact that he was in the army. She confirmed her mother died when she was young. He was telling the truth.'

He began tapping impatiently on the desk. 'Not only have we got this one wrong, we may now have put Ian Kellerman at risk.'

'He could still be the killer,' Pritchard offered.

'No,' Jack shouted, a little more forcefully than he'd intended. 'He's not the killer. But, if we aren't careful, he could be a victim.'

He pushed his chair back and began pacing. They'd been spectacularly wrong about Kellerman. Everything the man had said made sense. Jack swiped his desk drawer open and fished out some headache pills.

'You know,' Pritchard said. 'You should see a doctor about those headaches.'

'Look, I'm fine, I—' He stopped short. 'What did you just say?'

The old man shrugged. 'Go and see a doctor.'

Jack stopped pacing.

'What is it?' Watkins asked.

He shuffled some papers on his desk, located the file he was looking for. 'Peter Rutherford's mother said he'd been seeking help for his drug addiction, right?'

'Right.'

He finished chewing the tablets and continued. 'Let's put Gary Dartford to one side as we know he was an anomaly, okay?' The two men nodded. 'What do we know about Jessica Lisbie?'

'She was twenty-six, slim, dark hair...'

'No, what else?' Jack urged.

The DS paused. 'She had a recently broken nose.'

Jack nodded. The lightbulb was beginning to flash on.

'Where was Amy Drummond's part-time job?'

'The doctor's, right?'

Jack nodded. Realisation was dawning.

'The doctor's surgery?' Pritchard said.

He paused to look once more at the six murder victims on the whiteboard. 'We were right. The link isn't the people, it's the place.'

Watkins threw his chair back and stood. 'We have to get there now.'

'Wait,' Pritchard warned. 'What about Travis Kane?'

'There'll be a link,' Jack said. 'There has to be.'

By the time they'd reached St Oswald's Surgery, Jack had already called ahead to warn of their arrival. They parked up in the patient car park and the three of them made their way inside. The plush new build had cost millions in taxpayers' money. The press had had a field day over that. Still, he had to admit it was an impressive structure. They made their way into a seated waiting area, waded through the sea of sick people, coughing and spluttering until their turn to be seen flashed up on a digital screen. No matter how new it was, Jack noted, the stench of industrial-strength disinfectant was still overpowering.

'Gregory Liddell,' a small, suited man greeted them at the reception area. 'I'm the duty manager of the practice. Please, come with me.'

Jack shook the man's limp, clammy hand before wiping it on his jacket and following him to a back office. 'I appreciate you taking the time to see us,' he said.

'No problem,' he replied. 'We have been operating later opening hours to cope with demand. I've had our HR department here bring up a list of all of our current workforce. I don't suppose you can tell me what it is you're looking for?'

Jack smiled. 'No, I can't.'

'Is this about Amy? We're truly devastated by what happened to her...'

Watkins stepped forward. 'If you wouldn't mind, sir?'

'Oh, yes, of course,' he spluttered. 'I'll just be in my office if you need me. Sandra behind the desk can direct you if necessary.' He smiled a toothy grin and left.

They wouldn't be able to get any sensitive patient information, but Jack had Christensen ringing around the families to check which surgery each of the victims were a member of. Before his phone had even started buzzing, he was sure they had the right place.

'Christensen,' he accepted the call.

'Boss,' he said, a little breathless. 'I've been on the phone to Jessica's father and Peter Rutherford's mother.'

'Please tell me you have news,' Jack urged.

'I do,' the Scandinavian replied. 'Both were registered with St Oswald's as far as they know.'

He thanked the DS and ended the call, sending a nod in Watkins' direction. The two of them then set to work as a young, female HR worker brought up various images on the computer screen.

'It would help if I knew what it was you wanted to find,' she sighed, fingers tapping away impatiently.

'I'll let you know when I see it. Pritchard.' He turned to the psychologist. 'Thoughts on the manager?'

The old man shook his head. 'However, I've been proven wrong once already.'

Jack took note and focused back on the screen. 'I'm not interested in female members of staff, only the men,' he informed her.

One by one, the images of all the male staff flashed up on the screen. For each one, he had the worker print out three copies. Whilst she kept sending copies their way, Jack, Watkins and Pritchard studied the various staff members' faces. Jack was beginning to lose faith, when one image – a man he'd seen before – appeared before him. Dark, neat features, sunken eyes, not too unlike Ian Kellerman, faced up at him from the mugshot.

'Who is this?' Jack asked the girl, mouth dry.

She leaned over and took a look at the picture. 'Oh,' she said, eyes lighting up. 'That's Damien, he works as a receptionist here but he's also on placement as a counsellor.'

'Bring the manager back in.'

'What is it?' Pritchard asked as the girl scarpered from the room.

Jack motioned to the picture. 'I know this person.'

The profiler replaced his glasses and squinted at the image. 'It doesn't ring a bell...'

'What's wrong?' Gregory Liddell re-entered, followed by the flustered HR worker.

He handed him the sheet. 'What can you tell me about this man?'

'That's Damien Truman,' he said. 'He's a very popular member of staff here at the surgery,' he added, eyes flitting to the girl.

'What else?'

The man bristled. 'Look here, Detective...'

Jack interrupted him. 'Answer the question.'

The man eyed the three of them in turn, not one of them returning a friendly smile. As the silence stretched on, he cleared his throat and undid a shirt button.

'He's a receptionist,' he said. 'He's been here a couple of years now but he's been training as a counsellor, recently. He has a placement here at the surgery.'

He took another look at the image of Damien Truman. Jack could feel dread crawling up his spine. They had to act.

Now.

'I'll keep hold of this copy,' he informed the duty manager. 'And I'm going to need an address for him, right now.'

He motioned for Pritchard and Watkins to follow him, waiting until they were out of earshot before speaking further.

'What is it?' Pritchard asked.

Jack took out his phone, dialled the station. 'I've met him before,' he said.

'Who is it?'

Jack held a hand up for him to wait. 'Claire, I need you to run a check on a thirty-seven-year-old Damien Truman. Find out if he has any close family or friends, as well as any previous convictions.'

He finished the call to Gerrard and turned to face Pritchard.

'Seriously, Jack, what's going on?' the old man asked, eyes widening.

'It's been personal all along,' he said. 'He's been closer than we think. I have to contact Rosie, before it's too late.'

'What do you—?' Pritchard began before stopping short. 'Oh dear.'

'What is it?' Watkins pressed him.

'This,' Jack began, 'Is Rosie Lynne's boyfriend... only I don't know him as Damien.'

CHAPTER 38

Gerrard got back to him within ten minutes. That had given him plenty of time to bombard Rosie's mobile, house and work with calls. Each time the phone had rung off, or gone to voicemail, until a co-worker finally picked up on the third attempt. What they told him, though, had caused Jack's stomach to lurch.

Rosie hadn't been in for a couple of days.

They didn't know what was wrong, but she'd texted in to say she was sick.

Nobody had been able to reach her.

'Right, guv,' Gerrard speed-talked down the line. 'Last listed address for Damien Truman is seventy-three Iolanthe, Newcastle.'

Jack cross-referenced it with the printout from the surgery before handing it over to Watkins. 'What else can you tell me?'

'He's had the odd parking ticket but, other than that, he's squeaky clean.'

'What about family and friends?'

'Looking into it,' she continued. 'I know his mother was in and out of jail on a mixture of drug and prostitution-related charges until recently. I can't imagine he had a happy childhood.'

Parental issues. Was that the motive?

'Anything else?'

'Not right now.'

'Good work, Gerrard,' he told her. 'Keep me updated and tell Christensen to get out on the trail if anything comes up. Also, I want a squad car to head to Rosie's and scope the place out, just to be sure.'

'No problem, guv.' She ended the call.

'Get us to that address right away.'

Watkins gripped the steering wheel, the whites of his knuckles threatening to burst through his skin.

He glanced across at him. 'What is it?'

The DS shifted. 'You sure it's a good idea you go out there?'

'You got a better one?'

'It's just that you're emotionally involved and...'

He didn't have to finish the sentence. The possibility that Rosie was already dead hadn't left his thoughts since they'd come across Truman's picture in the surgery.

'I agree,' Pritchard piped up from the back of the car. 'It's a bad idea.'

Jack turned to gaze out of the window. 'It's a good job neither of you two are SIO then.'

Iolanthe Road was situated on the outskirts of Newcastle, a terraced street complete with a mixture of houses and flats. Damien Truman's place was an upstairs flat. The area itself wasn't too shabby, save for the odd bit of litter and low-level graffiti. Jack had definitely seen a lot worse.

'Just so you know,' he warned them. 'I'm going in, regardless.'

'What about the warrant?' Watkins asked.

'I'll sort it later.'

He turned and began the short journey up the concrete steps that led to number seventy-three. The door was an immaculate white, with the obligatory 'no salespeople' sticker plastered across the centre of the window pane. Lucky for Jack it was made of wood. Nothing untoward so far.

He pressed the bell and added a knock for good measure.

'Doesn't seem to be in,' Pritchard said.

He pressed at the bell again, holding it down for longer.

Nothing.

'We should get a warrant,' Watkins said.

'No time,' Jack replied. 'I'll deal with the consequences later.'

'Wait!' Watkins urged. 'Think about what you're doing, Jack!'

Jack pushed the two of them aside, lifted his leg and aimed a kick at the door, not quite shifting it. Pain shot up his leg, but his panic masked the throbbing of his knee as he sent another boot flying at the door.

Bingo.

The door smashed open. In an ideal situation, they'd have secured a warrant and used a battering ram. Using a ram would have allowed for entry on the first try, helping the response team get in nice and early. They didn't have that luxury, though.

'Police!' he shouted, sprinting up the stairs despite the searing pain in his leg.

'I'm right behind you,' Watkins shouted.

Jack turned right at the top of the stairs, entered into an open living room. Nobody there. It was also neat. Very neat. Just like the Open Grave Murderer.

Within seconds Watkins appeared in the doorway, his face almost as red as his hair. 'Anything?'

Jack shook his head. 'Not in here. You go check the bedroom, I'll look in the kitchen.'

He left Watkins to his search, but he already knew it would prove fruitless. Truman wasn't here.

His mobile buzzed indicating Gerrard was calling him. 'Guv, just a heads up, the squad car says all is quiet at Rosie's place. No sign of anyone around.'

'I didn't think there would be, thanks, Claire,' he said before hanging up.

As he headed through to the kitchen area, he was again struck by the sheer tidiness of the place. No dishes lying around, everything scrubbed to within an inch of its life. At the back of the kitchen, a set of knives rested in a block. A horrific image flashed through Jack's mind before he dismissed it. No, cutting wasn't this killer's MO.

'Seems all clear.' Pritchard appeared behind him, causing him to jump. 'You alright?'

He nodded. 'Now what? We can't damn well wait for him to come home.'

'He is tidy, isn't he? It's almost as if he isn't even living here.'

The snake in Jack's stomach slithered its way up to his neck, tightening its grip. 'That's because he isn't living here.'

'What?'

'This is his cover. He has another place. And I think I know just how to find it.'

'Jack... You might want to get in here,' Watkins called from the back room.

Jack ran through. 'What is it?'

The DS turned to him and tossed a set of photos onto the cream bedspread. 'Look.'

In front of him were gruesome images of each of the Open Grave murder victims. That wasn't the most disturbing thing, though. Newspaper cut-outs were plastered all over the walls. Pictures Jack recognised immediately.

Pictures of him.

CHAPTER 39

'Christensen is meeting us at the removal company office,' Jack told them, hurtling back down the stairs.

By now the neighbours had heard the commotion and were out in the street, no doubt wondering who had been breaking in to number seventy-three as afternoon turned to evening.

Watkins flashed his badge. 'Police, no need to worry.'

The downstairs neighbour was outside her flat, towel around her hair, eyes as wide as saucers.

'Do you know much about your neighbour Damien Truman?' he asked her.

'I...' she spluttered. 'Not really. He keeps to himself.'

'Do you know if he ever had company here?'

On the other side of the steps, someone snorted. 'Not him. He's weird, man.'

Jack turned to face an overweight man in an early nineties Newcastle United jersey. 'What makes you say that?'

He shrugged. 'Most people round here talk to each other. That fruit loop doesn't even say hello. He does come in during the middle of the night sometimes, though. Suspicious, if you ask me.'

Jack left the neighbours to gossip and headed for the car. 'I'll drive. Watkins, you stay here in case anybody goes up and tampers with the evidence. Pritchard, with me.'

'Why are we going to the removal place?' the profiler asked.

He stuck the makeshift siren on and began upping the speed. 'I don't think Travis Kane had anything to do with the surgery. I think he delivered something to Truman and that's how he targeted him. I want to find out whether my theory is right and, if so, whether or not the delivery was made to the flat or another place.'

It took less than twenty minutes to get to A & D removals. By the time they arrived, Christensen had already parked up.

'What's the latest?' the DS asked as Jack exited the car.

'Truman is definitely our man.'

'We sure?'

He swallowed his irritation. 'Yes, and we have pictures in the flat to prove it.'

'Okay.'

'We think he has a second location. He has to, in all honesty. He's not going to get away with murdering people in a street like that. I'm hoping the manager here can shed some light on that for us.'

The two detectives, and Pritchard, entered the small building that housed the workforce of A & D removals; a family business operating in removals and deliveries that had been going for some forty years. The reception area stank of sweat and stale coffee, various stains having worked their way up the walls from years of smoke abuse.

Behind a small windowed counter, a young man greeted them. 'DCI Jack Lambert?'

Jack nodded.

'I'll just fetch my dad.'

Moments later the manager appeared, a rotund man in his fifties, a horrific-looking comb-over giving him a stereotypical car salesman look. 'How can I help you gentlemen?'

'Travis Kane,' Jack cut straight to the point. 'I need to know if he made a delivery to somebody named Damien Truman?'

The manager cleared his throat. 'I don't know if I can release those details...'

He stepped forward. 'Yes you can. Trust me, you won't get arrested for it.'

The manager smiled a gold-toothed grin and invited them into his office before tapping away at a state-of-the-art Apple Mac computer. 'According to our records, there was no delivery to a Damien Truman, I'm sorry.'

'What about Alan?'

'Alan?'

'Yes. Unfortunately I don't know the surname he used.'

More keyboard tapping ensued before a brief pause. 'I'm sorry, Detective, we haven't made any deliveries to an Alan for over twelve months now.'

Both Pritchard and Lambert sighed in unison.

'Now what?' Pritchard asked.

Jack attempted to get hold of the panic that was eating away at his stomach. He had no idea how to answer Pritchard's question.

'We'll have to split up and get talking to people. Christensen.' He turned to the squat detective. 'Get yourself to the surgery and interview all of the staff who are still there, see what you can find out. Call Gerrard and take her with you.' He nodded. 'Pritchard, go back to the flat and see what you can find. I'll stay here and see what I can uncover.'

'I'm terribly sorry, Detective,' the manager continued. 'I really don't know how much help I can be from here on in.'

He felt the beginnings of a searing headache coming on. 'If you could get me a cup of coffee that would be a good start.'

He paused, obviously not used to being given orders from people in his own establishment. Then, after clearing his throat, left without comment.

Jack took the opportunity to look around the office. The furniture was ancient and cracked from years of use. The wallpaper was barely still attached to the mouldy walls. The only thing that looked under twenty years old was the computer.

'Here you go.' The manager returned, handing him a mug with the words 'World's Best Dad' written on it.

'Thanks,' he said. 'I appreciate you sticking around to speak to us this late. If you don't mind me asking, why don't you… you know… spruce the place up a little?'

The manager perched himself on the desk and chuckled. 'I know it's not great to look at, but my dad opened this place some forty odd years ago and, when he died a few years back, I just couldn't bring myself to change the place. I've thought about it, sometimes, making a clean start and everything, but I suppose I'm just not ready to do that.'

Making a clean start. Jack almost spat his coffee out.

'Is it too hot?'

'No, it's not that. Could you do one more check on the computer for me, please?'

The man shrugged and moved round the desk. 'What am I looking for?'

'Were any deliveries made to a Rosie Lynnes in the last few months?'

The silence was agonising as the manager studied his screen, pausing to clear his throat once more. 'Yes, we have made quite a few deliveries there in recent times.'

Jack placed his coffee on the desk and stood. 'That's all I needed to know.'

'What do you mean?'

Jack never answered the question, he was running to the car. He threw himself into the driver's seat and dragged his phone out. When he'd turned up drunk at Rosie's house, before Christmas, she'd changed all the furniture and decor. She'd told him she had made a fresh start. That's how Damien Truman knew Travis Kane. Was it possible that he'd been killing people right under her nose, in the house? Where better to hide than in plain view?

He was about to call Watkins when his phone began to vibrate. 'Hello?'

'Detective Lambert, didn't anybody tell you it was bad manners to ignore a phone call? I tried calling you earlier, but you must have been too busy. Well, I'm a forgiving person, so how about I give you the opportunity to make it up to me?'

He froze, his hands on the wheel as the cool, calm voice slithered in his ear. 'Is that you, Damien?'

'Ah, so you've finally started doing your job, have you? It took you long enough.'

'What do you want?'

The man laughed without humour. The kind of hollow laughter a psychopath would offer up. 'Why should I want anything?'

'People always want something.'

'I already have what I want, Jack. She's right here, why don't you say hello?'

He listened intently to the sound of muffled scrapes, before the rip of pulled duct tape echoed through the handset.

'Say hello to your darling ex, Detective Lambert.'

'Jack, I'm sorry, please—'

'That's enough,' the man returned. 'I'll make it easy for you, Jack. I'm at Rosie's place.' He laughed again. 'I've been here the whole time.'

His stomach turned. 'It's over, just let her go and give yourself up, Truman.'

He tutted. 'Jack, really? I thought you were better than that. This isn't over. We're just heating up. You are the next piece of the puzzle.'

'You expect me to just hand myself over to you?'

'You've already lost, Detective. Here are the options I'm giving you. You can come to the house in the next hour and we can finish our little game; I promise it will be quick. Or, you can refuse, and I will simply kill your precious Rosie in the most heinous way I can imagine. Oh, and trust me, Detective, I have a fertile imagination.'

Jack gritted his teeth and checked his watch – quarter to six. 'I'll be there.'

'Good,' he replied. 'Oh, and one other thing, if I even sense that you've brought anybody else along, I'll slit her throat for you and you can live with the fact that it was your betrayal that caused her death.'

Jack jabbed the 'call end' button and ground his teeth. He had to make a decision. Now.

He made it to Rosie's house within twenty minutes. The sky had darkened now, causing the house to look eerily secluded from the outside. Not bothering to indicate, he pulled into an empty space down the street from where the house was. Save for a man out walking his pet Alsatian, all was quiet. It always had been where Rosie lived. She'd picked the place for that very reason.

Jack stepped from the car. Although cold, he knew he was sweating. Slowly, he edged towards the boot, eyes not leaving the house. The dog walker passed by, paying him no heed. After several moments, he popped the boot and fished around in his kit bag until he found it.

Stepping away from the car, he pushed the metal bar into his waistband. The same bar he'd used on McGuinness's goon in the pub. The same bar he'd felt compelled to carry ever since he'd been attacked in his own home.

As he approached the house, there were still no signs of life, save for the odd flash of TV screens from distant neighbours. His instincts were urging him to inform the others about what was going on, but he couldn't risk it. Handing himself over was his best chance at trying to save her.

His knuckles were about to connect with the door when he noticed it was already open.

With an unsteady hand he pushed against it and entered the house.

Empty.

And silent.

Carefully, he closed the door, returning his gaze to the hallway. A chill pricked his spine as he stepped forward. It was then that he saw it. At his feet were clear footprints, leading directly to the basement door. Truman had deliberately trodden in muck to point Jack in the right direction. Jack couldn't help but wonder whether it was the same compost he'd used when burying the bodies.

He made for the light switch but was met with no response. He must have cut the power. Jack couldn't help but feel the odds tipping ever further away from him the closer he stepped towards the basement door. Squinting through the darkness he noticed something lodging it open. He was two steps away now. Following the dirt, he reached the opening and saw what it was.

A spade. The kind of spade you use to dig up graves.

'We're down here, Detective.'

CHAPTER 40

He moved down the rickety staircase, one unsteady step at a time, unsure of what would await him when he reached the bottom.

His eyes were beginning to adjust now, with wisps of yellow from a street lamp peeking in through a small window in the far corner of the basement. That and an old oil lamp, perched in the centre of the room, were the only sources of light.

The sound of laboured breathing caught his attention.

'Rosie?' he whispered, his throat dry.

'Ah, Mr Lambert,' Truman's slick, authoritative voice greeted him from the far side of the room.

As his vision adjusted, he found himself in the centre of the large basement space, an assortment of shelves and boxes littered about. The tall outline of Damien Truman stood opposite him, in military garb, knife pressed against Rosie's throat. Truman's eyes appeared black and inhuman. They had the same haunted look that Ian Kellerman's had. Jack couldn't help but wonder what horrors this man had lived through. His hairs bristled as the penetrating gaze of the serial killer bore through him.

'So this is it,' Truman spoke. 'I have to say I'm very disappointed.'

He had to keep him talking until he could figure out how to salvage the situation. 'What do you mean?'

Truman laughed. 'The famous Jack Lambert, nearly fifteen years of service, conqueror of the notorious Newcastle Knifer. Come on, Detective, I had expected better. Do you like my outfit?'

'I didn't realise you had a military background.'

'I don't, Jack. But I do know how fibre analysis works. I had to throw you off the scent for a bit while I made my preparations.'

'Very clever,' Jack replied, eyes scanning the room.

'Not as clever as using our beloved Rosie's basement here to conduct all of my... experiments. I should really be thanking you, Jack.'

'For what?'

'For breaking her heart. I'd go as far as to say you coming out as gay has made all of this possible. That allowed me to play the role of Alan, her dutiful boyfriend, and I've been killing people right under her nose all along. In the end, it was all too easy. We put all of your belongings down here and I put a lock on the door to help her forget about you.' He shot a look at Rosie. 'Unfortunately, I don't think it worked for her. And now it's too late.'

Jack took a small step forward. 'I'm not done, yet.'

Truman's face hardened, ever so slightly, his hand coming up to brush back a stray hair. 'Quite right,' he said, smiling once more.

'Nobody has to get hurt, Damien. Just let her go,' Jack urged.

Rosie stood, unmoving. Her gaze was on Jack and he could see she was scared but, being the strong person he knew she was, she wasn't going to show any fear to this bastard. Jack fought the urge to rush over. One wrong move and it would be too late.

Time to try a new approach. 'Is it all women you hate or just your mother?'

Truman's eye twitched. 'And what would you know about my mother?'

He took another small step forward. 'I know that she was in prison for being a prostitute. Did she bring her clients home when you were young, Damien? Is that why you kill people?'

Truman remained unmoved.

Jack decided to press harder. 'Is that why you got into counselling? Is it some kind of sick redemption for you, Truman?' He spat the surname, just to show disdain. This was a man who liked control. Jack wasn't going to give it to him.

'I'll tell you what, Detective,' he said. 'How about I just slit our beloved Rosie's throat right now?'

'Because that's not how it works. You don't like to get bloody, Truman. You're too neat. Hands round the neck, isn't it?'

Again he stepped forward.

'I'm willing to experiment with new techniques.'

Jack noted his voice was losing its steadiness.

'So, how does it work?'

Truman smiled, his tongue sliding across his lips. 'Like this.'

With that, he brought a large hand up around Rosie's throat. Her eyes bulged as she began to thrash about.

Jack made to move.

'Don't you fucking dare!' Truman screamed, holding the knife out in front of him. 'Now, get on your knees and turn around.'

Jack gazed at Rosie, twitched an apology, and did as he was ordered.

The smell of damp earth grew ever closer as Truman stepped up behind him.

'I want her to see,' he spat, aiming a kick at Jack's back. 'They always have to see!'

Jack coughed as he inhaled a thick blanket of rising dust from the concrete floor. 'What makes me so special?'

Truman laughed. 'Nothing. It was Rosie who approached me. She was so upset at the demise of your relationship that I had to listen to hours and hours of her sob stories about you. You see, the men always let them down. My father was the same. But, do you know what's worse than that? It's how pathetic the women become. That's why I do it and that's why she's going to watch you die first, before she gets to take her medicine. Don't worry, though, she can hold on to you once we are done. Then you can be together forever. Now put your arms behind your back.'

Jack heard the sound of ripping duct tape. He had to act.

Now.

As Truman made to grab his left arm, he sent an elbow at his groin. The killer grunted and fell back as Jack pulled the pipe from his jeans. He stood, turned, aimed a blow to the serial killer's body but Truman was too quick. Spinning away, he managed to get in between Rosie and Truman, holding his weapon out in protection. Beads of sweat dripped from his brow, stinging his vision.

'Now what?'

Truman shrugged. 'Your arrogance astounds me, Jack. Do you really think this was all about you?'

Jack felt his stomach lurch. 'What do you mean?'

Truman smiled. 'I think my work here is done. The two of you will find more pain in life now than you would in death. That is my gift to you. And this is my masterpiece.'

Without warning, the man known as the Open Grave Murderer raised the knife to his throat and slit it, his eyes betraying no emotion as he fell to the floor.

'No!' Jack shouted.

He lunged forward and tried to apply pressure to the wound. Blood spurted out over Jack's hands as Truman pulled him in close and grinned. He watched as his cold eyes glazed over. Jack fell back and let out a roar. It was too late.

Damien Truman was dead.

That was when Rosie started screaming.

CHAPTER 41

'Jack, do come in.'

He entered McGuinness's office and took a seat opposite the man they called 'the Boss.'

'Dorian,' he greeted him.

Feigned concern was etched across the mobster's face. 'How are you keeping after everything that has happened? A terrible business with that Open Grave nonsense.'

'There's no need to pretend to care, Dorian.'

McGuinness baulked. 'Is that any way to speak to the man who saved your life?'

Jack squirmed in his seat. 'How am I supposed to spin this?'

McGuinness stared at him over his tinted sunglasses. 'Spin what?'

He shook his head. 'I can't help but notice that Tank isn't working here any more.'

'Ah, it seems Mr Arnold was keen to explore opportunities elsewhere. As such, his employment has now been terminated.'

Jack paused. 'Am I going to find another body washed up on the banks of the Tyne in a few weeks?'

McGuinness motioned to one of his goons to leave the room before continuing. 'Mr Arnold is not my concern, nor yours, Jack. I'd have thought you would pay me a little more respect after what I did for you.'

'Dammit, Dorian, I'm a policeman. I can't just turn a blind eye when I know a crime has been committed.'

He fixed him with an icy stare. 'What crime? Let's consider what we both know. You attack one of my associates in a bar full of potential witnesses before running off and staking out one of my warehouses without proper clearance. Then you get yourself kidnapped and nearly killed in the process before I – your former employer no less – rescue you.' McGuinness paused, licking his lips. 'I'd be happy to tell this story to your associates if you like?'

Jack tugged at his collar and undid a button. 'I won't have you holding this over my head.'

'Jack, I'm worried about you,' McGuinness said, raising his considerable bulk up to a standing position. 'Perhaps police work isn't agreeing with you. Look, I'm a reasonable man, why don't you come and work for me again? We can always use a man with your... skills. I seem to remember you being pretty handy with your fists.'

He snorted. 'You need somebody to punch fish?'

The giant mob boss laughed, his voice booming around the room, before placing a firm hand on Jack's shoulder. He could smell the faint scent of sweet rum as McGuinness moved in closer. 'That's what I like about you, Jack, you always did have a sense of humour.'

McGuinness's hand remained on his shoulder as Jack spoke. 'What was going on in that warehouse?'

'Terrible things, Jack. Can you believe we found that criminals, foreign ones no less, had been using my property to peddle a supply of potent drugs? Naturally, we got rid of it all. I would hate for it to fall into the wrong hands.'

'And Liam Reed? What am I supposed to do about that? '

McGuinness remained silent.

He waited until Jack had left the shop before picking up the phone. Pondering his next move, he began tapping his ringed fingers on the mahogany table until he was sure of what to do. The phone was picked up after three rings, as always.

'Yes.'

'Dimitri,' McGuinness greeted the European. 'Has it been taken care of?'

'Yes,' he replied. 'Nobody will ever find him.'

'Good, I don't want any loose ends this time.'

'What about the detective?'

McGuinness scratched his stubble before continuing. 'Leave it with me; I haven't made a decision yet.'

'He could jeopardise the whole operation if he continues to sniff around.'

'Like I said, I haven't made a decision yet.'

'Your man should have killed him in his home when he had the chance.'

McGuinness ground his teeth together. 'Plans can change. Anyway, Lambert is more use to me alive.'

A pause on the line. 'If he finds out about Liam Reed...'

'I've made myself clear!' he hissed.

'I apologise,' the European replied. 'I'm merely concerned about my investment.'

He was about to continue when he noticed a small smudge on the corner of his desk. He'd have to remember to get somebody to clean it up. 'Don't worry about that. Now that we've taken hold of the goods in the factory there will be plenty to go around. You just make sure your people do their jobs.'

'He will retaliate.'

'That's what I'm hoping for.'

'Fair enough, Mr McGuinness, I'll be in touch.'

'Goodbye. Oh, and Dimitri?'

'Yes?'

'Don't worry about the business with Liam Reed. As far as Jack Lambert is concerned you were working for the Captain and most likely killed him to get to me,' he said. 'And you don't exist any more. Nobody will ever know the truth. Lambert thinks you are dead, along with Arnold Mohan. The business with Liam was... most unfortunate,' he said, mopping his brow with a silk handkerchief. 'Especially with a baby on the way. Unfortunately, you sometimes have to crack a few eggs to make an omelette. Without his death I would never have discovered the depth of Tank's betrayal. I thank you for making that happen.'

'And the decision to leave his body in such a public space?' the European asked.

McGuinness smiled. 'It's important I send a strong message on these matters.'

'Still, this detective seems determined.'

He laughed. 'The setup in the warehouse worked perfectly. Jack Lambert knows not to dig too deeply into my business now and David Robson will print whatever we tell him to. They belong to me,' he spat. 'You see, this business is like chess. Do you play it, Dimitri?'

'Yes, from time to time.'

'That's good to hear,' McGuinness replied. 'I like it when others play chess.' His tone darkened. 'As long as you remember that, in the end, I always win.'

The European paused. 'Yes, boss.'

They ended the call. Dimitri had played his role well. Yes, it had cost him nearly forty per cent to bring him on board, but by poaching such a strong ally from the Captain he had been able to secure his own interests in the North East – at least for the time being. He wasn't stupid, though. It was only a matter of time before the European betrayed him. He'd simply have to make sure he was the one to strike the first blow.

As for the Captain, he'd save a special kind of retaliation for him. Credit where it was due – his rival had been extremely clever, not even telling Dimitri about the high-level mole in the organisation. When Liam Reed had come to him, asking to leave, he'd known then that he had been betrayed. Liam had given up Tank's name in the end, allowing Dimitri to approach him as a faux-ally. McGuinness smiled. He'd made a strong start to the game.

Check.

CHAPTER 42

'Want to come with me?' Watkins asked.

Jack pulled the police car up to the kerb and shook his head. 'No, this was your good work, you can handle it.'

The DS made to speak but seemed unable to do so. Clearing his throat, he merely nodded and left him to it. As Watkins approached the house, Jack was struck by how, just two weeks before, he'd nearly lost his job. And life. Jane Russell had had some stern questions for him after all was said and done but with the return of Edwards, and the press having a field day with the hero angle, the department had decided to go easy on him.

It wouldn't do to have the PR Prince hauled up on a disciplinary. Yet.

He still hadn't spoken to Rosie since it had happened. He'd lost count of the number of times his finger had hovered over the call button, only to pull back at the last minute. Who knew where her head was at? All he ever seemed to do was make things worse for her. So space was what he'd given.

He watched as Watkins made his way up the path, a white double-glazed door standing before him, not unlike the one Jack had kicked in on Iolanthe Road. The memories of Damien Truman and the scene in the basement would stay with him forever. Another scar to add to his ever-growing collection.

When Becky opened the door, wearing her Blue Bamboo WKD work T-shirt, she didn't even seem surprised to see him. Jack noted the change in hair colour, blonde now. He watched in admiration as Watkins presented her with the facts. So consumed had he been by the Open Grave Murderer, he hadn't even registered the presence of anybody else on the CCTV footage in Mr Lynch's.

Watkins had, though.

Once all was said and done, the DS had pulled him to one side and shown him what he'd missed; namely Becky in an intense embrace with none other than Nell Stevens' boyfriend Shaun Armstrong. Jack had been taken aback but it turned out Watkins had already questioned Armstrong who had admitted everything. Besotted with Becky, a young girl with a vicious streak, the playboy had played his part in the harassment of the reality star, all out of some twisted idea of love.

Watkins hadn't even needed to seek Jack's advice.

Moments later he shuffled back into the car. 'All sorted.'

Jack nodded. 'Good work. She give any reason?'

'Apparently it all started with Gary Dartford. She was driven by jealousy over his fascination with the pop star.'

Jack remembered the Nell Stevens posters in Dartford's high rise flat. 'Do we think she'll back off now?'

'I'd say so,' Watkins said. 'Nell doesn't want to press any charges, but I've made it clear what will happen if she doesn't pack it in.'

Jack smiled.

'What is it?'

'Nothing,' he said. 'I just quite like this assertive Watkins. What have you done with my old DS?'

He shrugged. 'Nothing, I've just learnt from the best.'

'Does that mean you'll finally ask Gerrard out now?'

'What?' he spluttered.

'Don't worry, I won't say a word.'

They left a visibly hunched Becky on her doorstep, staring into the distance. Unlike Damien Truman's victims, her life would go on, just like everybody else's.

CHAPTER 43

It hadn't taken them long to find Truman's mother's house. She'd been living alone on the outskirts of Scotswood, not too far from the banks of the River Tyne. It was the smell that gave it away; a mixture of hard drugs and something that had become more familiar to Jack over the bleak winter period. Much like Truman's own death, his mother's killing hadn't been neat. When they found the body, it wasn't even immediately clear who she was, such was the damage done to her head. They found the hammer by the side of the mattress. When the pathologist's office got involved it hadn't been Rosie who came along but one of her junior colleagues.

Initially, he had struggled to put all of the pieces together. Surely he and Rosie hadn't been the ultimate goal? If they had been, why not kill them when he had the chance? Truman's suicide had troubled him until the discovery. The body had been found in the back bedroom, positioned on its side, with a picture of her son in her hands. It seemed Damien himself was the final piece of the jigsaw all along. Having built up to killing the mother who had abandoned him as a child, the only thing left to do was add himself to the list of victims.

Unlike Gary Dartford, they'd never know why Peter Rutherford and Travis Kane had been targeted by the killer. With regards to his female victims, that was much clearer. They had all suffered some degree of emotional trauma. Truman, using his counselling skills and position of trust, had got to know them all through his line of work. He hadn't come across Jessica due to a broken nose but because she'd sought help to work through her emotional issues linked to her family. Once they'd gained access to her patient records, they'd found that Damien Truman had been seeing her on a regular basis. It came as no surprise when Melissa Norman's name also appeared on his client list. Truman's infatuation with Jack stemmed from Rosie talking openly about the breakup of their relationship to the man she thought was beginning to love her. That man was Alan Davies, a fictional character plucked from his imagination.

With regards to how he subdued his victims, Rosie was able to offer first-hand testimony. It seemed Truman had been using chloroform. Toxicology hadn't picked it up due to a mixture of the substance moving very quickly through the body and the fact that he hadn't used it to kill his victims. The length of time that passed between administering it and the subsequent killing meant that the autopsies were unable to detect its use. It seemed Damien Truman had done his homework.

He finished up some paperwork before taking some time to himself in the office. Regarding the outcome, he'd liaised with Durham DI, Oliver Tomkins, given that two of the victims had been found on his patch. Despite mild disappointment that they hadn't been the ones to catch the killer, he was pleased that the case was now closed.

After a brief phone call to the hospital they had told him that his father was doing much better and that they believed a donor had been found. He polished off his coffee, searched for some paracetamol, only to realise his usual headache had disappeared. Perhaps things were looking up.

As he turned to face the wall, Truman's victims stared at him; lifeless, but a little more satisfied than they'd been just weeks before. There was nothing they could do to bring them back but at least they'd been able to secure some kind of justice. Getting him behind bars would have been preferable but Jack would settle for his death, given that it had put an end to the murder spree.

A faint knock brought his attention back.

'Hello, Jack.'

The bruises on her neck had faded, a little of the life behind her eyes diminished, but there was no mistaking the one woman who had meant more to him than anybody else in the world at one time.

'Hello, Rosie.'

She took a seat and began fiddling with a hanky. He couldn't help but notice she'd lost some weight since he'd last seen her.

'How are you keeping?' he asked.

She shrugged. 'So-so. I'm taking a bit of a sabbatical from work, just to get my head together, you know?'

He nodded. 'I understand.'

'How about you?' she asked, her eyes meeting his for the first time, before retreating.

'You know me, full on busy.'

'Are they not going to give you some leave?'

'They offered but I turned it down,' he told her.

She nodded. 'You love this job, don't you?'

He paused and gazed back over at the Open Grave victims. It hadn't been easy and, once the dust had settled, enquiries would be made into what had gone wrong during the investigation. Newly-installed PCC Nadine Guthrie had made that abundantly clear to him upon his return to work, stating her intention to follow his career progress closely. But catching bad guys was what he did. These days it was all he seemed to know.

'I do,' he finally said. 'Rosie, I—'

She raised a shaking hand, stopping him in his tracks. 'We should leave it there,' she said, her eyes watering. 'I have to go. By the way, I'm liking the new hairdo. And shaving that beard off has made you look much younger.'

He watched her leave, without replying to her observations.

'Bad time?' a voice called round the door.

'Come in, Christensen,' he said, motioning for the DS to sit down.

The Scandinavian detective duly obliged, placing a newspaper on the desk. 'I see you're famous.'

Jack scanned his image on the front of the paper. The article had been written by a recently returned David Robson. It seemed they had an uneasy truce in place. It wasn't the only relationship that had formed, though. Jack had noticed an article from the previous day coming out in support of Dorian McGuinness's plans to expand his business ventures onto the Quayside, written by none other than Robson himself.

Something caught Jack's eye. 'Do you make a habit of doodling on newspapers?' he asked.

'All the time,' Christensen told him. 'Always the same – glasses and messy hairdo. It's an old habit.'

Jack bit his tongue as a memory struck him, but he was unable to place it. It fizzled from his mind as Watkins appeared in the doorway. 'Come in,' he beckoned.

'There you are!' he said, sitting down. 'Has Pritchard left?'

He nodded. 'I don't think we'll be seeing much of him from now on.'

The memory of their final conversation was still fresh in his mind. Pritchard had been drained, sallow and withdrawn. He'd managed to convince the profiler to return to his wife and deal with his demons. The psychologist had smiled and advised Jack to do the same, minus the wife. Jack's decision to enter the world of Internet dating the previous day had filled him with both dread and excitement. Sick of being miserable about who he was, he had decided to move forward with his life.

'I'm liking the new hairdo,' Watkins continued. 'It suits you.'

Jack waved him away. 'Was there something you wanted?'

'What? No, I just wanted to let you know that somebody left a letter for you. I put it on your desk.'

He found the small brown envelope to his right. Tearing it open, he unfolded the parchment inside and began to read.

Detective Lambert,

I think perhaps we share a common enemy and, when my enemy has enemies, I'm keen to make sure we become friends. We have much to discuss. Don't worry about finding me.

I will find you.

The Captain.

Suddenly his headache was back.

Acknowledgements

There are a number of people who have contributed to the completion of this book. I'd like to thank Glenn Upsall for his continued support, feedback, and positivity towards my work, despite my constant pestering on Facebook Messenger.

I'd also like to thank Jaclyn Wrightson for her patience and willingness to answer the procedural questions I put to her.

As this book was nearing completion, novelist Tracey Iceton was extremely supportive towards me, offering advice and valuable insight on the process of publication.

Great credit must be given to Mark Hudson, my PGCE lecturer, for encouraging me to write many years ago and providing feedback on my early short stories. I've had a number of excellent teachers over the years and, although there are too many to name individually, I'd like to thank all of them for their support throughout my time in education.

To my editor, Ben Adam, and my proofreader, Julia Gibbs, thank you for putting up with my many emails, questions and queries. Your input was much appreciated.

I will also be eternally grateful to Betsy, and everybody at Bloodhound Books, for believing in this novel and giving me the opportunity to publish it. Special thanks to Heather Fitt for making the extra changes I requested.

Finally, I'd like to thank my parents for being willing to fund my early obsession with Roald Dahl and R.L. Stine books, the latter of which can't have been cheap!